LOVE
& OTHER
CARNIVOROUS
Plants

LOVE
& OTHER
CARNIVOROUS
Plants

FLORENCE GONSALVES

LITTLE, BROWN AND COMPANY
New York Boston

Little, Brown and Company
Hachette Book Group
1290 Avenue of the Americas, New York, NY 10104
Visit us at LBYR.com

First Edition: May 2018

Little, Brown and Company is a division of Hachette Book Group, Inc. The Little, Brown name and logo are trademarks of Hachette Book Group, Inc.

Library of Congress Cataloging-in-Publication Data

Names: Gonsalves, Florence, author.
Title: Love and other carnivorous plants / Florence Gonsalves.
Description: First edition. | New York ; Boston : Little, Brown and Company, 2018. | Summary: "Nineteen-year-old Danny returns home after a disastrous first semester of college as a pre-med student and struggles with first love, grief, identity, and self-destructive behavior" —Provided by publisher.
Identifiers: LCCN 2017018094| ISBN 9780316436724 (hardcover) | ISBN 9780316436694 (ebook) | ISBN 9780316436717 (library edition ebook)
Subjects: | CYAC: Best friends—Fiction. | Friendship—Fiction. | Identity—Fiction. | Eating disorders—Fiction. | Death—Fiction. | Sexual orientation—Fiction.
Classification: LCC PZ7.1.G65219 Lov 2018 | DDC [Fic]—dc23
LC record available at https://lccn.loc.gov/2017018094

ISBNs: 978-0-316-43672-4 (hardcover), 978-0-316-43669-4 (ebook)

Printed in the United States of America

LSC-C

10 9 8 7 6 5 4 3 2 1

For H

There is a crack in everything.
That's how the light gets in.

———————————

-LEONARD COHEN

PROLOGUE

No one wants to be *that* girl who locks herself in the bathroom on her birthday like she's on the brink of a nervous breakdown, but here I am, leaning my elbows on the toilet bowl, inhaling God knows how many private-part diseases, all in the hope of freeing myself of this birthday cake while freeing myself of my best friend's wrath. It's not that Sara's anger toward me isn't justified (I'm a Grade A asshole), but I thought maybe we could shelve that today, the one day of the year dedicated to my graceless exit from the womb.

There's a bang on the bathroom door so loud it

reverberates off every building on campus. "Dandelion Berkowitz, if you don't come out of the bathroom right now, I'm going to tell everyone that you're a shit friend who breaks promises and tells lies the size of her head, which has gotten pretty freaking big since you got into Harvard."

I do my best impersonation of a toilet paper roll, forgetting that, though Sara is all sorts of formidable, even she can't break a steel lock with drunken will alone. I'm about to weigh the pros and cons of unlocking the door when I hear a different voice.

"Um, Danny? I think you should come out and put Sara to bed."

"But I don't want to go to bed, *Maaaaaark*," says Sara.

"Stephen." He sighs. "It's Stephen, remember?"

I do eventually come out, smelling like whatever concoction they clean the bathrooms with, and Stephen helps me herd Sara back to my dorm room. "I've got her from here," I say, and tuck her in on the futon next to the trash can. When she's snoring those drunk snores that make you think it's gonna earthquake, I pretend none of this ever happened—not just Sara ruining my birthday, but the first few months of college altogether. I'm fantastic at putting things in a brain drawer and losing track of them entirely, so instead I pretend it's ten months ago, on our high school graduation day in June, when Sara was in her kitchen making us her famous grilled cheeses. She's not world-famous for them, just me-famous for them, but they can only be described as Hallelujah in the Mouth: three slices of bread, four types of cheese, truffle aioli, and caramelized onion. I have no idea what truffle aioli is, but *whoa*.

"Tell me The Plan," I'd said that day, and she launched right into it:

"Okay, two overachievers meet in kindergarten: one sporty, one super nerdy."

I flicked an onion at her. "Hey, I lobbied hard to have that word replaced."

"*Fine.*" She peeled the onion off her forehead and corrected herself. "One super *smart*. At first they can't get along, but soon they realize that unless they join forces, they'll destroy each other. So they make a solemn pact to never leave each other. They grow up and go to college together—"

"Which we're about to do now!" I interrupted her.

"One to be a professional tennis player, the other to be a surgeon. Then they marry their high school sweethearts—"

"Shit." I interrupted her again. "We totally didn't get high school sweethearts."

"I mean, I have Dave," she said, but by "have Dave" she meant she lost her virginity to him in his dad's Escalade. Driver's seat. Moonroof open.

"True, you *screw* Dave," I said, recalling that I got my

SAT scores back that same weekend. They were good, excellent even. "I, on the other hand, am as romantic as a spatula."

"You've been too focused on schoolwork," she said. "All that will change in college."

I hoped she was right—that as soon as I stepped into a frat party or whatever, I'd immediately stop thinking boys were uninteresting and magically know what to do with them.

"Watch, this is an easy fix." Sara cleared her throat. "Then they marry their *college* sweethearts—two brothers, lawyers, who love them stupidly—and when they end up widows they get a little house together with a big wall for all their accomplishments. Then they make grilled cheeses every night for dinner because there's no one to tell them there's such a thing as too much butter."

"There *isn't* such a thing as too much butter," I'd said, finishing my sandwich and sighing. Graduating high school was looking pretty good that day, before I knew we'd have to leave the safety of being in each other's corner.

For a few more hours at least the future wasn't *the* future, it was *our* future. Right up until I opened the letter that, in seven hundred words, ruined everything.

CHAPTER ONE

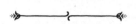

Ten godforsaken weeks after the worst birthday in history according to an informal survey done by HBS (Harvard Bathroom Stalls)

"Well, Danny, at least we know you've been eating!" my dad says as I get out of the car.

It isn't the warm welcome I was anticipating after being banished to a treatment center where my own father didn't visit me. Not once. Like, really, Dad? As oblivious as you are, can't you see how wildly insulting that'd be?

"So much for your smock idea, *Mom.*" I grimace, checking out my reflection in the car door. I had asked her to bring me something "roomy, yet flattering," but what she brought was missing the second, more important component, so I'm now the proud owner of the same ugly tentlike dress in eight different shades of Mom. And I'm going to have to wear them all summer. Well, I *could* wear my jean shorts if I don't button or zip them. But I'd also need to cut slits in the sides so my legs can circulate enough blood not to turn blue. It sounds like a fun DIY project and all, but I'm not the artsy-fartsy type.

"You look beautiful," my mom says. "We're so relieved you're home and safe and feeling better." Then she starts crying. *Crying.* While she blows her nose, my dad whips out my Harvard acceptance letter to remind me of "all the things I've accomplished," then tells me that per our deal, he and my mom had a great conference call with my doctors, therapists, and deans, and as long as I keep going to therapy this summer I'll be able to redo my second semester and return to Harvard in the fall. He points to the letterhead proudly as he says this, and I try not to let on that looking at the letter is making me feel sick. I would never elect to have my parents in on my craziness, but since they pay my tuition, I can't really be an asshole about it.

"Okay, I love you guys, but I can't be with you right now." I take the letter from my dad and fold it up. "We have all summer to hammer out these details, so if you'll excuse me, I'm going to charge my cell phone, turn it back on, and make myself available to the world for the first time since April. Unless it's died of malnourishment."

My parents shoot me a standard horrified-parent look.

"Oh, come on," I say cheerfully. "Eating disorder jokes

are funny for cell phones because *texting* is their nourishment. And they're getting plenty of that."

They don't laugh, but it's fine. I'm my most important audience member.

On my way into the house I trip on one of the plastic geese my dad puts around the garden, lest we forget he's an ornithology professor. When I put it upright again I think of a poem someone gave me when I first got to treatment, not that I like poetry *or* that "someone" who gave it to me, but some things have a way of staying with you.

"Wild Geese," I start, then cut myself off. What happens in treatment stays in treatment. I brush the soil off my hands, but the garden goose stares at me until I'm inside.

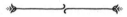

Even after two months of neglect my cell phone turns on immediately, no questions asked, which is how all friends should be. I ignore the 132 unread texts from people I probably don't want to talk to and call the only number I've ever memorized besides mine. And Papa John's, because come on.

After a few rings she yells, "Dandelion!" and I say, "Sara, how the hell are ya?"

"I'm good, kid, how the hell are you?"

We always greet each other in this over-the-top way, like two old gangsters reuniting for the first time since the baptism of their eighth child with their fifth wife. Then she drops her grandiose voice because we can only go on like that for a few seconds and says, "Are you finally home? Where are you? What are you doing? I can't believe you turned your phone off and finals kept you until *June*. It's practically a crime against summer."

I haven't exactly told her about my stint in treatment, so I'm like, "I'm a free woman now. Let's tango." To be clear, *tango* isn't a word I usually use, but it's been a long time since I've had a normal, nonfacilitated conversation.

"Let's go to the beach," she says.

"Absolutely not." I'm standing in the mirror trying to find a stance that makes me look more like how I used to look and less like how I look now. Success rate: zero percent. "I know your metabolism is run by do-gooding fairies, but you're going to have to take pity on those of us who fell victim to the freshman fifteen and then some."

"We won't swim, we'll walk."

I sigh and give up. Mirrors will have to be added to the list of things to avoid.

"Hey, Danny?"

I hold my breath because I can tell she's gonna bring up something unsavory. "Yeah?"

"We're fine, right? I know your birthday a couple of months ago was bad, but—"

I make the executive decision to cut her off. "It's water under the bridge." I even think I mean it.

"Is that one of those intellectual sayings you learned at *Haaaarvaaaard*?"

"No, I didn't learn it at *Haaaaarvaaaard*."

Everyone knows the water under the bridge saying, but the last thing I need to do is get Sara back into the mindset that I now think I'm better than everyone because of *Haaaarvaaaard*.

"I'm just teasing you," she says. "I'll pick you up in ten."

I catch an unfortunate final glimpse of myself in the mirror and tell the voice of body-loving reason to block its ears. "If you don't see me, look for the girl who looks like she ate the girl once known as Danny."

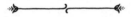

Fifty-three minutes later (Sara has her own world clock), a black Range Rover pulls into the driveway blasting country music. I run to her car door and Sara jumps out to give me a hug. She's taller than I am, so when she wraps her arms around me my ear smooshes into her neck and I eat a little bit of her hair, not because I'm hungry, but just by mistake.

"Ahh! I missed you so much!" she says. Immediately, everything from the birthday fiasco to the last two months of silence dissolves between us. She's wearing a white summer dress that shows off all the freckles on her shoulders, and I'm smiling because she seems to have gotten more beautiful since the last time I saw her, but probably I just forgot what she looked like. That happens, you know, no matter how beautiful you are, which is why I try not to get so hung up on beauty. It's the same thing as being ugly: You look at it long enough and it doesn't look like anything.

"How are you? Your hair is gorgeous! I like the highlights," she says.

I didn't get highlights, but whatever. "I'm so happy to see you. You're so beautiful that if we weren't already friends we definitely couldn't be."

She rolls her eyes, which is her signature move. "Stop, I feel like a mess. I just left Ethan's house." She leans in when she says it, and I can tell his name tastes good in her mouth.

"Who's Ethan?"

"Some guy I met at school. I'll tell you about him sometime, but right now we have way more important things to catch up on."

We get in her car and I hope she intends on doing most of the catching up for us. In addition to being emotionally exhausting, my last two months in treatment have been kept entirely secret, even from Sara, who thinks I was undergoing a grueling second semester instead. "How were finals for you?" she asks. "I finished a month ago and I've been partying nonstop since. I need to sweat out hella toxins later."

"Since when do you say 'hella'? And since when do you party nonstop?" I try to see through her sunglasses if her eyes are actually her eyes. "Doesn't that mess with your game?"

"Oh, it's fine," she says quickly. "Besides, I don't have training for a couple more weeks. And my tennis season went so well I deserve a break."

I don't know what to say, so I look out the window at the strip malls and coffee franchises growing over our town like weeds. I guess that's what happens when you leave a place alone. It goes to shit without you.

"Did I tell you my coach wants to make me captain next year?" she continues. "I was so shocked, but of course it'd be great for me. I love it there, Danny. The only thing that's missing is you."

A heavy silence follows.

"Sorry, I didn't mean to reopen old wounds," she says quickly, and I wish we would get to the beach already. "I just meant I miss you and it would have been fun to go to college together. But I'm so happy for you, really."

"It's fine," I mumble into the seat belt crossing my chest. "So who is Sir Ethan?"

It's probably not fair to distract Sara with her love of boys, but it's also not fair for vultures to eat a deer that isn't fully dead yet. I guess at the end of the day it's not about "fair"; it's about survival.

"Get comfortable. The Ethan story is a long one. Wait, no. Let me start with my sorority. Wait, no, tennis. Yes, tennis, okay, so…"

While Sara describes the most perfect freshman year of college, I take my sandals off and put my feet up on the dashboard. My toenails are chipped black from the last time I painted them, when I thought my choice in polish ought to reflect my soul.

"Enough about me," Sara says at last. She pulls into the beach too fast and we almost squash a dumb seagull with shitty reflexes. "I can't believe you turned your phone off for two months. I know you said you were turning it off to focus on school, but were classes really that intense? Or were you still mad about our fight? Maybe we should talk it out."

"You know how much I love to talk about feelings," I say sarcastically. I almost wish we had hit the seagull so we'd have something else to talk about, something *actually* dramatic to distract us from our own dramatics. *Just kidding*, I mouth to the seagull through the side mirror.

"Same, but I was reading this article that said married couples all end up having the same fight, like, their whole lives," she says, parking the car. "It might *seem* like a different fight, but if you boil it down, it's probably the exact same fight as last week and the week before that. They just keep having that one fight until they die. Or get divorced."

I peel a large strip of polish off my toenail. "Are you saying the college fight is going to be our fight?"

"It could be. But I don't want it to be. So I think we should nip it in the butt."

"Bud."

"Whatever."

I could mention that *she's* the one who brought up the fight that happened on my birthday this April, when she got the drunkest I've ever seen her, then slapped me in the face with a piece of pizza, forcing me to hide out in the bathroom stall like *that* girl about to have a breakdown. But I'm trying to be a better person, so instead I say: "I said I'm sorry. You said you're sorry. It's been over two months. I think we can skip down the yellow brick road anytime now."

She looks over at me, but I can't read her expression due to the enormity of her sunglasses. Besides, it's starting to feel like global warming in the car, so I open the door and breathe in the fresh beach air. I link my arm in hers as we walk from the parking lot to the shore, and she gives it a little squeeze. The thing about not having any siblings is that you have to be strategic about who you get in sibling-fights with. The most crucial factor is that they love you unconditionally. Otherwise you start saying ruthless shit to people and they think the devil lives in your asshole and you end up friendless and alone until your cats stage a coup and murder you. So really Sara and I don't ever *need* to apologize to each other. Sometimes it's good to say sorry, though, just as a formality.

"You still haven't told me anything about second semester," Sara prods. I know I should tell her about treatment, but honestly it's too nice of a day out.

"Classes were intense," I lie, picking up a flattish stone and feeling its weight in my hand. "Studying all hours of the day and night. At one point I thought about hiring a high schooler to pinch me every forty-five seconds to keep me awake in the library." I throw the rock at the ocean and pray for a smooth surface skim. "Finals were even more brutal. I had to keep a gallon jug of iced coffee by my bed and I grew, like, grocery bags under my eyes." Instead of skipping, the stone plunks anticlimactically into the water and I curse my parents for not giving me a single strand of athletic DNA. "Can we talk about something else?" I ask. "This is giving me PTSD."

"Oh my God, of course," she says, and it's the exact tone of Sara's I missed, the Everything Is Okay tone, regardless of what "everything" is. I breathe a sigh of relief knowing I can say anything to her because even though PTSD isn't technically a joking matter, she's about as politically correct as a drunk pirate.

"What about your friend? What's his name?" She picks up a flat rock too, and hers skips like an Olympian six times before disappearing under the water.

"Stephen." I undo my ponytail and try not to let on how absurd it is that she can't remember his name, even though we hung out with him my whole terrible birthday night.

"How is he? Have you two hooked up yet?"

"Ew. It's *Stephen*. Combined, we're about as sexual as a Styrofoam peanut." But I'm speaking for myself. Of the three times I've masturbated in my life, once was an accident. "We literally study together, eat too many snacks, then fall asleep drooling on each other."

"Oh, please. When I came up to visit I could tell he was totally in love with you."

"Yuck."

But then we're both silent. Sara's spring visit to Harvard for my birthday was bad, even before the big blowup. It's not that I was embarrassed to have my roommates meet Sara, but how could I have known she was going to become a vodka-guzzling sorority doll?

"So how come you didn't put on the freshman anything but I became the Pillsbury Doughgirl?" I say abruptly.

Sara laughs and we keep walking. "Danny, shut up. You're not even fat. You've gained, what, ten pounds since I saw you?"

"Twenty-five," I mumble, but I don't know the number now. Scales were forbidden in treatment due to my vague diagnosis: Eating Disorders Not Otherwise Specified, plus Bulimia, plus a dollop of General Anxiety Disorder, just for good measure. Still, any mention of numbers makes it feel like my thighs are rubbing together, which makes me seriously regret agreeing to this walk on the beach.

"Twenty-five pounds is nothing. Everyone gains weight in college, and now you have even better curves. But if you want, we'll play tennis every day this summer and it'll be gone in a month." Sara takes off her sandals and walks with a lightness I want to steal from her—not so that she can't have it, but so that we both can.

"Yeah, but I'm short so you notice it more," I whine. "Plus, some of it went to my nose or something and now my face is distorted. Do I look like a Teletubby? Be honest."

"Why don't you see a nutritionist?" she asks, as if I didn't think to see every possible specialist when I quickly surpassed the legendary freshman fifteen. I'd hoped to have a thyroid issue, but every blood test came back negative. Apparently I got this way purely of my own volition, which didn't concern the doctors at all. They called it "normal." It wasn't until I developed my own methods to treat the weight gain that the doctors got concerned and ordered me to treatment. Even now they don't seem to know what's wrong, and they won't know until we've spent a good many hours together with my feelings. I don't know how we're going to find enough of my feelings to fit into the hours of appointments I have scheduled with Leslie, the robot therapist, but I guess I'll worry about that later.

"*Obviously*, I've seen a nutritionist," I say, and Sara

16

stops walking to pick up a piece of sea glass. I could tell her that the big accomplishment of the last two months is that I don't skip off to the little girls' room after every meal anymore, so we shouldn't be worried about a few "vanity pounds." But watching her turn over the piece of glass I decide she doesn't need all this information, at least not right now. I settle it all by saying, "All the nutritionists want me to do is write down my food and why I'm eating, blah blah blah. It squashes the fun out of everything."

"Ew, yeah. That sounds so boring."

I pick up a piece of sea glass to add to the collection Sara's started in her hand, but it turns out to be regular glass that scrapes my finger when I touch it. "Dammit," I mumble. Going to treatment would've been a lot less unsettling if I knew *why* it all happened. The therapists say stress and needing an outlet for control and yadda yadda yadda, but it's unsettling how illogical and arbitrary it is.

"Don't worry," Sara says, closing her hand and seeming content with her findings. "I'll show you the workout my mom's trainer does with her and you'll get your confidence back in no time." I don't point out that Sara's mother is at least fifty pounds overweight. "And I'll set you up with one of Ethan's friends. I think you'd like John." She describes John: tall, loves dogs, sort of looks and acts like one.

We sit by the water and she picks up handfuls of sand. "God, I missed this," she says.

"Me too." The wind blows my hair into my mouth and it tastes a little salty as I brush it back behind my ear. "I just wish someone warned me how hard college would be. I thought it would be like *American Pie*—beer pong and sex in every room."

Sara's eyes light up and she grabs me by the shoulders. "Wait, have you finally had sex?"

I glare at her. "You say 'finally' like I'm forty and not nineteen. I have other priorities, okay?" There's a cracking sound near us as a shell breaks against a rock. When it opens, the seagull that dropped it eats it mercilessly, one large peck at a time. "To answer your question, *no*, I have not had The Sex yet. Even getting laid is hard. Classes are one thing, but c'mon. Sex was supposed to be easy."

"I know it's hard, Danny," Sara says, and I just know she *doesn't* know at all. "But we're back in action now. The Plan is right on track." She clears her throat and I wish the waves would drown out the sound of her trying to act like nothing has changed. "They reunite *after* college, marry two brothers, lawyers, who love them stupidly. And you know the rest." She puts her arm around me. "Oh, I meant to tell you, I'm having a party tonight. You're invited."

"Thanks for the last-minute invite." I semipush her into the sand.

"Come on, you didn't have a phone!" She semipushes me back. "No more sulking. Finals are over, it's summer, and we have party things to tend to. Okay?" She stands up and offers me her hand, but I almost prefer to lie with my nose in the seaweed, taking in its faint dead-fish smell.

"Okay?" she says again, and in spite of myself, I take her hand and let her help me up. She does have a point—I've been waiting for it to be summer since the last time it was summer. And I can't say no to Sara. I've only said no to Sara once, and we're still working out the politics of that decision.

CHAPTER TWO

"You're leaving again?" my dad asks when I come into the kitchen. They remodeled it while I was at college, and the steel accents give the whole place a hostile feel. "You just got here! We should hang out now that you're out of..." His face twitches, but I'm *very* perceptive. "...treatment."

I open the dark metal refrigerator for a diet any-beverage to avoid looking at him. He doesn't have to stumble over the T-word every time he says it, as if it's as hard for him to talk about as it was for me to go through.

"I'm surprised you even knew I was in *treatment*," I say,

accentuating the word even though I never say it in front of my mom, who insists on saying it all the time. "Considering you never stopped by."

"I know. I'm sorry."

I open the can of Diet Coke on the cold marble counter and a carpenter ant scuttles by. I wait for my dad to squish it, but he looks at me like I'm supposed to squish it. Obviously, the carpenter ant will die another day, when my mother is in the kitchen.

"Do you want to talk about it?" he finally says, and his voice is so strained I want to punch him. Instead I stomp out of the kitchen and grab his keys.

"I'm taking your car, okay," I say, because it sounds nicer than "forget it." I get that it must have sucked to watch me go from valedictorian to Occupy Depression all in the course of ten months, but the least you could do is kill the stupid ant for me, Dad.

Sara's house is always unlocked because her mother is always there, so I let myself in and up the stairs to Sara's room. I can smell alcohol in the hallway, and sure enough when I open the door she's standing over her desk, pouring two generous shots from a handle of vodka.

"I guess we're not frinking tonight?" I ask. I pull the sleeves of my smock away from the puddle of my armpits and notice how little has changed in Sara's room: same pink walls and white furniture and gingerbread candle no matter what season it is.

"No, I never frink anymore. I can't believe you still do." Her tone reduces me to something even less cool than head lice, which is totally unfair. Frinking, i.e., fake-drinking, is what Sara and I used to do in high school. It's stupid easy. You hold a red cup and dance aggressively and don't consume calories or ruin your chances of, like, becoming someone important in the future. I'd planned on frinking tonight, but I guess I can deal with being fat and unsuccessful tomorrow. Besides, I deserve a little fun on my first night out of captivity. "The most important thing I learned in college, well really it was in my sorority, is that it's way more fun to *actually* drink." Sara adjusts her boobs so they sit up higher in her push-up bra and then grabs one of the glasses. "Here, this one is for you."

"It's only more fun until tomorrow rolls around," I correct her, taking the glass from her hand and wondering why it is that Sara got fat boobs and I got fat everything else *except* boobs. "What should we cheers to?"

"To the two of us," she says, sitting under the white-frilled canopy of her bed and gesturing that I do the same.

"Okay. To the two of us." We sit facing each other and I cross my arm around hers.

"Going strong since the era of diapers," Sara says regally.

"You wore diapers in kindergarten?"

"Don't ruin my cheers with the facts, Danny."

We put the shot glasses to our lips and I cringe a little. The shot smells like pineapple and nail polish remover but I swallow anyway. As I start to feel like I might throw up, a singsong voice says, "Knocky-knock," but without physically knocking on the door.

"Come in," Sara says, and rolls her eyes in my direction. There's no way to prepare for Janet, who's one of those large women who gives generous hugs that leave you smelling like Chanel and not necessarily happy about it.

"Danny, darling, we missed you so much." Janet swirls the wine in her goblet. "How are your pre-med classes? I ran into your mother at the grocery store and she told you were studying so hard you turned off your phone."

I'm sure my parents didn't *want* to tell people I was at school when I wasn't at school, but the details of my treatment days aren't their business to tell. I clear my throat. "Mhm, yeah, been studying very hard. Pre-med classes are really good."

Pre-med classes really blow. The first semester I spent four hours three times a week in massive lab goggles that left a red ring around my eyes, which took an additional four hours to go away. Midway through the term my dinoflagellates all died (first they rebelled and then they killed each other), and I was so frustrated with organic chemistry that I threw the little tinker-toy study kit into the toilet, which I later had to fish out.

"Good for you, darling. We are so proud of you. Any boyfriends yet?"

"None that I know of."

"Well, good. You have so much tiiiiiime." She stretches out the last word to show the infinite nature of youth. "Did Sara tell you about her boyfriend? He's adorable. I haven't met him yet except on Instagram, but—"

"Okay, Mom, good to see you." Sara guides her back through the door.

"Don't you girls want me to help you get ready? I can do your makeup." Janet's tone makes me feel a little sad for her. "I want you to look good for Ethan, you may want to, you know."

She winks, but Sara says, "Absolutely not. Out with you, right now."

"Well, we've hardly talked about you and him at all." Her mouth forms a pout. "What about the s-e-x?"

"We can all spell, Mom." Sara tries to close the door, but Janet's face is in the way. "Thanks for the alcohol, though. You're such a good friend," Sara adds, and that pleases Janet much more than calling her *Mom* ever could.

The doorbell rings a minute later, and we run downstairs to open the door for Kate and Liz. We all squeal and hug a lot, and I'm surprisingly glad for vodka. Sometimes I need a little liquid help in these sorts of situations.

"Danny, we missed you so much. You disappeared off the face of the digital earth. How are you? You look *great*,"

Kate says. Or maybe Liz said it? They're such carbon copies of each other that I can hardly distinguish between them, let alone fathom how we used to be friends.

"Did your boobs get bigger?" the other asks.

"I think my head just got smaller," I say. "Which only makes it look like I went up a cup size due to the discrepancy in the usual ratio." Of course they don't get that I'm being an asshole.

"I'm so glad the Gems are back together," Liz says, and I wince internally. I thought we ditched that name in high school, but since it's not worth getting called out for thinking I'm better than everyone else, I smile and do my best impersonation of a party-loving teenager.

"More alcohol!" I say. Honestly, it's the easiest way to get everyone on your side.

We take the party into the backyard, where Janet has actualized every kid's dream. The pool-house bar has two types of tequila, limes, salt, and a bowl of very strong-smelling punch. The lights are off on the tennis court, making it an ideal spot for a hookup. There's wood for the bonfire, stuff to make s'mores, and a table with red cups for all the accompanying drinking games. Soon a lot of people Sara went to college with start showing up, and I try to count them all while she plays hostess, but it's, like, a lot of people.

"Jesus, how many friends did you make? 'Cause I'm pretty sure I only made one," I say to myself, which goes to show you that I'm a pretty lousy version of myself when

Sara isn't around. Danny with Sara = Danny. Danny with Danny = chubby, insecure, and chock-full of self-destructive coping mechanisms. I indulge my pity party for ten more seconds, then join in the tequila charade with everyone else: lime, tequila, salt...shit, no...salt, tequila, *then* lime. See? I can't even get the fun things right.

Meeting new people is arguably better than reliving stories of the high school glory days with the Gems, but I'm not drunk enough yet to enjoy myself. I'm certainly not drunk enough for the big introduction which is closing in in three...two...

"Ethan, this is Danny," Sara says, approaching me while clutching the arm of a guy who is all muscle and all tan, with teeth so white you sort of don't believe them.

"Danny, it's nice to finally meet you," he says, with so much warmth and enthusiasm that I feel I have to compliment him.

"Yeah, same. I...love your T-shirt?"

He looks down at his chest: SUN'S OUT GUNS OUT is written in huge block letters.

"I think it's a tank top," he says, and goddammit, he's right. "This is my friend John," he adds as another guy with a buzz cut walks up. He extends his hand and I think he's going for the shake but no. He wants me to pound it.

"I'm Danny." As I knock my fist against his, he opens his hand and clamps it around mine, yelling, "Turkey!" Then he starts laughing. "Gotcha."

"Isn't he hilarious?" Sara says, and the scary thing is I think she means it. "John, Danny and I met in kindergarten because we were the only two kids in the whole class who didn't have siblings to bring to Bring Your Sibling to Class Day."

"We've been subbing for each other ever since." Then I add, in a failed attempt to seem interesting, "We even made it official when we became blood buddies. Not with real blood 'cause that would make me vom, but with real red Kool-Aid, you know, the name-brand kind, not the grocery-store-knockoff kind."

"Actually we *drank* each other's Kool-Aid, which makes us more vampires than sisters." Sara puts her arm around me and I laugh too loudly, wishing I found it as easy to talk to people as to talk to inanimate objects.

"Righteous," John says, and his eyes linger on Liz's ass.

"And Danny's super smart. Graduated first in our class and totally abandoned me when she got into Harvard off the waitlist last June."

"Oh, yeah?" John sounds captivated for the first time since the conversation started. "My sister went there, but she said it was boring."

"Huh." I wish he could've picked anything else to suddenly get interested about.

"*I* think she just hated not being the only valedictorian in the room anymore, 'cause I guess Harvard has a shit ton of valedictorians, which is a catch-22 or something because

27

there should only be one." He laughs a little. "She's the smart one in the family."

"Oh, bummer. I love it," I say, then to avoid setting Sara off I add quickly, "So should we take shots?"

Rallying toward inebriation is a party trick that works every time.

As the tequila goes down (salt first this round) I come to the groundbreaking conclusion that 80 percent of the student body is as sneaky and eager to lie about Harvard as I am. The two hypotheses for this entirely arbitrary statistic that I just made up are 1) valedictorians live such boring, calculated lives that petty lies are their only excitement or 2) up until college, valedictorians have this disease called Valedictorianism, which causes them to think that they are not valedictorian of their high school, but valedictorian of the whole world, which naturally makes them feel like a louse when they realize there's hundreds just like them. To hide their disappointment, they have to lie to their friends and family about how small they feel because they are not the big cheese anymore, they are simply *a* cheese, albeit a fine one in a very overpriced shop.

And right when I'm feeling like maybe I've found a thesis topic that will win the Nobel Prize and whoa am I *ravenous*—cheese would be delicious, if only I hadn't made my thousandth vow to veganism this morning upon leaving treatment—I see her. My stomach does somersaults and I hope that I'm drunk and hallucinating but no. It's absolutely her. She looks exactly like she did before, with her red hair wild down her back, but I guess most people don't become unrecognizable from April to June. She's standing by the punch, not looking bored exactly but not looking quite like she wants to be here either. When she looks at me I feel a lump in my throat the size of a lime. Since I can't figure out how to disappear completely in a fraction of a second, I turn toward the house and consider making a run for it.

"Oh, hey." Sara nudges me. "My friend from yoga is here. How cute is her tutu? Danny, come meet her. I think you two would really get along."

Who in the hell makes friends at *yoga*? "Um, I was going to—" I rack my brain, but a lie hasn't developed yet.

"Well, whatever it is, can it wait a second? You're going to love this girl. I want you to come to class with us next week."

So they're an *us*? "But I told Liz I'd be her next beer pong partner," I say, grateful that the lie factory has resumed its operations.

"She's not even close to being done yet. And you hate beer pong. Why are you being weird? Come meet my new friend." Sara grabs my arm and pulls me over to Girl Red (who could also be nicknamed Code Red) while I try to keep all the contents of my stomach within my stomach. What are the chances of *her* being *here*, and why is the universe never Team Danny?

"I'm so glad you could come, Bugg," Sara says, and gives "Bugg" (I prefer Girl Red) a long hug.

"Thanks for the invite." She turns to look at me and I turn to stone, though unfortunately with my nervous system still intact. "Well, hey, you," she says, and I try to respond but my mouth won't cooperate.

"Oh, do you two know each other?" Sara looks between the two of us.

And here lies the problem with lying. Every so often the truth blows your cover.

"No," I say, but at the same time Bugg is saying, "Yes."

CHAPTER THREE

"I mean yes," I say, while Bugg is saying, "Well, not really."

Then I laugh nervously and try the only trick up my sleeve. "Should we take shots?"

"You guys are being weird," Sara says. "Am I missing something?"

This time I keep my mouth shut.

Bugg finally catches on and doesn't spill the proverbial beans. "You just look *so* familiar."

"Ditto," I say, looking at the pool where a multicolored beach ball is drifting slowly into the deep end.

"Well, Danny, this is Bugg." Sara puts an arm on each

of our shoulders, locking us into an interaction. "Bugg likes yoga and plans on spending her summer at some poetry class thing. And Bugg, this is Danny. Danny likes school and plans on spending her summer doing…school-related things?"

"Oh, *this* is Danny?" Bugg asks. My cheeks turn as red as one of the beach ball's triangles.

"I talk about you all the time," Sara explains, but I'm feeling quite claustrophobic now in the shrinking space between the ground and the sky.

"Good to meet you *officially*." Bugg smirks, and for a few seconds I'm worried she's changed her mind about the proverbial beans. Then she turns to Sara. "Do you still want some of the stuff?"

Sara's eyes light up and I try to figure out what "the stuff" could be. "Yes, hang on, I have cash for you." She reaches into her shorts pocket, but Bugg stops her.

"Maybe someplace a little less visible. It's a covert, *tiny* business," she adds to me, as if I know what they're talking about.

"Give us a sec, Danny." Sara motions for Bugg to follow her, and they disappear behind the pool house. They're gone for as long as it takes me to determine that Bugg was in treatment for some terrible drug addiction, which she's now passing on to Sara in the guise of fun partying, and I'm enabling it all by not calling the cops. When they get back I give Sara the wide-eyed we're-all-gonna-die look and she pats me on the shoulder.

"Relax, Danny, it's just weed. Totally legal."

1) Since when does Sara dabble in "just weed" and 2) just because weed is legal in this glorious Pilgrim State doesn't mean you can *buy* it from *whoever*. Whomever? GOD, I HATE LIVING IN MY HEAD.

"Either we're too drunk or not drunk enough," Sara says, cutting open a lime carelessly and drawing a little blood on her finger. "Ouch." She looks down, then shrugs. "Screw it. Shots it is."

"Can't. I'm DD." Bugg jangles her keys while I piece together that DD = Designated Driver. "But you two go ahead."

As we're about to tequila ourselves comfortable again, Liz yells, "Sara, you and Ethan are up now. John and I just lost."

"Sorry, I gotta go," Sara says. "Hang out for a second, okay? I'll come find you after."

"Nooooo," I want to shout, but instead I lick the salt on my hand and take the hit while praying a meteor strikes the earth and we all get wiped out in one fell swoop. I hate to sound apocalyptic, but I think it would be less painful than standing here like this.

"So this is a fun party," Bugg says after a few seconds of torturous silence. She sounds beyond bored.

"Yeah." I study the tiki torch behind her because I can't really look at her. "But I'm agreeing more with the tone of your voice than what you actually said." I feel her looking at me for way longer than is comfortable, and then she bursts out laughing.

"Do you want to get out of here?"

I look around to clarify that she's talking to me. She is.

"Um, with you?"

"No, stupid, with them." She jerks her finger toward the side of the pool house, where John is exploring Liz's skirt with his gropey paws.

I shudder. "Ew."

"Well, the offer stands." She takes her keys out of her pocket and gives them another jingle.

"But if you're DD, doesn't that mean you have other people to D?"

"Nope. I'm the chauffeur and the passenger. Designated to myself and myself only." She starts to walk up the lawn, which is wet with dew and maybe liquor. I try to do a quick pros and cons list, but the problem with being drunk is fuck it.

"Wait. I can't leave or Sara will kill me, but I need to make some food or I'm going to die a tequila death tomorrow."

Bugg turns around and the wind blows her hair into her face. "Well, does Sara have good snacks?" Her shadow is long and exaggerated on the lawn because of physics or whatever it is that distorts us. I step into her darkness and lead us toward the kitchen.

"Sara's cabinets," I say, pausing for effect because I'm

a stupid drunk, "put BJ's, Sam's Club, and Walmart all to shame."

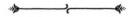

In the kitchen I pull supplies out of the cabinet and Bugg gives me the third degree. "So what was that all about? Have you not told Sara about St. John's? What's the net worth of your secrets?" She's not even whispering, which is totally disrespectful when I'm *clearly* trying to live my whole life in private.

As punishment I ignore her questions and their judgy undertones. "I should be asking you the same. Isn't it a little cliché for the girl who just got out of treatment to be selling weed to teenagers?" Her face doesn't register my insult. "I shouldn't be eating this, by the way. Do you know how many calories are in a single whiff of a single loaded nacho?" I hold the bag of Tostitos to my chest. "I can't resist the scoopable kind, though. You gotta admire man's ingenuity."

"Hmm, the calories in a single whiff?" Bugg sniffs the bag. "Maybe fifty-five? But if you picture yourself eating one, probably more like ninety-five." I make a face and she throws one at me.

It hits me in the chest and falls on the counter to crumble. "Ow."

"There's no way that hurt and I can't pretend for very

much longer that we don't know each other, so let's shoot the elephant before it sucks all the oxygen out of this room."

Her hands are on her hips in an undeniable power stance, so I put my finger to my lips in an exaggerated plea for her to shut the hell up.

"Oh, come on," she says incredulously. "No one is around."

I go about suffocating the chips in beans, cheese, and other sorts of heaven—veganism will still be a worthy cause tomorrow—then put the nachos in the oven and set the timer. We stand facing each other in silence so thick it almost takes away my appetite (and virtually nothing takes away my appetite or I would pay anything on the black market for it).

It's a relief when she laughs. "Well, this is a little awkward, but I felt like we knew each other, even though I guess we don't really. Maybe it was the nature of the place, or passing notes or something. Anyway, I'm sorry, it's definitely so weird that I'm still here. Enjoy your nachos. It was good to see you again, Danny." She turns to leave and I grab her tutu.

"No," I say quickly, surprising myself maybe as much as her. "Don't go. It's fine. Just strange to see you in the real world, I guess, or whatever this is." I hear a splash outside and see Sara stripped down to her underwear, jumping in the pool after Ethan. I let go of the tulle and pull my smock down self-consciously.

"When I saw you I felt like I had to say something, but as soon as Sara introduced us I knew you didn't want to talk about it with her around."

"Honestly, I don't want to talk about it, period." I start washing the dishes in the sink so I'll have something to clank around.

"Well, I wanted you to know that you being there and having someone to share poems and shit with made it all bearable for me," Bugg says. "After I left I was kicking myself for not introducing myself. Or saying bye."

I turn my face to look at her, and the water gets so hot it burns my hand. "Yeah, you disappeared." I try not to sound wounded about it as I blow on my finger.

"I should have said something. It's one of those things where I wasn't in there to make friends, even though we were sort of friends, you know? Friends who didn't talk or know anything about each other but were in one place in the same way. It was kind of sweet," she says, and the look on her face seals me off from the rest of the world entirely.

"It *was* sweet," I mumble.

Then the timer goes off, startling me a little, and I put our culinary feat on the counter to cool. "It's hard to know how to navigate anything there or after."

We look at each other silently and I try not to blush. *Embody the cabinetry, embody the cabinetry,* I chant.

"So how much longer were you there after I left?" she asks, and I take it upon myself to look at her, you know, in an objective way. She's chubby in all the good places—soft exactly where it counts.

"Six weeks." To keep myself from gaping at her, I proceed to stuff my face with nachos. They're the best things I've eaten in sixty days. "I just got home this morning," I say, but it comes out *ji jug sgot grome gis smorning*.

"Easy there, champ. No one's gonna take it away from you." She removes a nacho from the bottom of the pile like we're playing Jenga. "So I caught you at the beginning and you caught me at the end."

I swallow. "Yeah, I guess so. It's so stupid, though. I gained three million pounds because of their goddamn meal plan and having to keep it all down."

She grins. "Yeah, I was totally estimating your weight to be around three million pounds."

"You have a keen eye."

"And you have cheese on your mouth." Before I can die a quick death of embarrassment, she walks over to me and wipes my lip with her thumb, as if there's no such thing as personal space or, I don't know, *diseases* spread through skin-to-skin contact. "So that's what you were in for? Bulimia?"

I wipe my mouth where she wiped my mouth and lean against the stove for support. The skin on my face is starting to hurt, which is probably how an onion feels when it senses someone is trying to peel it.

"Beep," I say. "Beep . . . Beep . . . BEEP . . . BEEP."

Bugg starts laughing. "Oh my God, you are such a weirdo. What are you beeping about?"

"The machine is threatening to combust."

"*Such* a weirdo, but fine. I'll leave it alone. For now." She helps herself to another nacho, and I look back into the yard.

"I think we should go back out to the party and pretend this sort of thing is fun for us, like normal nineteen-year-olds."

"Ugh, you're so young." She sounds wistful, but I can tell she likes to say things like that.

"I'm not *so* young." I try to look her up and down casually, but I'm positive I'm terrible at it. "Why, how old are you?"

"Twenty-one." The way she says it, it sounds like the epitome of youth, like the oasis at the end of a teenage desert where everything is yours to drink and nothing is a mirage—

But then Sara bursts in soaking wet, disrupting my drunk interlude and igniting my nervous system again. "What's going on in here?" She's breathless, leaving a Sara-size puddle on the floor.

"Nothing," I say quickly. It's too weird having them both in the same room. Like, no one would make Harry Potter enter the Hunger Games, not because he couldn't do it, but because some worlds need to be kept separate.

"Oh my God, nachos. I'm sooooo hungry. But I need a

towel stat." She runs to the closet for a pile of them. "I'm *so* glad you two are getting to know each other."

"We're trying," Bugg says, and I face-stuff more nachos. "I should go, though. I have one more thing to do tonight."

"Aw, okay. I'd give you a hug but I'm dripping wet. Danny, come back out with me. We're about to play flip cup." She wrings her hair out in the sink and then tries to pull me back out with her.

"In a minute," I say, and make like the nachos will be offended unless I finish them all.

When she leaves, I walk Bugg to the door, not that she asked me to, but I guess because I want to. "To answer your question from a million seconds ago, no. I haven't told Sara any of this and you'd get the acquaintance trophy of the year if you didn't either."

Bugg adjusts her tutu and leans against the door. "Isn't she your best friend, though? How could she not know you were at St. John's?"

I wince at the name. I think we should agree to call it You-Know-Where. "It's complicated. I *am* going to tell her, just not yet."

Bugg looks like she wants to say something, but then she leans in and hugs me. It gets hard to breathe because she smells so good, like cinnamon and cigarettes, and I don't even like cigarettes. Or cinnamon, for that matter. "But you should talk to her soon, Danny. The longer you wait, the more bad stuff builds up between the two of you.

Secrets are nasty. If you don't come clean, they fester and fuck up everything."

I blink at her. "Well, does she know *you* were at St. John's?"

Bugg shuffles her keys from one hand to the other.

"*No*, but we're *acquaintances*, not best friends for life."

I cross my arms over my chest. "Is that what you call someone you sell drugs to?"

"I do not sell drugs! I give a couple of people weed, and if they feel so inclined they give me money for it."

"Exactly."

Bugg's watch starts beeping, and she looks down at it. "Twenty-two hundred hours," she says, then looks up at me as if I'm supposed to know what that means. "You coming?"

"I'd kind of planned on lying down upstairs and letting these nachos work their way through my digestive system for the next eight to ten hours."

Bugg gives me a look and I go a little unconscious.

"Danny, it's twenty-two hundred hours on a summer night in your nineteenth year." She opens the door into all the possibilities of the night. "You can't squander your youth *digesting*."

CHAPTER FOUR

"All you have to do is deliver the package," Bugg says. "Do you think you can do that?"

We're in her car, a Volkswagen convertible from when cars were really old. My legs start sticking to the seats and I feel a serious case of swass (formally known as sweaty-ass) coming on. I put my seat belt on for ultimate safety. "Uh, what kind of package? This isn't some drug thing, is it? 'Cause I'm cool and all but the kind of cool that doesn't do drugs."

"I'm starting to think it was a bad idea to let you in on my side business," Bugg says, playing with the radio tuner, but it all comes in as static.

"It's not a bad idea, just a felony." I look out the window. Either because we're driving fast or I'm drunk, the streetlights blend into the house lights, making it hard to say what's what. Luckily sometimes you can find comfort in the blur.

"So are you in or not?" she asks indifferently.

It's not like I dream of spending the next few years in juvie, but for no apparent reason, I say, "I'm in."

We cross the town line and stop at a pizza place. She leaves the car running and hops out. "Stay here. This'll only take a minute." Sure enough she comes back in about sixty seconds with a pizza box and a pack of M&M's. "Take this."

"Uh…" The pizza is hot in my lap, and the smell, despite how full I am, is one that makes me believe in a cheesy God.

"Open the M&M's and use them to spell out the word 'thanks' on top of the pizza," she says, and I do as I'm told, even though I haven't washed my hands since I can't remember when. "And don't use any yellow ones. She hates the yellow ones."

"Can I ask—"

"No." She laughs and turns down a street, parking between two houses. She reaches into the back seat and hands me a Papa John's polo. "Here, put this on."

"Where did you get that?" I ask, licking my finger after I put the last M&M in place. I'm no artist, but it looks pretty good, if I do say so myself.

She ignores me entirely and puts her finger against the window. "See that house up there? I need you to ring the doorbell, make small talk with the girl with short blue hair for as long as possible, then walk up to the top of the street and I'll pick you up. Any questions?" I'm about to open my mouth when she says, "Good. Ready. Set. Break."

We open the car doors and get out quickly. The Papa John's polo is almost as long as my smock, and I think it's fair to say I look ridiculous. I walk up to the doorbell with my heart racing and pizza in hand, wondering what it is that I've gotten myself into. My anxiety is exacerbated when from the corner of my eye, I see Bugg run through the side of the yard and disappear around the house. I ring the doorbell once, then a second time. Finally, I hear footsteps and the girl with short blue hair appears.

"I didn't order a pizza." She's opened the door enough to fit her face through, and I try not to look like a deer in the headlights. Bugg in no way prepared me for this.

"It's complimentary," I say, the lie coming out surprisingly easy, or maybe not so surprising, considering my propensity for the nontruth. "Every month we choose someone at random from our list of delivery contacts."

"I'm a vegan now," she says and the porch light above me is so bright I wonder how long it will take my forehead to start perspiring.

"Oh really? Me too!" Except for the nachos I just ate. "Well, I've been *trying* for, like, eight months, ever since

I took this class about nutrition and animal rights, but it's harder than it seems." She must sense that my excitement is genuine because she opens the door fully. "But I'm sure that starting tomorrow my willpower will be stronger than cheese power, which honestly rivals solar power."

She gives me a half smile. "Don't be too hard on yourself. You have a shit job for trying to go vegan." She reaches into her pocket to hand me a few dollars, which makes me feel like a pile of dog doo.

"No, no, I get paid plenty by the hour. Thanks, though." I hand her the pizza and avoid her tip. I'm about to sprint off when I remember that Bugg said to stall. "We're, uh, trying to rally to join the union, raise the minimum wage, have equal pay for women, and stuff, so it'd be a break in values to accept tips."

"Well, good luck with that." She has as much hopefulness in her voice as I have for my personal future. "The patriarchy's a bitch."

As the door slams I walk away quickly, hoping that she doesn't open it again before I've disappeared. When I see Bugg's headlights up ahead, I start running.

"Wooooooooo!" she hoots as I open the door and get in, sweaty and panting. "Mission accomplished!" She smacks my knee a little too hard and I try to steady my hands.

"What exactly did we accomplish?" I ask, taking the stiff shirt off and throwing it into the back seat.

"This is good shit, Danny. GOOD SHIT," she yells out

the window, then reaches into the console and pulls out a small pipe shaped like a dragon.

"But what is it?"

"Um, only my good luck charm, which my ex-girlfriend stole from me, then refused to give back when I was released from St. John's. I've been *destitute* without it."

My heart hops to the right at the word "girlfriend" and I let all of that sink in. "Wait, am I *enabling* you?"

She snorts. "Danny, relax. Weed is basically better for you than Tylenol. But I wasn't in treatment for smoking weed. You helped out a friend is all." She looks over at me with a smile on her face that makes the magnetism in the car nearly sickening. That, or the tequila has finally caught up with me.

We get back to Sara's and Bugg thanks me for my help. By the sound of it, the party got on fine without me and Bugg doesn't seem to need me anymore, so I start walking toward the house, trying to figure out what the hell just happened.

"Hey, Danny," she calls.

Calm down, I tell my heart because it can't be healthy for a pulse to accelerate so quickly. (On the plus side, I might get my cardio in every time she says my name.) When I'm ready to turn around I'm really not ready to turn around. Her chin is leaning against the car window and she looks beautiful, in an objective way.

"Do you want to come to the poetry thing Sara mentioned on Thursday?"

I tug at my smock and try not to look too much at her. Even though I haven't agreed to anything, she scribbles something on a piece of rolling paper and holds it out to me. "Meet me at this address at one o'clock on Thursday." It dances a little in the wind, slips from her fingers, and starts to blow away.

I chase it down the driveway and step on it. "What should I—" I start, because obviously I'm incapable of saying no, not to her or to Sara or to anybody, but she's already backing out of the driveway. She sticks her hand out the window, I guess as a sort of good-bye.

The second her car disappears I feel the dullness of the regular world and count the hours left in the four days before I see her next.

CHAPTER FIVE

"You can touch it," she says.

"Okay." My heart is beating fast because I'm kind of into it, and not like I'm into peanut butter Twix bars. I'm *into* it. I reach my hand out and touch her long red hair. It slips like silk through my fingers and I get the chills. I'm about to lean in and smell it, which is probably creepy, when she starts yelling, "Danny! What the hell are you doing? I need you to hold my hair back, not scalp me."

I blink my eyes open and try to figure out where I am. Then it all comes into focus—the pink walls, the death grip I have on Sara's ponytail.

"Oh, it's you." I'm too sleepy to be embarrassed, though I'm sure that'll come soon enough.

"Well, yeah, who did you think it was?"

I rub my eyes. The tequila is definitely to blame, but it's still not a good look to wake up stroking your best friend's head. I manufacture a lie.

"My mom. I dreamed that, uh, she was sick. And I was taking care of her."

"*I'm* the one who's sick." She holds up her trash can full of pink and orange vomit. "I thought you heard me puking and were consoling me. God, I'm hungover."

I sit up, feeling the solid brick of guilt and dairy in my stomach, which is reason number a million why finally committing to veganism today is imperative. At the rate I'm digesting, I'll be lucky to poop before I'm twenty.

"Don't worry, I'm sure the pool people will be able to clean the puke out of it."

"I threw up in the pool?" Sara props herself up on one of her twenty useless decorative pillows.

"Oops. I thought you remembered." I pull the sheet over my head to avoid the smell of vomit and try to wish the hangover away.

"I don't remember much past seeing you in the kitchen." She sounds totally unfazed by this, which is good, because I have enough anxiety about it for the two of us.

I've only blacked out once, and once was enough for me: I seemed totally functional, albeit louder and stupider, but then I started broadcasting my secrets to anyone who would listen—including my college roommates, who then told my dean, and then, well, the rest is history.

"So you met Bugg through yoga class?" I ask casually, my voice slightly muffled by the sheet.

"Mhm. My coach recommended it. She's a cool girl. Definitely a little weird, like one time she asked me seriously if I believe in fairies, but something about her reminds me of you. I'm glad you got to meet because we're totally going to hang out all the time now."

I'd rather feed on live mice for the next few months than hang out with the two of them together, but it's impossible to dissuade Sara once she has an idea. And I do want to hang out with Bugg, not because the dream meant anything, but because maybe it *would* be good to talk—not necessarily about *treatment*, but about *something*.

"Are you okay?" I ask Sara, and I almost add, *because it seems like you're drinking a lot, and since when do you smoke weed?* but then I remind myself that everyone in college drinks this much and also probably smokes weed. I was the only one who seemed to hate both things, which then got me dubbed Fun Suck on Campus. Not that anyone ever called me that, but sometimes I can read minds.

"Yeah, I'll be fine," Sara says, and I wish I could see her face, but that would require me to emerge from the safety of the covers. "My sorority sisters taught me a great hangover cure."

"Cool."

I hope I don't sound jealous because I'm not jealous. I am lying in bed with the sheet over my head because that's what my highest self would do.

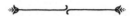

When my mom gets home from work that night she's very concerned about whether I'm readjusting to civilian life okay. I wondered the same thing about her when she realized that being an aging hippie wasn't going to sustain her emotionally or monetarily so she went back to school to be a real-estate agent. It's still funny to see her in slacks and blazers when she used to wear ripped overalls and two long braids, but I guess at some point we all have to grow up.

"How are you, sweetie? How was your party?" she asks, adjusting her watch on her wrist. I hate that she looks so concerned. It's definitely the worst part about all this. It was easy to say college was dandy via text, but I lost a lot of credibility when I could only use the hospital phone.

"Fine and fine," I say, with semiforced chipperness. Even though it's nearly dinnertime, I'm still a little woozy, either from last night's tequila or the Bugg interaction or both.

"Glad to hear it. Also, this came for you in the mail."

She hands me a thick envelope and I roll my eyes. It's from You-Know-Where.

"What did they do, put this together and send it before I even left? What bastards," I say, throwing it down on the counter.

"They're dotting their i's and crossing their t's, sweetie. Honestly, we paid too much money for them not to."

I grip the counter for support, but still the guilt seems to pulse from the marble. I feel lousy enough for spending the last half of spring semester at the equivalent of a well-decorated loony bin, far from the Ivy League college where my parents dropped me off. Is it also necessary to know that my subpar coping mechanisms cost them their next three vacations?

"I'll deal with it tomorrow. Right now I have to start looking for med-school-worthy internships. I'm going to apply to at least fifteen between today and tomorrow, and also I'm going to a poetry class later this week." The last thing I need is for my parents to think I'm becoming a blob in addition to a screwup.

"Oh, how wonderful! I didn't know you like poetry." She starts getting stuff out of the refrigerator for dinner, a meal I hope she doesn't think I'm partaking in.

"I don't like poetry."

"Then why are you going?"

Unfortunately I can't give her a good answer, at least not one I'd want to admit to her or myself. The only time I've been interested in artsy-fartsy stuff was when Bugg passed me poems on a series of dirty napkins during our riveting time in treatment. Not that that says anything about poetry. It was so boring in there that I often painted my nails just to watch them dry.

I give my mother a knowing look. "Life begins outside your comfort zone," I tell her, which is something they loved to say in treatment.

My poor mother, though, never realizes when I'm being an asshole, so she takes her blazer off, freeing her arms to hug me harder. "It'll keep your brain well greased for when you go back to Harvard in the fall," she says, pulling away to peer into a Styrofoam container of leftover grossness. "Do you know how lucky you are to be there? Thousands of kids would kill for your experience."

"No kidding." I almost add that I feel like I'm killing myself to have it too, but that seems like an unnecessary contribution to an otherwise sunny conversation.

As I'm about to excuse myself on account of needing to chew my fingernails down to stubs, a carpenter ant comes out of the woodwork and my mom slams her palm down on it. "I'm so proud of you," she says, flicking it into the trash.

I smile, even though my insides are recoiling. It's not that she could've used a paper towel to do her murdering, it's that "proud" isn't remotely close to the adjective I'd use to describe myself.

Later that night I start half-heartedly filling out an application to volunteer at the local hospital. I can answer my age and education fine, but I feel like a fraud saying I'm capable of having someone else's life in my hands; I can hardly keep my own life in my hands.

I give up a few minutes later and lie in bed with my journal out. Technically my journal is a diary, but I can't call it that because it's bad for my image. Journaling was one of the activities You-Know-Where mandated I do to glue my soul back together, but I've come to find out I like it a lot, mostly because of the unlined pages. As a recovering Goody Two-shoes, it feels so deliciously wrong to write anywhere I want on the page that I often consider becoming a full-time badass instead of a full-time life saver or however doctors refer to themselves. I have the journal divided into two sections: other people's poetry and personal entries. The poetry section is labeled with sticky notes that say things like "Look here if your soul is as empty as Walmart the night before Christmas," or "Read me if you're feeling as worthwhile as a recyclable bag of flaming dog shit." Then below the sticky note is some work of sheer poetic brilliance (passed along to me by Bugg because I hate poetry) that I've hand-copied, word for word. I don't type any of the poems or print them off the Internet because that's cheating. I don't know why it's cheating, but I'm certain it is.

Today I flip to my personal entries mostly because I want to see what I wrote about Bugg. I tighten my ponytail and prepare to be thoroughly embarrassed as I read the section labeled "The Dark Ages":

4/23 (In the Bathroom by the Dining Hall):
You'd think that upon damning me to eating disorder rehab my dean would mention something about the social hierarchy in places like this—like, say, I don't know, THAT THERE IS ONE. The cliques here are worse than middle school, high school, and college combined. If you don't fall into the right one by day ten, you're screwed out of the good activities. And if you don't fall into one at all, you can flush away your chances of a normal, healthy life altogether (pun not intended). Whatever. If Sara were here, she'd stage a rebellion and become Queen Bee herself, then I could be her faithful sidekick. If I learned anything in college, it's that a sidekick is pretty useless without its mainkick. Hypothesis: If we'd stayed true to The Plan, I wouldn't be in this predicament. Also, do you know that every meal tastes like it was meant for somebody's cat? No vegan options (I'll have to resume veganism when I'm out) and I have to eat it all in a certain amount of time and then they

watch me after. Like I'm going to vom in a public bathroom. Please.

4/24 (After Dinner):

Located another lone wolf. She stares at me a lot, which is a little unnerving and also flattering. Either I'm way more gorgeous than I've been giving myself credit for or she knows I'm not cut out for Clique Life either. We went to the same activity today and I watched her glue a feather to a piece of construction paper. It's goddamn kindergarten up in here except everyone's crazy. When lunch was over she threw this napkin at me and at first I thought she confused me for the trash, which would be totally understandable, but then I realized she wrote two words on it: WILD GEESE. I've spent the last hour googling "Wild Geese" like it contains the cure for cancer. It doesn't, but Mary Oliver's poetry does seem to help a certain malignancy.

4/28 (Kind of Giddy):

Girl Red and I communicate nearly entirely with looks, besides the eighteen napkins she's thrown at me, each containing a line of "Wild Geese." I'm afraid to talk to her because I think it'll ruin the whole mute thing we've got going on. Meanwhile the therapists say I'm doing great. My pants feel tight but at least this legging-as-pants trend is still trending.

4/29 (Dispatch from the Dining Hall):
There's been contact with a foreign object: looked like a hand, felt like life from another universe. Occurred east of the white rice and west of the mixed greens. I was holding the tongs used only for the green beans when Girl Red put down the white-rice spoon and then . . . contact. A stirring. (Of the food, mainly.)

4/30 (In the Middle of the Night):
Just woke up after a very disturbing dream about Girl Red. Need to wash my underwear ASAP. Like, who am I? Is it normal for a freshman in college not to have had a boyfriend? Ugh, I'm the last person who'd ever be chosen to draw boundaries on the map "Normal."

5/1 (In Bed with Headlamp):
Code Red. Where's Girl Red? She didn't have to say good-bye, but she could've at least waved.

I close my journal and sigh. There's no point in denying the hunch I have when I'm around her, which is that the big hunger, i.e., the worst kind of aching human hunger, will be satisfied if I can touch her. Because, see, the big hunger isn't anything celery or even cheeseburgers can fix. It's the grumbling emptiness of needing to kiss another person, but not *any* person. My prom date, Billy Taylor, was "any person," and everyone else in the world is "any person" too.

Well not *everyone* else. I'm counting on there being one exception.

CHAPTER SIX

I spend the next few days madly applying to hospital internships and volunteer positions and want ads for lab rats. Each time I start an application, though, I run into the same problem I did before and so have about sixteen documents listing only my name and age. The issue with planning your future is you have to plan for it before it's already happening.

When I'm taking a break from applications to torture myself on the elliptical in the basement, Sara texts me about coming to a yoga class with her. I agree to come if she buys me a juice, which is how we end up at the Coffee

Place with her getting our usual: French toast bagel with hazelnut cream cheese. It's all I can do not to get it too, but then I remind myself how gloomy the prospect is of wearing a smock for the rest of my youth.

"A green monster, please," I say at the counter. There's an illuminated doughnut sign on the wall behind the register, and the air is so thick with buttery gluttony it's hard to breathe. I force a smile when I'm handed a large cup of green sludge.

"Doesn't that taste like ass?" Sara asks, with her mouth full of bagel.

"Yeah, like a tight ass."

She rolls her eyes at me and I don't tell her she has cream cheese on her mouth.

"You're beautiful, Danny. Don't make me bully you into believing it." I turn around to leave and she pinches my butt so hard I nearly choke on all my liquid vegetables. I pinch hers back and the person behind the counter looks at us like we're twelve, which is exactly how old I feel. She jumps on my back and I carry her to the car.

"You've muled the last two times. It's my turn next," Sara says when I deposit her at the door. I lean back to catch my breath, and the metal of the car is hot on my back.

"No, thank you. If we wanted to break your back, we could do it in much more interesting ways."

While we drive, Sara talks my ear off about Ethan and

their fancy date last night and how they drank champagne and how now she has a champagne headache.

"You poor thing." I frown dramatically in her direction. "Last night I talked to my air conditioner until three a.m."

"We're gonna find you a boyfriend," Sara says matter-of-factly, and I wonder if it's ever occurred to her that I might not want one. "This summer is gonna be *the* summer. He'll be sweet and smart, and we'll finally have a place to put your V card." I look out the window and count the pieces of visible litter on the side of the road, wishing I didn't always feel like I was carrying another Danny on my shoulders.

At the studio Sara hands me her extra yoga mat and starts talking about "connecting with my body." In spite of the yellow-polka-dot walls and tired aphorisms stenciled in glitter, I'm the tiniest bit interested. I've never heard Sara talk about anything this way; she's not competitive about it and doesn't want a lot out of it like she does tennis and guys. As we lay our mats in the back corner of the room (upon my request), I start thinking that maybe Sara and I can't ever be who we were before, but we can be someone older.

I'm about to try to nap when Bugg walks into the room, causing my stomach to drop into my pelvis. There's no staying cool as Sara waves her over—there's something too unsettling about the two of them together. I know the definition of a fake person is someone who acts differently depending on who they're with, but how else am I supposed to know how to be? Luckily, the instructor comes in and tells us to lie down and shut up, well not quite like that, but either way it saves me from a three way. Like, a three-way conversation with Bugg on my left and Sara on my right.

"Never thought I'd see you here, Danny," Bugg whispers, then leans over me in a huge wave of cinnamon and cigarettes. I wonder why Bugg thinks she's above the lie down/shut up message. "Sara, what sort of sexual favor did you have to offer her?"

My face heats up like a bad idea.

"Terrible, terrible things have been promised," Sara whispers back, then pokes me. "Just kidding, I asked nicely. That's the best thing about Danny. She only pretends to be against everything, but you can get her to do anything."

I throw one of the blocks at Sara and the instructor looks over at us with a very nonpeaceful, nonyogic look.

"What? It's a good thing that you're a chameleon!"

The class gets going and it's not as terrible as I expected, but it's definitely not something I feel I need to do again before I'm fifty. The piece of linguine teaching the class has us putting our bodies in all sorts of positions, which makes my stomach rise up out of my yoga pants like pizza crust in the oven, expanding and expanding, so that my tank top comes up. I peek over at Bugg's mat and realize the same thing is happening to her except it looks *good* on her, sexy even, maybe because her face looks so happy. I don't want Sara to think I'm checking Bugg out so I look at Sara too, and make like I'm confused about what to do (which isn't inaccurate). Sara, on the other hand, looks like a yogic angel, bending over herself like bones are nothing. At one point I end up sitting down on my mat and looking around at everyone wondering what it is that I like to do, because clearly this is not it.

As we pack up to go, Sara and Bugg are talking and I figure I should make a quick getaway, in case Bugg is telling her all of my secrets. It's not that I'm threatened by their friendship; I just think I'd sleep better if they didn't know each other. I walk over to them armed with an excuse about having to jog home to work out a kink in my hamstring so that I can help my parents clean the garage.

"Still see you tomorrow?" Bugg asks, and I don't know why I'm so horrified that Sara might know we're going to a poetry class together, but she's engrossed in her cell phone anyway. I praise Jesus for modern medicine, i.e., technology, then nod and sprint for home. Well, maybe sprint is too strong a word for it.

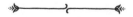

At one o'clock on Thursday I arrive at the Yellow House Studio. I hate to be critical, but considering it's a place dedicated to creativity, I think the Yellow House Studio, which is a *yellow house* and a *studio*, could have been a little more creative with its name. I look around for Bugg but don't see her, so I approach the porch, where a woman with a long neck and purple lipstick is sitting.

"Hello, dear," the woman greets me, as if we've been searching the ends of the earth for each other and have finally met after a hundred years of separation.

"Hi, I'm Danny, here for the poetry class? I'm not enrolled or anything. My friend...well, she's *sort of* my friend, told me about it and—"

"Danny, yes, don't worry, Bugg mentioned you might show up." She stands to give me a hug and I wonder why she's wearing an apron, especially such a violent one. The cartoon carrots, beets, and broccoli are spurting blood and tears, and the knife that's drawn to look like it's coming from her pocket is dripping green, orange, and purple.

"I'm Cynthia. I'll be leading the poetry workshop." Her voice is soft and doesn't fit the vegetable-serial-killer tone of the apron at all. "Tell me, how do you like your eggs, Danny?"

"Sorry?"

"You can tell a lot about a person by how they like their eggs."

"Oh...usually I'm a vegan." Well, *usually* is a bit of a stretch. "But scrambled, I suppose."

She grins and takes a tube of lipstick from the pocket of her apron. It looks sweaty and displeased to be uncapped. "Interesting. I eat mine nearly raw." Visions of salmonella swirl in my head while she applies the lipstick, still making direct eye contact with me. I think it's some sort of test and I shift from one foot to the next, wondering if I've passed.

"Here, I have a name tag for you." She puts the lipstick away and hands me a sticky piece of paper from her other pocket that says DANDELION. I want to ask how she knows the horrendous legal name my parents gave me back in their hippie days, but that seems rude, considering the time she's taken with it. The letters are curled, and in the top right corner she's drawn a yellow flower. I put it above my left boob, which, frankly, is the nicer of the two.

"Come on in. The classroom is in the back. You're going to love our group." She goes on to tell me in a humble way how her dad was this famous poet-slash-professor who died a couple of years ago and wanted his estate to be a place for writers. "I'm doing my best with it."

I tell her it's great because it is. The ceilings are tall and the walls are papered with tiny white flowers. Plus, it smells like pie. Score. Then we get to the back room and there's a large wooden table with people seated around it. My heart does this weird fluttery thing when I see Bugg. I feel like I have to do something, so I do the worst thing imaginable and give her two thumbs-up. *Two thumbs-up.* She sticks her tongue out at me.

"Welcome, everyone," Cynthia says, taking a seat at the head of the table. "This is my favorite class to teach because we're going to dive deep into our creative and emotional selves over the next eight weeks. If you all don't cry at least once, I will consider myself a failure."

She winks and it isn't corny. Even though I'd rather sever my taste buds than cry in a room full of people, I have to admit there's something nice about her, despite the dystopian lip color, vegetable-serial-killer apron, and strange little haircut. I sneak a look at Bugg. She's also looking at me. Where do you find velvet overalls and how is she not sweating herself into an aquatic life-form?

"To write the perfect poem, you have to be perfect, then write a poem," Cynthia continues. I gulp, hoping perfection is a metaphor. While she describes the methods of achieving said perfection—lots of writing prompts and a mandatory thirty minutes a day of journal writing—I look around at the people who *volunteered* for this: an older man with thick-framed glasses, a younger guy with gauges, and a nervous-looking woman with gray-streaked hair. "Poetry isn't strictly poems. It's about taking your raw material and cooking yourself," Cynthia explains, and I shiver despite the heat. That explains the apron...sort of. "Over the next few weeks, you'll be writing to develop your voice as a writer in preparation for the final assignment, which will

be a credo you write to yourself. I'm not going to say anything else about it because I don't want to ruin the surprise,
but keep in mind that you're working to get closer to your
truest center. Now let's do introductions."

Everyone in the room smiles and shifts in their chairs.
My stomach starts to feel queasy. How am I going to get
through eight weeks of this artsy-fartsy emotional stuff,
especially in the company of Bugg?

"How about your name and why you write," Cynthia
suggests, and we start going around the table. The introductions are as awkward as you would expect given the cast
of characters, and I wish I had a Life Saver or something to
occupy my mouth. Bugg and I are the last to go.

"I'm Sally Bugg." She pauses and pulls a little bit at one
of the curls hanging by her waist. "I write," she says slowly,
"because it's the one thing I've never felt I could lose."

Bugg's sleeveless blouse is buttoned up all the way
under her overalls, and her arms are husky and very white
except for a few doodle-like tattoos on her wrists. She has
a small brown leather notebook in front of her and a pen
with a fuzzy end like you get at the second-grade book fair.
It's not that I didn't notice this the other night or a couple
of months ago, but it's worth saying again that she's beautiful. And I can say that because any human can acknowledge the beauty of another human, just like a ceramic pot
can acknowledge the craftsmanship of another ceramic
pot. Chances are it's not sexual. It's *artisanal*.

"Lovely," Cynthia says. "Absolutely lovely." I can tell she's going to be saying that a lot. "Danny?" She turns to me and it's so silent I can almost hear the sun cast shadows on the table.

I make intense eye contact with a water stain a few inches from my hand, and begin. "Um, I don't really write. I keep a journal but it's not literature or anything, and I'd probably have to take someone hostage if they read it. But sometimes when I'm writing it feels less like I'm drowning—only slightly less, but less." In my peripherals I see a few people nod solemnly. I have a feeling they also paint their toenails black to properly reflect their souls.

"Lovely," Cynthia says again. "Let's get started, then." She takes out her notebook and we all do the same. I can't believe I've taken my journal into the public domain, but it'd feel wrong to write in anything else. When she dumps a pack of sharpened pencils onto the table, we each take one then look at her expectantly.

"Let's go for fifteen minutes and the prompt is 'Things that make you cold.'"

The room becomes silent except for the sound of pencils scribbling. I look at mine impatiently then tap it on the table, wondering how I ended up with the constipated #2. I start nibbling on the eraser, which I haven't done since fourth grade when Sara enumerated the ways it was not only gross, but likely to give me an oral infection.

A few minutes pass. I write a thing or two down, wonder how many calories there are in the granola bar I packed, feel a pimple forming on my chin.

"Three minutes," Cynthia warns.

As I add my last bullet she points to me. "Read for us, my dear."

I blink. Where was the call for a volunteer? Surely this is a violation of workshop etiquette. My face is very warm. I think my upper lip is sweating. I clear my throat in an attempt to get more air into my lungs and begin.

"Things that make me cold: One: car rides to unfamiliar places. Two: ice cubes, ice storms, and ice hockey. Three: when my therapist brings up my eating habits, which are subpar at best, but better than they were when they were worse. Four: the thought that bones are alive. Five: department stores with too much AC. Six: people with very white teeth. Seven: vegan promises I can't seem to keep." I go on for a little bit longer, feeling more and more embarrassed, which must show in the unprecedented amount of blood that's rushed to my face.

When I'm done, my hands are trembling but there's an unfamiliar lightness in my body. Cynthia thanks me for letting her put me on the spot. "Free writes are great for revealing our subconscious thoughts. Reading them is good too. Embarrassing of course, but it'll make you more confident writers." She smiles her purple-lipped smile. "Are you set to share your poem this week, Bugg?"

Bugg nods, then starts. "September." Her voice is husky and she speaks noticeably slowly, not like she doesn't have enough to say but like every word is important enough to not be swallowed by the next.

> *As far down as Virginia*
> *they turn and fall*
> *there's nothing human about them*
> *but their scent*
> *is there any scent as sweet*
> *as dying leaves?*

She looks up and we make eye contact because I'm too slow at looking away. Cynthia sets the timer for fifteen minutes and the workshopping begins. Philip, the younger guy, thinks the title could use more work, Larry wants her to play with line breaks, something about the enjambment not working, and Irene loves it. Simply loves it. As for me, I alternate between staring at her and the water stain on the table and then back at her again.

"Danny, is there anything you want to add?"

Gotta appreciate Cynthia's effort to throw me a line. "Nope, it was baller." Which is a word I've never said before and immediately regret saying now. "Particularly the ending."

"Baller, yes, excellent. Well, I think that's good for

today. I made lavender lemonade if you guys want to hang out outside for a bit and get to know each other."

I would like nothing less, but sometimes social duties call. Besides, when I end up failing this class I'm going to need something to guarantee my A.

You're not getting graded for this, idiot.

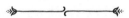

Outside, I stand apart from everyone else and drink my lemonade and wonder how long it'll take Bugg to come over and talk to me. The yard is lush and smells nice, like grass and cherry blossoms, but I'm too nervous to enjoy the world in bloom.

"So what'd you think?" Bugg asks from behind me.

I turn around and she's standing there in her velvet overalls looking impossibly cool. I probably just look impossible.

"It was interesting." I smooth out my smock and drain my lemonade. "Definitely not as cringeworthy as I expected it to be."

She doesn't say anything for a few seconds, so I start counting the birds in the tree above us. I get to six when she says, "You know, my horoscope said I'd have a coincidental chance encounter that would change the shape of my whole summer. This might be it."

"I don't do horoscopes. And this wasn't a coincidence. You *invited* me."

She kicks off her Jesus sandals and has a seat in the grass. "I was thinking about the other night," she says, plucking one strand of grass at a time and collecting them in her palm. "And I think you should know I'm not a weasel. If you want to pretend St. John's didn't happen, then I'll pretend with you, but I do think it's messed up."

"Thanks, Friend Police. But you don't know Sara like I know Sara. You don't know the pressure that comes with being her friend." I crush my plastic cup and a forgotten drop of lemonade falls to the ground. It's just like Sara to magically befriend the only semi-friend I made without her. I extend my pinky in Bugg's direction. "Promise to keep it on the DL for now?"

She hooks her pinky in mine and we hold each other to it for a few seconds too long. Finally, she reaches into her leather fringe bag and takes out rolling papers and tobacco, then starts to make a cigarette.

"The list you read was nice." She works with her thumb and pointer finger, pinching the tobacco from the pouch and sprinkling it evenly onto the paper before rolling it back and forth until it forms the cigarette shape. When she runs her tongue along the edge to seal it, she looks up at me and I get an uncontrollable case of goose bumps.

"Thanks." I clear my throat a little too loudly. "I liked your poem a lot."

"You think? I've been trying to write it for a few years. I finally gave up a few months ago, and then last week I was scrambling an egg but I didn't have any clean forks so I had to use a spoon and then it came to me." She takes a lighter to her finished work, then blows the smoke in my face.

"Ew, can't you massacre your lungs someplace else? Things that can kill you don't belong in the sunshine."

"Of course they do. Death is the most brilliant part of life. And no, I can't. I'm too comfortable right here." She tilts her head back and her hair falls into the grass. I nearly have to sit on my hands to keep myself from touching it, which I guess is leftover muscle memory from my ridiculous dream. "Okay, I've been thinking a lot about it over the past few seconds, and here's what I've decided: We don't have to talk about the past if you insist upon it—"

"I insist upon it."

"But you can't argue that we had something special. Sometimes fate puts two people together once, and sometimes fate puts two people together twice. Maybe this is our second chance."

I frown in her direction. "I'm going to gag if you keep talking about fate."

She bites her lip between drags, and I start thinking about suspension—not the kind where you get to miss school, but the throbbing seconds between two outcomes: This versus That, so-called fate taken or so-called fate missed.

"Come over tonight. I'll make you dinner."

I hesitate. But I can tell I've already begun to fall.

"Okay." I hope my voice sounds more confident than I feel. "But I'm a vegan today."

She gets up and pats my shoulder. "I was a vegan once too, until a piece of bacon saved my life."

CHAPTER SEVEN

I feel too excited about dinner at Bugg's to focus on anything, but right now I don't have a choice. Part of the reason I got to come home from treatment was that I agreed to be "cooperative." Cooperative means that my parents are in constant communication with my therapist and doctors and dean so that we can all be certain I'm ready to go back to Harvard in the fall. Cooperative also means filling out this stupid survey that came in the mail, which I can't even do online. Hasn't anyone at You-Know-Where heard of e-mail before?

I sit down at the kitchen table with the packet, wondering

what fun thing Sara is doing with Ethan while I struggle through the prime of my life.

First question:

Pick your unit.

I can do this. I can do anything as long as it's multiple choice.

a) Eating disorder recovery, b) Mental illness recovery, c) Alcohol & drug addiction recovery.

Well, how many questions are we talking? I flip through the pages and feel a pit growing in my stomach.

How did you find the food? Was there too much free time? Too much support group time? Too much one-on-one time? Would you have preferred a separation of units at mealtimes? At free time?

Jesus, if I wanted to relive the whole experience I'd have asked for a permanent residency. I put the packet down. Thinking about treatment makes me feel like I can't breathe—not because there's not enough air in the room, but because I'm suddenly allergic to it. I'm getting itchier and hotter, so I wander into the bathroom and get on the scale for the first time in two months. I don't mean to take it out of the cabinet and stand on it, but I also never mean to jerk my leg when a doctor taps on my knee. Unfortunately, some reflexes are more harmful than others.

I get off the scale and want to throw it out the window. No, I want to throw up. I don't even want to. I *need* to. *It's just a thought; you're not your thoughts.* I can't throw up. I can't throw up because a) I haven't done that in two months and b) I'd like to not spend two more months in the place that got me to stop doing that for two months.

Instead, like the A+ Recovered Patient that I am, I go into my room and try the breathing exercise Leslie, my therapist, has been teaching me. It's touted for being "simple and accessible," but it's nothing more than a deep breath they've invented a complicated term for: Three-Part Pause-and-Go Stress Reduction Breath. I lie on the floor like the therapy junkie I've yet to become and picture the air filling my stomach, then my ribs, then my chest, all the way up to my collarbone. I pause at the top and notice the parts of my body making contact with the floor: back of the skull, scapula. *One, two, three.* I exhale slowly. By the time I'm twenty-five they'll have found a way to sell my own breath back to me.

I still feel anxious, so I open the e-mail Cynthia sent us with the writing exercises for the week. They're optional— maybe everything in life is—but it couldn't hurt to do a couple. I take my journal out and write according to the prompt, losing track of time until my dad interrupts me.

"Danny?" he says, opening my bedroom door and poking his head in.

I close my journal quickly. "Definitely don't knock, Dad. It's not like I change in here, or, I don't know, have a basic right to privacy."

"Sorry, sorry, you were so quiet I didn't even think you were home."

He seems too tall for the doorway and he keeps turning the knob nervously, making an annoying rhythmic squeaking. He could've at least brought some WD-40.

"Here I am. Home. In my room." I stand up so we're at least closer to eye-level, brushing bits of debris from the floor off my legs.

"And we're so happy you're home. How are you, kiddo? You adjusting okay?"

I've never seen a face want something so much. It makes it hard to be mad at him for going MIA. Not that I needed him in treatment, but it would've been nice to know that he could show up for both my high school graduation *and* loony bin visitor hours—you know, the good, the bad, *and* the ugly.

"Yeah, I feel fine," I say coolly. And I am fine, minus gaining ten more pounds than freshmen usually gain, but finally committing to veganism and regular sessions on the elliptical will take care of that.

"Good. Your mother and I are here for you, Danny. I'm sorry I wasn't more there physically; it's hard for me because—"

But I don't need to hear how jarring it was for him to discover that I'm light-years from perfection. "Don't worry about it." I make my way past him into the hallway. "I forgive you or whatever."

"But—"

"No, really. As much as I'd like to have a heart-spilling session together, I have to go meet a friend."

I stare him down until he closes my door and the click of the latch tells me I've won. "Well, tell Sara I say hi."

"It's not Sara," I say incredulously. "Is it so unbelievable that I'd connect with another human being besides her?" Maybe sensing that he can't say anything right, my dad resorts to taking off his glasses and cleaning them with his dirty T-shirt. I don't outwardly acknowledge the pointlessness of this exercise. I have my own menagerie of nonsensical habits to tend to. I walk down the hall into the kitchen, where his car keys hang on a hook sculpted into the tail of a mockingbird. The rest of the bird is stenciled around the hook, I guess to make it seem like the bird is looking back at you, but the mix of two and three dimensions is remarkably unconvincing.

"Is it cool if I take your car?" I ask, but this is a pity-ask. Not only is he into biking these days, but I overheard him telling my mom that he feels so guilty about never coming to visit me that he might give me his car for the summer. And that is the glory of capitalism: the exchange of material objects to cover up our shortcomings.

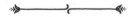

When I show up nervous and sweaty to the address Bugg gave me, I feel like I should be wearing a ball gown, not the smock in mom-salmon. I think Sara's house is big, but Bugg's house looks like it ate Sara's house and is now pregnant with it. I lean out the window of my dad's car and press the buzzer that's located on the sidewalk. "It's Danny."

"Coming!" The crinkled sound of Bugg's voice through the intercom makes me grip the steering wheel harder. The gates open and I drive around the fountain, the *fountain*, in the middle of the driveway, and Bugg comes running out in her velvet overalls. Not that I know anything about it, but she looks like the antithesis of girls who live in places like these.

"Sorry, I meant to unlock the gates before you got here. They're *so* obnoxious." She leans her elbows on the open window, where my elbow is also leaning. We're close enough that I think maybe our arm hairs are exchanging follicle secrets.

"They're not obnoxious. They're *elite*." I turn the engine off and wish my nerves would power down too.

"Exactly." She opens the door for me. "Come inside. The chili is almost done. And don't worry, it's vegan."

We enter the walk-in refrigerator that is her house, and I take my shoes off. As I follow her into the kitchen, my bare feet make sticky noises on the floor, which doesn't help my self-consciousness in the least. To drown out the suction sounds I launch into a robot-esque spiel about the importance of veganism. My strongest point, which I try to frame as purely original and immensely profound, is that animals have feelings whereas plants do not. Bugg debunks this immediately while snipping bits of cilantro into the large pot on the stove.

"I call bullshit. Plants sense danger all the time and send distress signals to each other through the dirt or the air or, like, on messenger bees. They totally have feelings, but people don't care 'cause plants don't have *faces*."

I scowl. What is she, the Jane Goodall of kale?

Bugg puts two bowls of chili in front of us and we sit at the island, or she sits and I try to sit, but the stool is so tall that I have to pull it way out then climb onto it, then grab hold of the counter to scoot close enough to reach my elbows on the marble.

"You got that?" she asks, and I like when she smiles, even if it is at my expense.

"Totally." My foot brushes hers by mistake and goose bumps start at my feet then creep toward my stomach. "Except now I feel like an asshole eating all these plants."

She whips her hair around so that all the red curls fall over her other shoulder. It happens for me in slow motion, and I have to remind myself to close my mouth and look away to keep from eye-eating her. "So what's your deal?" she asks. "I moved to Scituate with my parents in January, but I haven't seen you around until recently."

I stir my chili nervously, occasionally holding a kidney bean under the surface to see if I'll receive its distress signal. Predictably, the only distress signal I receive is my own. "Well, I just got back from You-Know-Where, as you know, and before that I was floundering my way through my freshman year of college."

"As all freshmen do," Bugg says knowingly and asks which college.

"Just a small school in Cambridge."

She rolls her eyes. "I hate when people call it that. If you're worried about being pretentious, go to a different school." She looks at me. "Sorry, I can say that. I went to Brown and everyone always tried to pull that same shit: 'Oh, just a small school in *Providence.*'"

"Really? You went to Brown?" I hope I don't look surprised that a tutu-wearing, cigarette-smoking, low-key drug-dealing girl made it to an Ivy. "What year did you graduate?"

She makes a dismissive gesture with her hand, then scrapes the last of the chili into her mouth. "I never got around to graduating. Not that dropping out of a top-tier school is recommended. My parents sort of want to murder me, but only after they disown me." She smiles, but there's something in her face that isn't smiling. "Luckily, they're traveling this summer so I get their humble abode all to myself." She grimaces as she looks around the kitchen, and I become aware of a faint burning smell.

"Do you smell that?" I'm always afraid that I'm making things up, which makes it very relieving when someone else is in on my reality.

"Yeah?" She hops off the stool and goes over to the stove. "Damn, I dropped a bean in the flame." She turns off the gas and waves a towel up and down at the smoke alarm preemptively. The motion gives me a live-action cleavage shot and I find myself looking far longer than necessary at what is clearly a situation under control. The conversation turns back to Harvard, and I tell her the piece of The Plan that includes going to med school, becoming a surgeon, saving lives, making money, blah blah blah.

"So did you like it?" she asks, then points to my bowl and asks if I'm done.

"Yeah, it was delicious."

"No, I mean Harvard."

She takes our bowls to the sink, and for whatever reason I don't feel I have to pretend with her. "No," I finally say. "It was awful. Like, I was pretty disappointed when I was eleven and realized I was never going to Hogwarts, but Harvard was at least five hundred percent more disappointing than knowing I'm going to be a Muggle my whole life."

She snorts. "Because everyone was an elitist asshat?"

"Sort of?" I start ripping my paper napkin into confetti. "I think it was more that I wasn't good at any of the stuff I used to be good at, so studying wasn't fun anymore. No matter how hard I tried, I couldn't get anything higher than a C." It feels good to talk about something real with someone besides my therapist. Especially since I mostly lie to my therapist.

Bugg rinses the last dish and leans on the counter across from me, which brings up the cleavage issue again. "That's the problem with being a high school all-star. You're an addict for praise and good grades and all that bullshit. The second you stop getting them you go into withdrawals, and within six to ten weeks, you fall apart."

I look at my sad pile of ripped-up napkin, wishing I could reassemble it again, and continue. "Plus, living with roommates is total bullshit. They eat all your cereal, ask you nosy questions that you sometimes get drunk and answer, and if they hear you throwing up, like, *one time*, they tell your dean, who tells the school psychologist, who sends you off to treatment, like you're crazy, which *I'm not*. I mean, a little angsty, sure, but—"

She reaches across the counter and puts her hand on my hand and we have a moment: skin-to-skin contact, eye-to-eye contact, and something else too.

The thing is, I like her. Like, I like hanging out with her.

I move my hand away before my cheeks give away my feelings. "Anyway, I'm rambling. Why did you drop out?"

"I want to be a poet, not another bullshit egomaniac who gets off on being a hamster on an expensive wheel. It made me sick watching everyone compete for consulting jobs, living in their own screwed-up world but pretending everything is great. No one wants to admit that we're all there out of lucky circumstances. No one *deserves* to be there."

"It's not *just* luck," I say defensively, though truthfully I spent the last year thinking they meant to let someone named Shmandelion Burpowitz in off the waitlist, but accidentally sent the letter to me instead.

Bugg chews her fingernails thoughtfully. "All I know is that it screws you up being in a place like that, and I'm plenty screwed up on my own."

I study the squiggly tattoos on her wrists, wondering why anyone would go through the pain for nothing more than miscellaneous shapes.

"Since I was a kid all I wanted to do was go to an Ivy," I tell her. "I guess after wanting something for so long it sucks to face the reality of it."

"And what's the reality of it?" She inches closer to me, or I'm hallucinating. Honestly, I don't know which would be more petrifying.

"I don't know, a clusterfuck of disappointment, confusion, guilt, and all the other shit emotions we aren't tuned into enough to name."

She wraps a curl around her finger. "It's so funny to get exactly what we want. Because then we realize happiness has nothing to do with such shitty things."

I nod, even though I think happiness has everything to do with getting what I want. Then, without any warning, even though I've probably consumed an entire cooked onion, she puts her hand on my shoulder and leans in close.

"What are you doing?" I ask, trying to turn away from the feeling that's deep inside my stomach and very alive.

"You never thought about this at St. John's?"

"Well...yeah, but I figured I was sooooo bored, what with all the therapy sessions and group talks and stuff."

"Gee, thanks." She sounds a little hurt, but she doesn't pull away.

"No, I don't mean it like that. I've just never really been into other girls, so I figured I needed a distraction, you know?" My hands are so sweaty I could give a fish swimming lessons. Usually I'm a spectacular liar, but judging by the smile that's playing at the corner of her mouth, she's not buying it. "Not that I don't think you're beautiful and sexy and *very* cool—way cooler than I am, which would probably end up being a point of contention—but I can't picture us being *together.*"

She puts her other hand on my other shoulder and we're so close that looking into her eyes is like being inside a kaleidoscope: crazy repeating patterns of green and brown, punctuated by an iris as alluring as a black hole. The problem with lying is sometimes you can't sustain it anymore. The good thing about lying, though, is it eventually leads to the truth. Key word being *eventually.*

"And on top of that," I continue rambling, "you can't

kiss me out of the blue with no warning because I'm a very anxious person and I need time to put on lip balm and stuff."

"Fine." She takes one hand from my shoulder and places it on my bare thigh. "What if I ask first?"

But it isn't a question I can answer dishonestly anymore, not when I have a heartbeat in places I didn't know I could get a pulse. I say nothing, having been officially rendered mute, and look at her, trying to take it all in and make sense of it. Unfortunately, all rationality has gone shit out the window, so I nod stupidly, then she tilts her head slightly and leans in so that her lips are only a few centimeters from mine. My stomach feels like a bed of Pop Rocks. *Close your eyes, idiot.* And I do.

CHAPTER EIGHT

Lips.

That's what it feels like to kiss her. That and something I don't recognize but I trust, as if everything that was out of place is not. The big hunger is gone and for however many seconds there's clarity, the blissful sensation of her mouth and my mouth. Then the buzzer rings and the moment gets ripped off like duct tape, exposing me.

Bugg gets up and presses the button to listen. "Bugg? It's Sara. Are you home?"

I nearly fall off my chair, but just in my head. "Shit." My voice is squeaky with nerves. "She's going to see my car."

"So? It's okay for us all to be friends." Bugg clearly doesn't get the stakes here.

"Well, yeah, but friends don't make out in the kitchen." Or I'm desperately hoping I'm right and Bugg doesn't do this with everyone she invites over for dinner. "Don't say anything about this to Sara, got it?"

She nods, but I want more than a nod. I want a verbal agreement and later a signed contract. Bugg presses the button to open the gates, and I wipe any remnants of her kiss from my lips. A few minutes later Sara comes into the kitchen.

"I knew that was your dad's car! What are you doing here, Danny?" Sara gives me a kiss on the cheek, and I try not to seem flustered. The last three minutes have been a lot of lip-to-face interaction for me.

"Just eating some dinner." I wonder if she saw me and Bugg kissing through the windows or if the bushes are tall enough to keep our secrets.

"Well, I was kind of hoping to talk to you." For a second I think Sara's talking to me, you know, her best friend since kindergarten, but when I look up I realize she's talking to Bugg. "We can talk later, though," she says, then smiles at me.

"Couldn't we all talk?" What would Sara have to say that she couldn't say in front of me? A) I'm a fortress when it comes to secrets, especially my own. And b) I'VE BEEN HER BEST FRIEND SINCE KINDERGARTEN.

"It's yoga stuff," Sara says, and I get the distinct feeling she's lying to me. "I know how much you hate yoga, Danny."

"I don't *hate* it." What I'm starting to hate is this triangle thing we've got going on. "I just think that if I'm going to work out, I should *work out*, not roll around the floor like a chubby baby stuck on her back."

Sara and Bugg laugh and it kind of pisses me off. Three's a crowd, to be honest.

"Well, I'll let you two talk, then. My parents probably need a third in Scrabble anyway. Thanks for dinner," I say to Bugg, while trying to tell her with my eyes not to tell Sara anything that happened with our mouths.

"Danny," Bugg starts, but I wave her off and get out of the kitchen fast. My whole body is sweating when I get in my car, but I can't bring myself to leave yet. It's dark and quiet and I can feel my lips vibrating nearly imperceptibly. Whatever happened back there before Sara barged in, I want more of it. Infinitely more.

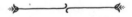

I'm too wound up from the kiss to sleep that night, so after ordering an MCAT practice book and filling out a few internship applications, I get in bed and finally address the 132 unread texts from the last two months. Nineteen of them are from Stephen, each more panicked than the last. It's the least I can do to give him a call.

"Danny, wow, hi," he answers. "How are you? How's medical leave treating you?"

"How do you know about med leave?" I ask incredulously.

"Well, when I came by your room for the fiftieth time demanding where you were, your roommates finally told me. I think they thought that I thought that they were keeping you tied up in the closet or something."

"Still, isn't that a violation of a person's basic right to privacy?" I grumble.

"Hey," he says quietly. "It's just me."

I shrink more under the covers, as if anything material can keep you hidden. "Right, well, how was the rest of your semester?" I ask.

"Pretty weird without you. I had to join a new lab-partner team 'cause you can't be lab partners with yourself."

"Oh, shit. Sorry." I switch the phone to the other ear so that both sides of my face can get equally sweaty.

"Yeah, *asshole*," he says jokingly, but Stephen is so nice I can tell it pains him to swear at me. "I'm glad you're taking care of yourself. Also, I've been so excited to tell you this: They fired that dick of a TA, the one who told you that you should try a different career path if you hate chemistry so much."

I sit up and immediately picture shoving pie in that TA's face, not that I'd ever waste pie like that. "Thank God. That guy was the reincarnation of Gollum. And even if it does feel good to know that he got what he deserved, the emotional damage he did is irreparable."

Stephen chuckles. "You're going to be a great doctor, don't worry." Then there's something resembling an awkward silence as if we both know maybe that's not true. "So, you *are* taking care of yourself, right?" he finally asks.

"Yeah. I am. As soon as I left campus I felt better. Like, all the pressure of being there went away. I'm probably just allergic to the chemicals they wash the bathrooms with."

"You're coming back, though, aren't you?"

"Yeah." I almost add, *I should be ready for the slaughterhouse come fall,* but the problem with Stephen is he's like most people I met at school where he's the puppy and Harvard is his master. Not in a bad way, I guess, but it's definitely where he wants to learn his tricks.

"And how's your friend Sara? Still pissed at you?"

I squint at the collage of her and me that's been accumulating on my wall for longer than half of my puny existence. "No, I think we're fine. We have a lot to talk about still, but we will. Summer just started."

"Well, hey, if you want to hang out sometime, I think I'm only an hour and a half from you. We could talk about nonchemistry things." He goes on to tell me about the books he's reading, but I haven't read a book outside of class since eighth grade, which I tell him when he invites me to join his book club, current membership: Stephen.

"I don't know about a two-person book club, but maybe we could hang out next week or something." Then I add quickly, "Just to warn you, though, I got more chubby, because apparently getting healthy means putting on a shit-ton of weight. But if you wait a month, I'll probably be half as chubby." I'm playing with my stomach under my T-shirt, pretending my belly button is the one saying all of this.

"I'm sure you look beautiful."

There's a pause and I decide to go for it. "Hey, do you ever think that maybe you got into Harvard by mistake?"

There's an even longer pause in which I hate life for not coming with a rewind button.

"Not really," he finally says. "Both my parents went there. And my brother."

I sigh. Of course they did. "Well, I'll let you know about next week."

"All right. It's good to hear your voice, Danny." I can almost see him through the phone deciding if he should say more or not. "Really good."

"Okay, bye." I hang up quickly.

As I sit there holding my phone I realize he's probably the first guy who's shown any interest in me since I showed up on this planet nineteen long years ago. And even though it feels good to feel wanted and even though he's cute and nice and smart, I don't think about his lips the way I think about, say, Bugg's fingernails. I like Stephen, or at least 82 percent of things about him, but I just don't want to see him naked.

CHAPTER NINE

Morning comes especially fast because Sara decides to call me and shout into the phone, even though shouting into the phone does not have the same effect as shouting in person, which everyone younger than seventy-five knows.

"COME GET MIMOSAS WITH US!"

"Who, you and Ethan?" I say groggily. "Because, as much as I like tricycles I'm not trying to be the third—"

"No, no, I stayed over at Bugg's and we want you to come drink with us."

I feel a pang in my stomach. "You stayed over at Bugg's?"

"Yeah, I smoked some weed and drank some wine and

totally passed out. I'm a little hungover, but nothing fixes that like a splash of more alcohol."

"The sun isn't even up yet."

"Yes it is. Open your blinds, Danny."

"You open yours," I grumble, but I end up agreeing to meet them at the only bar in town that serves both breakfast and minors.

The whole ride to the bar I wish to God or Whoever that Bugg and Sara did not make out. Sara's never outwardly expressed an interest in girls, but then again neither have I, so really you can't rely on something as unreliable as how people seem.

By the time I get there they're already sitting down in a booth with fake leather seats.

"Do you want a drink, Danny?" Sara asks, holding up a champagne flute as I slide in next to her and across from Bugg. "I brought this just in case but they didn't even ID me." She waves a fake license in front of my nose that I've never seen before.

"Grapefruit juice would be nice."

"What's it like to be so *boring*?" Sara asks, and Bugg holds up a glass of OJ in my direction.

"It's not five o'clock anywhere in the world, let alone here." I feel weird and nervous, and unfortunately my white smock displays my over-functioning underarms. Also, I think I smell, but there's no way to check this discreetly.

"You okay, Danny?" Bugg asks. I've been trying not to

look at her because looking at her makes my heart do an Olympic floor routine, but I do. Her hair is piled on top of her head and some of the curls are falling around her face. She looks really, really beautiful in a way that makes me want to kiss her again. Or for her to kiss me again, because I have the chutzpah of an ostrich, the creatures best known for sticking their heads in the sand.

"Yep, all good. Just hungry." I grab a menu and skim over it. "Do they have acai bowls here?"

Sara snorts. "You and your health craze. Ever since you took that nutrition class last fall you've been a psycho about how there's cow pus in milk and maggots in hamburgers. Remember in high school when you ate Slim Jims for breakfast? I liked you better then."

"Well, sorry my metabolism shit the bed. That must be soooo hard for you." The waiter brings over a glass of water and I take the paper off my straw to blow at Sara's face. "Besides, I can't be a doctor and promote good health if I'm going to clog my arteries in between patients. It's inconsistent."

She returns the favor by licking the paper and rolling it into a ball, then preparing to load her straw.

"Don't you dare. This is a respectable establishment." I gesture toward some scruffy men who look like they've been here since last night. "Besides, everyone's a psycho about something. Your thing happens to be tennis."

Sara and Bugg look at me in this funny way, which

makes me feel like I'm the one who's missing something. I trace my finger over the red-checkered tablecloth, hating everything about its plastic sheen.

"I don't know why everyone is so afraid of inconsistencies," Bugg says, breaking the awkward silence and tying her shoelace-choker tighter around her neck. "I do yoga and smoke cigarettes and sell the occasional plant of marijuana. I like to think it keeps me human." She pauses and her voice takes on the qualities of an old white guy. "Like Whitman said, 'I contain multitudes.'"

Just as I'm starting to think that maybe the three of us can hang out without me developing an aneurism, Bugg's phone goes off.

"Sorry. I should've put it on silent." She looks at it for a few seconds longer, then hits DECLINE. "It's my ex-girlfriend, the one you met." She nods in my direction, which signals my armpits to start pooling again. It's not that my pizza mission with Bugg was a secret, but I don't see why Sara has to know everything about me and *my* friend Bugg. Or why Bugg has to know everything about me and *my* friend Sara. Doesn't anyone else know how to compartmentalize?

"I didn't know you were into girls. I'm learning so much at this little brunch," Sara says to Bugg. She sounds totally unfazed by it, which shouldn't be surprising, but you never know. It's not as if Sara and I hammer out our sexuality over mocha lattes every morning. "And now I feel so stupid! You should have told me to shut the hell up when I

97

kept telling you about that friend of Ethan's I wanted to set you up with."

Bugg swishes OJ in her mouth then swallows. "Just because I'm into girls doesn't mean I'm not also into guys." Bugg grumbles something about the fallacy of the binary, and I feel that terrible bean of ignorance settling in my stomach. "All you need to know about me and my sexuality is it's not dependent on penises, vaginas, or other related organs. Even if I *were* solely into guys, I could never stomach John. He's such an asshat."

"I agree," I say, relieved to have something to contribute. "I think Liz found him palatable enough, though."

"Hey, I like him," Sara says. "But whatever, I'm so curious about this. How did you know? I'm sorry, have you been asked this six thousand times?"

Bugg shrugs and plays with a sugar packet from the holder at the center of the table. "It's fine. I started making out with girls because I knew it'd freak my parents out, but then I realized I felt something. So then I went for it. My last relationship was with a girl, but before that I dated a guy. I don't know, it's whoever I connect with." When she says this she looks at me, and we make eye contact like I've never made eye contact with someone before. My eyes probably fall out of their sockets like those creepy Halloween googly-eye glasses.

"I always thought bisexual stuff was just indecision," Sara says, swirling her glass thoughtfully. I consider reaching across the table and stuffing her napkin into her mouth. It's easy to hate people who are overtly homophobic and much harder to know what to do with your closest friend, who doesn't know shit about what she's talking about. Bugg and I share a look, and she puts the sugar packet back.

"I think that's my cue to leave," Bugg says, checking the time on her phone. "Did I tell you that I intern for Cynthia?"

"Who's Cynthia?" Sara asks, too deep in her mimosa to realize much beyond her glass.

"She teaches this poetry class we're taking," Bugg says coolly. "I'm helping her organize her father's writing and stuff, and in return she helps me with my portfolio. She wants me to keep writing because she thinks that's good enough. And she introduced me to Mary's poems right before St. J—"

I start making this egregious fake coughing noise.

Bugg gives me a look that says *Oops, sorry*, then recovers. "Are you okay?"

"Wrong pipe," I gasp and drink some water.

"Another mimosa," Sara tells the waiter when he passes. "I have no idea what you guys are talking about when you talk poetry."

I feel so relieved to have avoided a treatment reference that I chug some ice water and guide the conversation far away from me and Bugg. "You really want another?" I ask Sara.

"Hey, don't judge me." She looks playful, but there's something about her tone that isn't playing.

"Just don't go and do something stupid like drive," Bugg says. "Otherwise drink to your little heart's content, maybe call every lousy ex-boyfriend you've ever had, steal from large corporations, and so on."

"I'll cart your drunk ass around," I offer, like the A+ friend I am.

"Jeez, you guys are like my mother." Sara thanks the waiter for the drink and gets started on it right away.

"Actually, your mother would be on the mimosa train," I point out.

"Okay, bye, guys." Bugg gets up and places her hand on my shoulder as she leaves. "Danny, I'll text you later. Also, now would be a great time to tell Sara that thing we talked about."

My jaw nearly drops with the betrayal. She smiles and I say *Fuck you*, but only with my eyes.

"Ooh, tell me what?" Sara asks as Bugg disappears in a swirl of cinnamon, cigarettes, and one very unapologetic wave.

"I had this idea for a poem," I lie.

Sara rolls her eyes. "Come on, Danny! It's *summer.*"

"You're right. I'll tell you later."

Luckily, she drops it. With Bugg gone, Sara and I fall back into the old dynamic of being Danny and Sara pretty quickly. I swear Sara has a magic power that sucks me into her world so fast I don't even leave behind a shadow. She tells me about Ethan and I listen and nod and let her dominate the conversation. We don't end up ordering any food because it's all factory-killed grossness (Well, that was my reasoning; "I prefer to drink on an empty stomach" was Sara's), but it feels *normal* and that's something I haven't felt in a while. Really that's the best thing about Sara, and one of the reasons that I can't tell her any of the unfortunate developments that happened while we were apart: It feels too good when she makes me feel okay.

"Okay, I need to go sleep this off," Sara says, handing the waiter her mother's credit card. Oh, right, it feels entirely normal *except* that she's moderately tipsy at noontime. "You didn't even look at my fake ID," she pouts, holding her wallet out to me.

"Are you sure everything is okay life-wise?" I ask hesitantly. I figured the last few times Sara was drunk—like at my birthday and at her party—it was a fluke incident, typical college stuff. But day-drinking with a fake ID is some next-level shit.

"Totally. This is a classic hangover remedy." She points to her empty glass. "I feel *great.*"

"If you say so. But you'd tell me if something were wrong, right?" I don't want her to think I'm prying, but more importantly there can't be anything wrong with Sara or I'll have to blow up in solidarity.

She looks at me for a second. A foreign look flits across

her face, but when she says, "Of course I would, Danny," I believe her.

"You should come over for grilled cheese night when I come back from tennis camp. Did I tell you I'm going to tennis camp? I don't think I did. It's going to be awesome, lots of drills and so great for my game." Sara signs the slip, and as we get up from the booth I decide that even though Bugg went about it in an asshole way, I *should* tell Sara about treatment and maybe about the kiss too. "Say you'll come to grilled cheese night when I come back! We need more *us* time, Danny." She drapes herself on my shoulder as we walk from the dark bar into the sun-soaked parking lot.

"Of course," I say. Because I will go to grilled cheese night and because she's right. We do need more us time.

CHAPTER TEN

Over the weekend I spend a lot of time writing in my journal and doing Cynthia's prompts. It makes me want to read real poetry, so I gear up to unpack my treatment bags, but sifting through the contents of the last two months ends up being more taxing than I thought it'd be. Worst of all is finding the mostly full bottles of pills that I stopped taking because each medication the doctors pushed made me feel terrible. (Losing faith in medicine is yet another reason why I'm going to be a terrible doctor.)

I stuff the pills into a pocket of my suitcase and find the plastic bag with the used napkins inside it—which sounds weird but I swear I didn't treasure the meals at You-Know-Where so much that I had to take home a souvenir. I unwrap the first one and smile at Bugg's sloppy handwriting. I open the others and lay them out on my bed so that they form the full poem:

Wild Geese

You do not have to be good.
You do not have to walk on your knees
for a hundred miles through the desert, repenting.
You only have to let the soft animal of your body
     love what it loves.
Tell me about despair, yours, and I will tell you mine.
Meanwhile the world goes on.
Meanwhile the sun and the clear pebbles of the rain
are moving across the landscapes,
over the prairies and the deep trees,
the mountains and the rivers.
Meanwhile the wild geese, high in the clean blue air,
are heading home again.
Whoever you are, no matter how lonely,
the world offers itself to your imagination,
calls to you like the wild geese, harsh and exciting -
over and over announcing your place
in the family of things.

Mary Oliver

I touch them softly, then wish I hadn't because it kind of makes me feel like a serial killer. I take a picture and text it to Bugg: Thanks for passing me your dirty napkins. I appreciated it so much I took them home with me. Then I add self-consciously, I'm not obsessed with you, I swear. Just with Mary Oliver. But, that doesn't seem good enough either. And you're okay too. I enter into a staring contest with my cell phone and wait for the three dots to appear. When she finally starts typing, the excitement I feel rivals Christmas morning circa age five.

Pretty cool to have a bond like that without ever speaking to each other.

Speaking's not the only way to talk, you know. I said things to you all the time. In my head.

Creepy. Then a few seconds later, JFK!

What's JFK?

Just fucking kidding.

I want her to ask me to hang out or something, anything that acknowledges our sixteen-second kiss happened and I didn't hallucinate it. When you haven't kissed anyone since prom because it was so weird inside Billy Taylor's mouth that you were afraid all mouths were like that, a kiss is a big deal. She's probably had lots of kisses, though, because she doesn't respond. I distract myself for the rest of the afternoon by doing the elliptical until I'm about to turn into someone's pet hamster. I get off after one hundred and twenty-five minutes, then touch my face for whiskers.

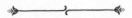

Later, as I'm trying to fall asleep, I see the blinking light of a tiny pink helicopter outside my window. At first I think I'm having visions of the past, but when I get up I see actual Sara actually standing there. The moon gives her skin a bluish tint, and she's holding the helicopter's controller with two hands. I open the window and try to take it out of the air, but she makes it fly a little to the left. Out of instinct I reach for it and nearly topple out of the window. She giggles.

"Asshole," I hiss. "Hey, is that my T-shirt?"

"Shit, is it?" she says with faux bewilderment.

I give her a look. The T-shirt is two years old from the kids section of some department store and says WHY BE PRINCESS WHEN YOU CAN BE PRESIDENT—not exactly a difficult T-shirt to keep track of.

"You gonna let me in or what?" she asks, finally directing the helicopter into my hands. I leave the window to unlock the front door, opening it quietly and putting my finger to my lips as we tiptoe back to my room.

"Wow, I haven't been here in so long. What're those?" She kicks her flip-flops off and points to Bugg's napkins lying exposed on my bed.

"Nothing." I gather them up quickly.

"Aren't you going to throw them away?" She's looking at me like I'm being weird, which I'm *not*.

"Yes, Trash Police." I hover over the basket by my desk. If I throw them away, they might get ruined by peach pits and apple cores, but I don't want to draw any more attention to myself. I place them as gingerly as I can on top of the basket and tuck my journal safely into a drawer.

"So what's up? You haven't sent the tiny pink helicopter of distress in a while." I get into bed on the far right side, leaving space for her.

"I know I could've texted you," she says, pulling the Harry Potter blanket back and getting in next to me. "But that would be sacrilegious."

Sara started sending her helicopter when Janet's drinking got so bad she tried to make the toothbrushes in the bathroom do karaoke. Sara knows how to handle Janet now, but sometimes nighttime is still scary, darker even than when you were a little kid.

"I tried to walkie-talkie you, but *someone's* walkie-talkie wasn't on," she adds, then opens a drawer in my nightstand, rummages through some stuff, and finally finds what she's looking for.

"You can't just go through a girl's nightstand," I say, taking the walkie-talkie from her and trying to switch it on. "You never know what you're going to find in there." I flick the switch back and forth a few times, but the green light doesn't come on. "I guess the batteries are dead."

She takes it back and frowns at it, brushing the dust

from the speaker aggressively, as if it's the walkie-talkie's fault for not being self-sustaining.

"We have to get new batteries, then. Remember that huge snowstorm in tenth grade when we lost power and this was our lifeline? And the hurricane senior year?"

"We'll get batteries tomorrow," I promise. As we lie there blinking into the dust I wonder how long it'll take her to tell me why she's here. "Janet getting to you?" I finally say. But I don't think it's Janet.

"Nah, she passed out at eight and was surprisingly nonintrusive." Sara takes her shorts off and throws them on the floor. I look past her to the pink helicopter and see it for what it is: a toy. If we want to get to each other, we're going to have to be more serious about our distress signals. "The thing is I had a burrito for dinner and I thought you might like to be in the company of my farts before I'm gone for a couple weeks." She gets into typical Sara sleep position, curled on her left side with her right leg up like a frog.

"How considerate of you, but I better fall asleep before the orchestra starts." I roll onto the side that doesn't face her to protect my sense of smell. "Did you at least take a Beano?"

I can tell by the way her breathing is clogged that she's already asleep. I close my eyes and try to sleep too, but every time I drift off I see Bugg's face, feel her lips on my lips in the quiet darkness. I'm petrified I'm going to say her name in a dream and wake Sara up with my biggest secret.

I end up tiptoeing to the couch and lying facedown with my nose pressed into the suede cushion. It's a terrible sleep, especially with the contributions from my dad's cuckoo clock, but not more terrible than the alternative.

CHAPTER ELEVEN

While Sara is at tennis camp, Bugg and I spend a shit-ton of time together, melting the days of summer away like a Popsicle you can't keep up with. She insists we do all her favorite things, which all have one thing in common: making out. Since I haven't heard back from any pre-med endeavors (I did finally finish four applications), my lips and I are more than happy to oblige.

We go to the aquarium one day where we try (unsuccessfully) to find the octopus's beak, then make out in the last row of the OMNI theater, crouched down during a remarkably uninteresting exposé on the green puffer fish.

On the Fourth of July we go to the fair, where we ride something called the Spin Cycle. Afterward she pushes me into a Porta-Potty and kisses me amid the piss and fumes in a way that makes my stomach drop even more than it did when I was upside down two hundred feet in the air. I even come with her while she "doesn't sell weed," which brings us to a house party a few towns away where there's alcohol in a trash bag and we each take big gulps of it.

"I've never seen you drink," I observe as the red liquid sloshes against the sides of the bag and into our cups.

"I'm not supposed to be drinking after treatment," she admits, "but this doesn't count." We drink so much we pass out on the trampoline in the backyard, only to wake up at five a.m. in nothing but our underwear. It'd be thoroughly appalling behavior if it weren't so goddamn fun.

Besides kissing, the best part about hanging out is going to poetry class together. I do the exercises Cynthia assigns every week in preparation for our final project and my poems come out terrible, but God, it's thrilling to be so bad at something and still like doing it. In one exercise Cynthia tells us to describe our inner world and I decide mine is a piece of land with everything bulldozed off it. It smells like rubber and dirt and no one can sleep because of the tractor noises, but in the far corner two weedlike flowers are growing closer, apparently thriving despite the mayhem. I'm not even jealous that Bugg's poems are as wonderful as mine are terrible. It's worth it to be around her. I don't know what we're doing, but I like not knowing and doing it anyway.

The only time it occurs to me that I might need to know what we're doing is when Sara gets back from tennis camp in July and invites me over for grilled cheese night. She demands that I wear our matching leopard-print onesies, so I show up nervous, reluctant about eating a grilled cheese and, true to my word, wearing the footie pajamas Janet got us last Christmas. "If you girls can't be together at school, you can at least wear the same adorable sleepwear while FaceTiming each other good night," Janet had said, after like, six spiked eggnogs. She opens the door now and smothers me in a Chanel hug.

"Come right in, Danny. You look *fabulous*," she says.

"Me-*ow*," Sara confirms when I enter the kitchen. Janet got our onesies a little big, but now mine hugs every place on me that I never wanted to be huggable.

"You are one sexy cat, Dandelion. Come here and hug me." Sara reaches out to me with her hands full of butter and cheese. "If you stopped wearing those tent dresses, you'd notice how hot you are."

"I prefer to call them *smocks*."

"Fine, have a grilled cheese." She dangles the sandwich in front of my face but I wave it away. "Come on, you're not going to have one of my famous grilled cheeses?" Sara looks so insulted I nearly question my decision, but it's not worth breaking my veganism streak.

"I just ate." My stomach growls. *Pipe down*, I hiss at it.

"Why the hell would you *eat* before grilled cheese night?" she asks, putting the grilled cheese in my face again and nearly inducing a sensory aneurism. It's unfair for something to smell *that* good.

"I know, I haven't had one since last June—" I start to say, but thinking back on high school graduation day—the day before I got the Harvard acceptance letter—makes me want to throw up. Everything was easy then, when Sara and I were still Sara and I and a grilled cheese was just a grilled cheese, not a number that translated to a number of grueling minutes on the elliptical.

"I can't wait to tell you all about tennis camp," Sara says as I follow her upstairs to her room. "It felt so good to lose myself in the game again—total topspin consumption."

"You know, that's how I've been feeling about poetry class. It sounds touchy-feely and terrible but—"

"Wait, before we get into all of this, do you know what I was thinking about today?" She pats the spot on her pink ruffled comforter where she wants me to sit. "The day we made our house. Look." She reaches under her bed and pulls out the cardboard house we made together the summer before eighth grade.

"Would ya look at that." I touch the cut-up Popsicle sticks we used for the roof and feel a wave of nostalgia flood my body. The summer we made the house was when we started hanging out with boys and Sara kissed one of them and I watched, but not in a creepy way. We had sleepovers every night, and her bed was always fluffy and cool from the AC. I secretly wished her parents would adopt me because they had all the normal cereals and didn't make Sara read any books before bed like my parents did. Plus, if my parents signed me over to Janet and Cal, Sara and I would be more than Kool-Aid blood sisters. We'd be *legal* sisters and that seemed more legit.

"Do you remember the day we made it?" Sara asks, taking hold of the cardboard me.

"Duh. We got your dad to drive us to buy paint and glue and cardboard."

We got dollhouse furniture too—a bed, a sofa, a thumb-size toilet—then we sat on her deck and drew lines and cut things out and labored our future into existence, complete with stand-up mini-cardboard people that we'd taped pictures of our faces to.

Sara picks at the peeling sunburn on her arm, then looks up at me as if she wants to say something touchy-feely.

"I've missed you, Danny," she finally says. "Not just while I was at camp, but this whole year."

"Me too." When I shift my weight on the bed the cardboard house rattles as if it's experiencing a mini earthquake, but nothing falls.

Sara steadies the house, then moves the cardboard cutout of herself around the kitchen. "I wish shit was as easy now as it was then."

I put my arm around her, noting that I do not feel anything when my skin touches Sara's skin, which makes me think that my reaction to Bugg is just a Bugg thing. That or I'm immune to Sara the way you are with everyone else in your family.

"It was a shit thing to do, to know for a whole month that you weren't going to college with me and not tell me," Sara says quietly. "I felt like an idiot for ordering all that stuff from PBteen. You should have told me right when you got the letter. I could've handled it." She rearranges the tiny furniture in our tiny pretend room.

"I know, I'm sorry." I pick at my toenail polish and wish words meant more in times like this. "Sometimes I forget that I can't actually make shit disappear by ignoring it hard enough."

"That'd be the best superpower, though."

"Why call Wonder Woman when you could call the Blind Eye?"

She hugs me and I feel that she forgives me—either that or she's going to cry. I let my body relax into hers, but no tears come so we sit like that, holding each other up in more ways than one.

I'm of the school of thought that friendship is like a river in that it's different in different seasons. Sometimes it's an August river, all dry and shrinking from the banks, and sometimes it's an April river, rushing and overflowing the dam. She and I, we've been in both places, but today the stuff between us is a good old July river, quiet and content, ambling through the summer.

"There's actually a couple of things I want to talk to you about," I say, and even though I'm not psyched about it, I know telling her about treatment is the only way to keep our friendship from turning into a memorabilia piece, a useless relic of the past. I take a deep breath, but Sara interrupts me.

"There's something I've been meaning to tell you too." The foreign look flits across her face like it did at the bar when I asked her if she was okay.

It's only fair to let her tell me first. "What is it?"

Slowly she turns her butt toward me and lets out a loud fart, approximately five inches from my face. "IT'S TIME TO WAGE A FART WAR." Then she jumps on top of me and puts her hand over my mouth, which forces me to inhale her fart directly through my nostrils.

"SWEET JESUS MARY MOTHER OF GOD," I yell, meanwhile my eyes water at the stench. You cannot judge a book by its cover when it comes to pretty girls; they have the most lethal farts. When she hops off of me she's laughing so hard I think she might pee herself, which has happened on exactly four occasions during a fart war. I try to summon something of my own, but I haven't eaten enough to come up with anything so I wave an imaginary white flag: "You win," I gasp. "I surrender. I have no ammunition and I'm weak in the head after that one."

She wipes tears of laughter from her eyes, and when we lie back on her bed I almost forget that Sara and I aren't thirteen anymore. It makes me hesitant to bring the moment back to where we are now.

Sara props herself up on her elbow and asks, "So what was it you wanted to tell me? I should've let you talk, but I felt the fart gathering steam and then I couldn't resist waging a tiny—" She's interrupted by her own phone ringing. "Sorry, it's Liz. Do you mind if I get it real quick?"

"Not at all. Take your time." Frankly, I'm grateful for the excuse to postpone telling her about treatment.

"Hey, girl." I can't hear Liz, but I know she's telling Sara something good by the way Sara's eyebrows are moving. "Oh my God. Get out. I can't believe it."

"What?" I mouth, sitting up.

"Wait until I tell Danny." Sara plays with our cardboard figures and accidentally knocks me over. "Okay, yeah, I'm gonna tell her right now. Bye."

"What?" I ask again, leaning over Sara to try to stand cardboard me back up, but I'm out of reach.

"You're never going to guess who came out on Facebook." Sara's voice is juicy with gossip, and I instinctively put a hand on my stomach to keep it from somersaulting. "Bridget Carr," she says before I even try to guess.

"From the high school tennis team?" My voice cracks a little.

"Yeah, isn't that so weird?" Sara picks up her cardboard

cutout and fixes its taped-on clothes. "We all used to change together in the same room. Do you think she was into me? Because I thought one time I saw her giving me the look—remember I told you about it—but then I forgot about it, but now that I'm remembering it, she was *totally* giving me the look." She's being all cavalier, as if this is another piece of gossip to exchange instead of something real and hard and life-changing. I hate the smug look on her face, as if there's a prize for knowing something about Bridget Carr's sexuality before Bridget Carr did.

"You're kidding, right." My voice is so harsh that Sara fumbles and drops her cardboard self. The closeness I felt toward her before the phone call now feels like a distance that nothing but anger can cross. "She finally gets up the courage to come out to, like, seven hundred of her closest friends, and all you can think about was whether or not she thought *you* were hot?" Even though the AC is on blast I'm starting to feel like I'm overheating, and it's all I can do to keep the steam from coming out of my ears.

"Danny, I obviously think it's great that she came out." Sara crosses her room and selects a lipstick from her makeup desk. She swipes it on and smacks her lips in front of the mirror. "I'm just saying I felt like I *knew* that. Don't be so dramatic—"

"I'm not being dramatic!" I tell her reflection. She's looking at herself and not at me. "You're so...so...in your own bubble. Do you get that there's a world outside of yourself?" Something bad is happening. All the anger I didn't know I was hiding for the last year suddenly wants out. I grab the cardboard cutout of myself and take it from the room that Sara's cardboard cutout is in. I try to control my voice but it's a fairly useless exercise at this point. "Bridget Carr being a lesbian has nothing to do with you, but you're too self-absorbed to know that because you're so self-absorbed that you could make a line of fine sponges that would put Bounty, Scotch-Brite, and Swiffer all out of business." Tears stream down my face and I grip the cardboard cutout of myself harder.

Sara smacks her lips together again and swipes the dash of red off her tooth. "I see what you mean," she says slowly, finally looking at me through the reflection in the mirror. "About how you've gotten a little fat."

CHAPTER TWELVE

"Unbe-fucking-*lievable*," I say to my cardboard cutout as I run down Sara's stairs with it safely in my grasp. "She can have the house." My cutout nods in agreement, but I still vow to eat, like, three carrots for the rest of my life.

When I get in my dad's car I text Bugg to meet me at the Coffee Place. I'm driving too fast, but if I run over a squirrel it's the squirrel's fault for not having learned a single lesson from its roadkill ancestors.

"I'm glad you suggested this. My blood-gelato levels are low," Bugg says when I pull into the parking lot next to her. She's wearing a short blue sequined dress and fingerless gloves. "Wait, have you been crying? And why are you wearing footie pajamas?"

My hands are shaking slightly with adrenaline. "Sara and I had a fight. Blood was shed. Not real blood—friendship blood. I guess you could say Kool-Aid was spilled."

Bugg puts her hand on the small of my back and guides me toward the small brick building. "Come on. Gelato will fix you up."

Inside, people stare at my ridiculous outfit, but I ignore them and give Bugg most of the details of the fight. I leave out the part where I related Sara's potent self-absorption to that of a drugstore sponge because it's not the light I'd like to paint myself in. Besides, Sara will probably tell her the next time they're having some lame bonding experience at yoga.

"Yikes, sorry, dude." Bugg looks between me and the chalkboard of gelato flavors on the Coffee Place's wall. "I think you needed to have a blowout fight, though. That's the best way to relieve tension."

She approaches the gelato scooper and says, "Pistachio, please," like it isn't the worst flavor invented.

"And for you?" the bored-looking guy asks me. I look into the tub of offerings and realize the frozen crystals on the sides of the containers are probably cow tears.

"All set, thanks."

"Oh, come on, Danny! Live a little." Bugg takes her cone of animal cruelty and licks it.

"What about the cows?" I ask, and she gives me a look. "Besides, Kate Moss or someone in her BMI range said no food tastes as good as skinny feels."

"Oh, please." Bugg points the cone in my face like a microphone. "What about gelato, *Kate*?"

I end up with a cone of something that tastes like Nutella and Bugg kisses me on the cheek *in public*. I get as frozen as the freezer while she goes on about how "There's nothing more boring than complaining about your body. Bodies are beautiful. It's an inherent thing, not a weight-contingent thing."

When I turn around to get some napkins, I notice Liz and Kate are standing in the doorway staring at us and whispering to each other. When the hell did they get there?

"Um, hey," I say to them, waving my hand a little rudely in their direction. I grab a fistful of napkins too aggressively and a few hang out of the canister.

"Oh, hey, Danny!" They have this look on their faces that sends my paranoia into high gear. They absolutely saw Bugg kiss my cheek. They're going to tell everyone they've ever spoken to in real life *and* on the Internet about it, and I'm going to have to live out the rest of my youth debunking rumors or finally squaring away what it is Bugg and I are doing.

"Well, bye," I say and pay for Bugg's gelato to get the whole thing moving faster.

"What's the rush?" Bugg whispers as I bump a chair

in my haste to get out. "Don't you want to stay and talk to your friends?"

"No, I don't want to stay and talk to my friends." I pull her safely outside, and the bells of the door jangle as I slam it shut. "I've only been back here a month, and I'm already so tired of everyone and their gossip and their pea-size lives."

Bugg takes hold of the back of my footie pajamas. "Come here."

"No!" But I turn around and let her pull me back toward her. Her smile spreads like the flu and I haven't been immunized yet. "Don't you get that I can't cuddle with you in the middle of the parking lot, where people are probably spying on us from the bushes?" I look past the hot tar to where two severely dehydrated, perhaps clinically depressed bushes dream of water.

"No one is spying on us because no one gives a shit about us. You're lucky you're cute or this avoid-each-other-in-public thing would be way too annoying." The wind blows her blue sequined dress up a little too far. "Wait. I'm getting a really good idea." She holds her eyes closed with her thumb and pointer finger. Meanwhile her dress gets more carried away with the wind.

"What is it?" I'm trying not to look, but I end up entirely looking anyway.

She's silent for a minute then snaps her fingers. "Run away with me."

I blink at her, and some of my gelato dribbles into my thumb crease. "Come again?"

"Run away with me!" Her voice rises with excitement. "We'll live like villains. Do everything we think we're not supposed to do. It'll be *fun*, Danny. Do you remember fun?"

I resume my licking and try to think. "Vaguely? It might've made an appearance last summer before high school graduation?"

"Exactly. Before I fired my therapist she told me," she says, and she takes on this mocking voice, "'Not everything is supposed to be fun, Sally. Some things in life are boring and hard work and blah blah blah.' She calls me Sally 'cause she sucks and I don't let her use my nickname, but anyway I totally called bullshit on her. I said, 'Listen, *Marjorie*, life is already full of so much sadness and bullshit that fun is an entirely mandatory part of living. Otherwise we might as well become wax figurines and wait until the harshness of the world melts our faces off.'"

She tries to clean up her cone by taking a big bite off the top, then ferociously licking the sides, but drops of green are collecting on the pavement by our feet.

"I agree with you, I think, but I can't run away with you." I squint into the last of the sun, watching the door nervously and wondering how long it'll be until Kate and Liz come out. "My parents would send a search squad for me, and it'd be a poor use of tax dollars."

"How about just for the weekend?" She tucks a piece

of rebellious hair behind my ear. "Think you can swing two days?"

"Depends. Where do you have in mind?" I ask it as if I wouldn't go anywhere in the world with her.

"I know of this great moon festival down the Cape. If you go home right now—"

"But I haven't finished my gelato."

"—and pack a bag full of the items I text to you, we can leave in an hour."

"I'm sure you came up with a perfectly sound plan in the last one hundred and twenty seconds, but I'm not much of a surprise person, so if you tell me where we're going I can make sure that I have things like—"

She grabs my shoulder, smudging gelato from her fingers onto my onesie.

"Danny? Look at me."

"Yes?"

She pauses and I try to hold her gaze. The problem is that looking at her is like looking into a megawatt light-bulb; I'm just so human and she's just so bright.

"Trust me."

When I get home, my mom grills me about wearing footie pajamas in ninety-degree weather, then inundates me with updates from my therapist while my dad is engrossed in his bird watching. It's all good things to report, surprisingly—Harvard is looking like a go come fall.

"And this came in the mail," she says, beaming as she hands me my MCAT practice book.

I hold it against my chest with equal parts love and disdain, then break the news to the two of them as gently as I can. "So I'm going away with a friend for the weekend. Only two nights." I figure it's best not to ask them for permission because that would be an opportunity for them to say no.

"What? Where?" my mother asks. I wish I could do something to decrease the levels of worry in her voice, but alas, everything I do seems to have the opposite effect.

"I'll text you the address as soon as I know. It's a surprise," I add, "which is fun or something."

Usually when my dad has his face pressed into his binoculars he only contributes things to the conversation like the migratory patterns of wood warblers, but today he seems to be listening for once.

"Sara wouldn't tell you where you're going?"

And my mom prods, "Yeah, she must have some more information." Her BlackBerry goes off but she doesn't even blink, which is how I know she's entering mama-bear protective mode.

"I'm not going with Sara." I slam the MCAT book down on the counter. I know I shouldn't be short with them when I want something, but come on. "I have other friends besides Sara, you know."

My dad tears himself away from the window, and he and my mom share a brief look.

"No need to be snappy," my mom says in the tone she uses when she's speaking for both my dad and herself. It's a tone she uses frequently lately, if you want to know the truth.

"Sorry, the heat is getting to me." I unzip my onesie a bit and sprawl out on the suede couch. "It's my friend from poetry class. The whole class is going for team building." I don't know why I add the last part. Every liar knows that the easiest way to get caught fibbing is through unnecessary elaboration.

"Team building in *poetry*?" my dad asks, letting the binoculars hang from his neck.

"Yeah, we're going to embody words and probably play... Scrabble."

They're both very quiet, and then my mom's eyes narrow.

"Is there something you're not telling us?"

I tap my thumb on the pointy end of my dad's key and rack my brain for something more plausible. Her Black-Berry starts ringing and it's that song from *Annie* about how the sun's gonna come out tomorrow. She frowns down at it and picks it up. "This is terrible timing, but I have to take this. I'm supposed to meet a client in five minutes. Jim, can you handle this, please?"

My dad says yes, but he's already glued to the window again. My mom answers her phone as she leaves the house, and I try to scoot out too.

"Just a second, Danny."

I turn around and face my dad. I can tell he feels awkward, so I try not to look at the rings the binoculars left around his eyes.

"I meant to tell you that your dean said we have to fill out some paperwork this week to make sure you can go back in the fall, now that we have the therapist's approval."

I feel my face morph into a visage of dread.

"You *do* want to go back in the fall, don't you?"

I blink at him. Neither he nor my mom have explicitly asked me that. I don't know that *I've* explicitly asked me that.

"Of course I want to go back," I say, playing with the zipper again so I can listen to the plastic teeth clack. "Just because I had one hard term doesn't mean I'm going to throw it all away."

"That's my girl." Something flies past the window, and he whips his binoculars into position.

"I'm gonna go meet my friend now, okay? I'll text you when I get wherever we're going." He gives a distracted-sounding yes, and I thank the universe that my parents each have *something* else to do besides worry about me.

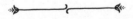

I should feel guiltier about the fight with Sara, but I'm excellent at tucking things into a brain drawer and not opening them for a while. So instead of worrying about how we're going to come back after the shit-storm of things I only partially meant, I do what Bugg texts me to do:

Be outside your house at 9:45 with a
backpack (it must be a BACKPACK) full of:
- a bathing suit
- tongs
- something very personal
- six tampons
- two EpiPens (one is probably enough
   but just in case)
- the extract of vanilla

I wave good-bye to my dad and wait on the porch steps with my knees together to avoid exposing my granny panties. (As a side note, Sara never wears granny panties, just lace thongs that never get period stains on them.)

When I see headlights my heart flutters.

"Get in," Bugg yells, opening the door of her ancient VW convertible and driving slowly along the curb.

"If you slowed the car down, it'd greatly decrease the chances of me breaking my leg by trying to get in." I walk quickly beside the car and the straps of my backpack chafe my shoulders.

"Come on, this is your female equivalent of a James Bond moment."

"Well, I guess I could try—"

"Oh my God, Danny, no! You just failed your first test of the night. You can't do things other people tell you. THINK FOR YOURSELF! BEING YOUR OWN PERSON IS THE ONLY WAY TO HAVE FUN!" She speeds the car up slightly, and I pant past another house that looks just like the last.

"Stop! I can't take the pressure! Is this what hazing feels like?"

Smiling, she stops the car. "I'm just kidding. I promise there won't be any more tests for the whole weekend."

I breathe a sigh of relief. "Good." I take my backpack off and get into the passenger's seat. She leans over and kisses me hard on the lips, which sends my heart into overdrive again.

"Watch out!" I lean away from her and the door digs into my back. "My dad is probably dressed up as a curtain trying to see what we're up to."

She rolls her eyes and peels away from the curb. "Danny, you are way too paranoid. We're, like, five houses away from yours and besides: No guts, no glory."

"I don't have any guts."

"Yes, you do. You just have to stop ignoring them."

CHAPTER THIRTEEN

"Okay, are you ready for the manifesto of the weekend?" Bugg asks when we make a pit stop at a creepy gas station. The pumps seem a hundred years old and the ice cooler looks like a place to store dead babies—babies killed by the girl in charge of the cash register, who's staring at us and twirling an unlit cigarette with her acrylic talons.

"Uh, I think so." I skirt a used condom that's stuck to the pavement like gum.

"Good. Twizzler?" Bugg holds the pack out to me while she fills up the tank. I nod and take one, then she reaches into her back pocket and starts reading from a piece of notebook paper.

"The manifesto goes like this: During this trip there will be no body whomping, body wishing, or body whining. There will be no talk of the future and the amorphous garbage heap that appears to be our adult lives. There will be no mention of failure in the conventional sense, which prohibits talk of pre-med, pre–college degree, pre–fun sucked out of the rest of your life. Failure may only be mentioned in terms of failing to give a flying fuck about everything everyone else cares about. And lastly, most importantly, anything not fun is banned, strictly prohibited, exiled, and so on. In the extremely unlikely event that we do encounter something not fun, you brought the EpiPens, right?"

"You mean a hypothetical EpiPen, right, for our severe, hypothetic allergy to things that are not fun? Because if you have an actual allergy to something, we're going to be screwed. All I have are these."

We get in the car, and from my backpack I take out the two Bic pens I labeled EPI #1 and EPI #2 with Sharpie.

Bugg clutches my makeshift medicine to her chest. "You're my kind of girl, Danny." Even though it makes no sense because objectively speaking I'm very dull, I'm starting to believe that somehow, miraculously I *am* her kind of girl. As she pulls out of the gas station, I decide that unless there's some hidden excitement I can't see in myself, it's safe to assume that girls like Bugg and Sara need someone like me: a flat surface off which they can shine.

When she's back on the highway I happen to glance at the dashboard. "Do you have any idea what the speed limit is here? This isn't the autobahn, you know."

Bugg lets her hair out of its ponytail. "We have to drive fast while we're young because our nucleus accumbens will never be this large again."

I watch the curls swirl around her like a frizzy aura and try to figure out what the hell she's talking about.

"Did I mention I was a neuro major before I dropped out?"

"You didn't, but I invite you to use normal terms."

"The nucleus accumbens is the pleasure center of the brain," she starts, as if a nucleus accumbens is as well known, as, say, an elbow. "It's biggest when you're a teenager but after about twenty-five it starts to shrink. So basically nothing will ever feel this good again. Not driving fast, not having sex, not eating pistachio gelato. *This* is our time, Danny. You have to let it consume you."

"I don't know if I believe that." I'm certainly being taken over by one part of my brain, but I don't think it's the nucleus incubator or whatever. "Besides, I'd sincerely like to believe that *this* isn't the prime of my life."

"Google it if you don't believe me. It's also why, as a cohort, we're more likely to take risks. It's not that we don't know any better. It's that our rewards are greater."

I tighten my seat belt and wish she'd put hers on.

"One day I'll have to stop smoking cigarettes and selling weed and living off my parents' money, but now is not that time. Right now *fun* is the only worthwhile objective. We hardly have the cranial capacity for much else."

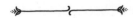

We finally get to the house on the Cape where we're apparently going to be having all this fun. We park in the driveway, which is paved with crushed shells, and Bugg takes a big suitcase out of the trunk.

"How long are we staying again? Because if I recall, you insisted I bring only a *backpack*."

"Relax, Danny. I had to bring more supplies than you did, being the master planner and everything." She gets the key to the house from under a fake rock and we go inside. "Home sweet second home," she says, turning the lights on, and I try to take it in without seeming provincial.

Every room is full of weird, expensive-looking art, particularly the living room, which houses a nearly life-size sculpture of an octopus. The ceiling and floors are wood, which makes the whole place smell like a log cabin but in a nice way. I keep my mouth from gaping open and follow Bugg upstairs to the master bedroom, where there's a hammock swing hanging from the ceiling. She plops down in it and opens the window so we can hear the ocean.

"This place is perfect," I say, then walk over to the wall behind her and squint at a photo in a thick gold frame. "Is that you?"

"Sure is. Right before my parents made me go to fat camp."

"I wish my parents would send me to fat camp."

Bugg plants her feet on the ground and says sharply, "You think you have it hard, but there are people in the world who are more than ten pounds overweight. Having been one of those people, it sucks when you complain about being fat when you're not."

I want to grumble that it's still hard. That part of what makes it so hard is that I don't technically have anything to complain about. Everything wrong with me is entirely in my head. I look at my feet, shifting back and forth on my heels.

She goes on. "I'm not ashamed that I'm still overweight, or that I used to be more overweight, as if it's some moral failing not to be a size six."

"Obviously it's not a moral failing," I agree, but isn't that how I've been treating it?

"People should mind their own business about other people's bodies, including their own body."

"Okay, okay, I'm minding mine."

It feels like our first fight but without the satisfaction

of her doing anything wrong. Fights are stupid when you're the only one to blame.

Just as it's starting to feel like this trip won't be much fun after all, Bugg gets up and opens the French doors onto a roof deck. "Come on, this is the best part. It's only big enough for two people and maybe a bottle of wine, which I happen to have." She goes into her suitcase and takes out a bottle and cups. "Not that I drink, but this is a special occasion. Look."

We take our shoes off and I tilt my head up. There's no light pollution, just stars and lots of them, like someone dumped a jar of sugar onto the sky. I hold my cup out as she opens the bottle and pours me some of the pink bubbly liquid. Then I take a sip and try to get my eyes to adjust to infinity.

"It makes me feel so small, but I love it. Every time my parents try to guilt me into getting a 'real job,' I remind myself that they don't have all the answers. They're just as tiny as I am."

"That must suck. My parents smother me with unconditional love, so I take it upon myself to lay the pressure on."

She pats my head and I don't think she's angry anymore, though her voice is thick with condescension when she says, "Being driven is an ego trip, Danny."

"Well, sorry I'm not enlightened yet." I pace back and forth, and the shingles are scratchy under my feet. "You know what, fuck enlightenment. I'd just like to have one pleasant afternoon."

We sit down and she crosses her leg over mine, giving me the chills. "Let's play a game." She doesn't wait for me to respond. "How about truth or dare?"

I take a gulp of wine. "Truth or dare gives me anxiety. What's the point in playing a game you can't ever win, but have ample opportunities to lose?"

"Because it's *fun*. If you don't do the dare or don't answer the truth, you have to drink, okay?"

"But sometimes wine makes me throw up."

"*Okay?*" she asks again.

"Fine."

She perks up, and really it's very dangerous to be around someone so beautiful. "Truth or dare?" She scoots closer to me, giving me minor heart palpitations. "Truth or dare, truth or dare, truth or dare?" she sings.

I don't know which is worse. I'd do a pros and cons list but it'd probably end up being a list of cons. I go ahead and tell her something true to loosen me up. "I feel like I do this great impersonation of an onion and it works well with most people, but you're so determined to cut through every last layer."

She wrinkles her nose. "Onions are gross. Can't you be a layer cake instead?"

"The metaphor doesn't work like that. Plus, cake makes me hungry." I'm about to say more, but in light of our recent conversation, I figure I can spare us both the self-deprecation. This is going to take some getting used to.

"*Fine.* But you still didn't choose. Truth or dare?"

I can't wriggle free from her gaze, but if I'm being honest with myself, I don't want to. "Truth."

"Wrong choice," she says, swirling her wine then tilting her glass back.

"You're not the Goddess of Truth or Dare. You don't get to determine my truth-or-dare fate." She inches closer to me and my lips tingle where she's kissed them maybe a hundred times total. Not that I'm counting. I drink a little more and the wine makes me feel warm and relieved, sort of like when you pee yourself, but without the damp embarrassment.

"Dare, then," I say and try to get a full breath in. The energy between us is charged and it's about 96 percent sexual. I'm a little afraid of it: hands shaking, chewing at the inside of my lip scared of it.

"I dare you." She pauses for suspense. "Tell me the whole story behind St. John's."

"That's not a dare! That's a truth."

"I know, but I thought I might need to dare the truth out of you."

I feel a pinch on my arm and slap a mosquito trying to suck me for my last drop. "Can I have more alcohol first?" I ask. "This is the sort of game you need to warm up for."

She looks into her empty cup. "Screw it, let's do it."

We go downstairs and she steals wine from her parents'

wine cellar—*wine cellar*—as well as a mega straw from, like, 7-Eleven. She plops it in the bottle and offers me a sip when we're back outside. We go sip for sip until the bottle is halfway done, and when we're nice and tipsy she goes, "I think I told you a few weeks ago that I'm not technically supposed to be drinking? It's what landed me in St. John's both times. Well, technically attempted suicide got me there, but I wouldn't have tried anything if I weren't drunk."

"Oh, shit," I say, instinctively taking the bottle from her hands. "Should we stop?" I do recall that she said *technically* she shouldn't be drinking, but how was I supposed to know that *technically* meant she had a serious alcohol problem? And technically, does that mean I'm a bad influence on her because we're drinking now?

"No, it's fine. Drinking and depression is just a bad mix sometimes."

I try to get a read on her, but the light from the house isn't enough to see much. Plus, when you're tipsy everything serious seems much less so.

"This past time was my second time at St. John's, because I got insanely drunk and threatened to jump out of my ex-girlfriend's window, apparently. I was blacked out so I don't remember it."

I swish the wine in my mouth, not knowing how to respond to something like that. "Er, the one I met?"

"That's the one." She takes the bottle from my hand. "And before that I tried drinking a cocktail of Benadryl and highlighter fluid."

"But why?" I look over at her and try to figure out which part is the messed-up part so I can take it and save her from herself.

She shrugs. "I wanted to see if I could glow in the dark." Her eyelashes are casting a shadow on her cheeks, and I try to see her pupils through the darkness.

"But how could you ever not want to live? You're so beautiful and smart and talented." For the first time I realize I'm kind of lucky, in a screwed-up way. Though at risk of rotting teeth, nothing that got me into St. John's was a matter of life or death. I was sick of myself, sure, but I never wanted to not be a self at all.

"It's so stupid," she says, looking away from me and bringing her knees into her chest. "Like I was built with a self-destruct button."

"I know what you mean." I feel around my chest as if I can locate mine. "It's crazy how the little rotten part can go in and spoil the whole fruit."

I try to keep myself from blinking so that I can really see her, see all her hurt and all her light and how they're not separate things. "You're staring at me so intensely," she says, laughing, and for the first time she looks something that I can't quite place.

"Sorry! I'm trying to be a good listener." She tilts her head and I decide that what she looks is fragile. I look down at the bottle of wine with the straw sticking out of it. "Are you sure it's fine that we're drinking? You're not gonna pull a Virginia Woolf and go walk into the ocean, right?" Suicide jokes probably aren't in high demand, but I don't know how else to talk to her about something so serious.

"Nah, I'm all better now," she says, chewing on the straw. I look at her dubiously. "Seriously. Besides, I need a little depression or my poems are cotton-candy shit. All artists need darkness, don't you think?" Bugg pulls a pre-rolled cigarette from her pouch of tobacco.

I watch her light it and sort of want to try a little. "That sounds like a bullshit excuse, but I don't know. I don't do 'art.'"

"Sure you do. I've seen you scribbling in your journal, and the stuff you've been working on in Cynthia's class is getting good."

The smoke is thick as it leaves her mouth. I try to watch it disperse, but by the time it enters the night it's wispy, then gone.

"I don't know what my thing is," I say. "Nothing stands out as my hokey new-age passion like writing does for you and tennis does for Sara. I guess I've been too occupied trying to be Valedictorian of the World. Also, can I try that?"

I ask, and she gasps theatrically. "What can I say? You're a bad influence."

I take over her cigarette, inhaling, exhaling, and suppressing my nausea. When I realize I'm not going to throw up, I kind of like the buzzy feeling in my head.

"My turn with the cigarette and your turn with the St. John's story," Bugg says cheerfully. I shake my head and she takes a last drag then puts the cigarette out, scarring the gray of the roof darker. "How about a new dare, then?" She doesn't wait for me to answer, which I'm seeing as a trend. "I dare you to kiss me."

My heart short-circuits, if that's a thing a heart can do. "That's even worse than sharing loony bin stories," I say, not because we haven't done it before but because I've never initiated anything. I'll probably miss and nab her in the lower jaw and be sentenced to my virginity for the rest of my unarousing years.

She pretends to clutch her heart. "Ouch! Well, fine. Have it your way. I'm going to change into pajamas."

I watch her go and try to talk my heart out of beating so fast, but all that goes to shit as soon as she comes back out wearing this maroon satin nightgown thing that makes it impossible not to look at her.

"That is *not* pajamas," I breathe. She sits down next to me and her cinnamon and cigarettes smell mixes with what I hope is my shampoo smell and not my sweaty armpit smell.

"What's going to happen tonight? 'Cause like I said before I'm not very good with surprises and I think maybe we should talk first or wait, no, let's not talk, maybe—"

She puts my hair behind my ear. "I'm going to kiss you now before you talk yourself further up your own asshole," she says. "Okay?"

I nod and close my eyes. She puts her lips on my lips and I fall into the dream of her.

CHAPTER FOURTEEN

It's nothing like the times we've kissed before. I mean, it is, because it's the same parts and stuff, but being in an unfamiliar place makes it feel like I'm someone unfamiliar too. It's the sort of kiss you lose all sense of time and place in, where space bends around us and leaves us to ourselves, whoever we are.

"Come on," she whispers.

"Where are we going?" I look around the roof at the two empty bottles of wine and realize I'm quite drunk.

"To the bed, silly." She pulls me back into the house.

In what's probably her parents' bedroom, I wrap my

arms around her neck and draw our bodies closer together. Her back is soft and smooth and I try to undo the hook of her bra, but I'm starting to think my fingers have become lobster claws. She takes pity on me and unclasps it, then in a gracious survey of the situation, takes her nightgown off too. I'm left with the very manageable task of turning out the lights. We sit on the bed side by side.

"Take your dress off," she says.

"It's a smock," I whisper, but I'm kind of buying time. Normally I try not to be naked even around myself.

"Are you okay?" she asks. "Do you want to stop? None of this is mandatory."

"No, no, I know." I'm trying to figure out how you tell someone they're about to swipe your V card. She traces the outline of my lips with her fingers and I notice they're trembling a little.

"Don't worry, it's second nature. We'll go slow. But if at any time you want to stop, the code word is 'stop.'" I love the logic of it enough to actually believe sex could be second nature, though all of my personal evidence points to the contrary. She fidgets with her underwear and I sense she wants to say more. "But just to warn you, vaginas are not like flowers," she blurts out, pausing with her underwear around her knees.

I try not to look bewildered, but I have no idea where this is coming from. "Who said vaginas were like flowers?"

"No one ever said it *explicitly*, but people are always

equating women to lovely things and pushing flower-scented period garb and—"

"I *have* a vagina, remember?" I strum the strap of her underwear playfully and it slaps against her skin.

"I'm just *saying* it might be different if it's not yours—you know, like, how people always hate other kids but think theirs is an exception? You might not mind *your* vagina but yours might be the exception, so when it comes to mine—"

"What are you even talking about?" I try to make out her face in the dark. "Wait, are you *nervous*? I think you're really nervous!" It delights me to think I'm not the only one who's on the verge of a panic attack.

"Well, it's a lot of pressure to be someone's first for everything," she says incredulously. "You might be wrong about wanting to do this with a girl, so I'm saying it's fine if you change your mind. It'll only feel like we're going to die of embarrassment for about thirty seconds, but then we'll—"

I cut her off. "This is a very sweet pep talk and I appreciate you wanting me to feel comfortable, but I think if we stop talking about it, we'll be much better off."

I take everything off and get under the covers as if they're a bomb shelter. My heart is the loudest thing in the room and when she touches me my body shudders, not because it's cold but because whoa. She pushes my legs apart and that's when all my nervous thinking stops. Nerves become nerves, millions of them responding to her lips, saying yes, this is how

I exist. Because sex is where the thinking stops so that the single best thing that's ever happened to you keeps happening and keeps happening until you think you might explode. And then you do. It's only after, when your sweat is drying and you're regaining the feeling in your toes that you realize you're some sort of miracle. What else do you call going to pieces without falling apart?

We lie on the bed afterward and all the nervousness I didn't feel before creeps in.

There's no big hunger in my body anymore, but should the moment feel more momentous or something? I lick my lips wishing I could consult Sara, who was arguably more invested in losing my virginity than I was.

"What are you thinking about?" Bugg faces me by propping herself on her elbow, but it's too dark to really see each other. I point to her body.

"Pubic hairs?"

I shake my head.

"Fire crotches?"

I laugh and shake my head. "I was thinking that you're right about vaginas not being remotely related to flowers. They don't smell the same or feel the same, and they're not pretty in any way that would make you want to put them in a vase in your kitchen."

"See? That's everything wrong with the patriarchy and all that scented tampon shit. Vaginas aren't *supposed* to look like flowers or smell like flowers or be fucking flowers."

"Hold up, I'm not saying they can't be in the flower *family*, just that they can't be a lily or a daffodil. If they *had* to be a flower, since you've planted this idea in my head, then they'd be an anomaly-type flower, the badass ones that eat flies."

"Venus fly traps!"

"Exactly." I close my eyes, liking how it feels to have our bodies pressed together without anything confusing like clothing in the way.

"So are you disappointed?" she asks quietly.

I take the strand of hair that's fallen across her cheek and kiss it, which is hands down the daintiest thing I've ever done. "Not even a little."

"Come on, we're going swimming," Bugg says the next morning, then throws a red-striped towel at me.

I don't think I'm awake yet. "What time is it?" I ask, squinting into the sunlight that's coming through the window. The room is a lot bigger than I noticed last night, with ocean-blue walls and mahogany furniture.

"Time to have fun. Come on." She starts rapid-fire kissing my face.

"Okay, okay, let me get my bathing suit."

"You don't need a bathing suit. I only told you to pack one so you'd anticipate going swimming, but obviously no one goes swimming unless they're naked."

I'm about to protest, but there's no arguing with her, particularly not with her naked body, so I try to cover as much of *my* naked body with the towel as I can. When we run out of the house and down the path to the beach the sand is warm under my feet.

"See, there's no one here!" she says when we get down to the water. And I have to admit her observation skills are on point. She takes her towel off and runs squawking into the waves. I try to form the sign of the cross, but I was never baptized so instead I run in squawking too. The thrill of being naked in broad daylight and letting the water carry me makes me feel ecstatic. It's the sort of thing Sara would love to do if we didn't hate each other right now.

Bugg and I lie on our backs so our nipples poke through the water, and somehow I'm trembling with the whole universe, sensitive enough to know the vibration of everything, like a perfectly operating human seismograph. And that's when I get my most brilliant idea ever.

"I've just had the most brilliant idea ever. I'm not saying I'm Thomas Jefferson or Ben Franklin or anyone like that, but we should lead a revolution." I feel the excitement building in my voice, and as I talk a flock of geese flies toward us, the V getting larger when they fly above us. I detail how this revolution will be against all the bullshit in the world, which there happens to be a lot of.

"You're right," Bugg says, floating closer to me, and her wet hair tickles my arm. "And we'll call ourselves something good, something that tells people we're not playing their game, something like the Venus Fly Trappers of the Revolution—"

"Except more pithy and less obvious."

"How about just the Trappers, then?" She turns onto her stomach and looks at me excitedly. "I'll write poems and you'll do anything you want, 'cause obviously you don't want to be a surgeon. And the only objective will be to feel like this every day." Her pale skin is flushed either from excitement or an early onset sunburn.

"We'll live by your manifesto and I'll keep one of those cooking blogs, the ones by very chubby, very happy, rosy-cheeked women," I say, and my stomach growls. "I'll give up on veganism once and for all and make meat pies and eat them without a single fuck about it."

"And we won't care about having a lot of money or what people think of us."

"Or worry about being skinny," I add, just for fun.

She grabs my hand under the water and I let my body move with the current. The best thing about being a Trapper is you can sense exactly what you're looking for, at the exclusion of everything else. When you finally catch the right thing, well, you just know.

"I think maybe Sara and I have been holding each other back for a long time," I whisper, but as soon as it's out of my mouth I feel guilty. I'm relieved that Bugg was underwater for the entirety of my confession.

"I'm ravenous," Bugg says when she comes up for air. "What would you have for breakfast if you could have anything in the world?"

"Bacon," I answer immediately. "Eight different types of bacon and maybe a pancake. With real maple syrup."

"Perfect. I know just the place. You're going to eat your little heart out."

And I do. Because in nothing short of a religious miracle, for the first time in nearly ten months I sit down at this random diner in this random town and actually *enjoy* a meal: no guilt, no inner peanut gallery, just Bugg's fork and my fork crisscrossing each other's plates.

"You might be onto something," I say, with my cheeks in full-on chipmunk-status. "Bacon may very well be saving my life."

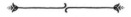

That afternoon Bugg has to pick up a mother lode of weed from some guy in town, enough to supply her clients for the rest of the summer. I'm not allowed to come because it's "too sketchy," so I wait nervously for her by the window, wondering how the hell I got myself tangled up in this, and noting that she did *not* mention any criminal activity when she suggested we run away.

She comes back an hour later with a suitcase full of more illegality than I've seen in my life: The bags are still vacuum-sealed, and it makes the trunk of her car smell like a greenhouse. "Don't ask, don't tell," she says and invites me to come with her while she makes a few deliveries, but I decline. As much as I'd love to get caught with what looks like several thousand dollars' worth of weed, I do have some sort of future to uphold.

After her weed errands are complete she reminds me that there's a party in town celebrating the full moon. Usually I forget the moon is a thing, but Bugg promises it's going to be fun so I help her make moon cookies—the circular ones with the black-and-white frosting. She cracks an egg into the batter bowl, and I pass her the vanilla extract from my backpack.

"So these aren't vegan, I take it."

She scoops some dough from the bowl with her finger and holds it out to me. "Lick it," she commands, and I do. It's a very sexual exchange of cookie dough. I end up eating six cookies before we leave the house for what Bugg promises is the greatest night of the summer: dancing in the street, people reading palms, and vendors selling moon juice, which is a purple drink that tastes a lot like gin. Bugg wears some shawl thing with beaded tassels and carries the cookies in a basket marked FREE. I for one would never eat a stranger's cookies, but I follow her wearing an unceremonious smock, though I at least choose the white one, for attempted solidarity.

The main street is closed off and there's a band playing on an open lawn and people are milling about in their summer skin: relaxed, giggly, a little tipsy. Lanterns hang from the trees, illuminating the faces we pass, and Bugg and I hold hands in public for once. At first I feel naked in a bad way—exposed and vulnerable—but then I feel naked in a good way—exposed and free. Just as I'm starting to feel like Bugg and I should relocate so we can reinvent ourselves and stay this way all the time, I see a face I recognize.

"Hey, isn't that your...ex-girlfriend?" I subtly turn Bugg in the direction of the girl with short blue hair. Bugg nods, and as she does the girl looks up at us, her face morphing into an angry frown. She starts coming toward us, staring intently at Bugg, and I feel myself shrinking into the peripherals of this interaction.

"What are you doing here?" the girl demands. She has a laughing moon painted on her left cheek that starkly contrasts with her mood. "You know the moon festival is my territory."

Bugg grips my hand and steps closer to me.

"Veronica, this is Dan—"

Veronica cuts Bugg off. "I don't care who it is. We agreed that I got the moon festival and I wouldn't steal back my pipe." My mind flashes back to Bugg cradling the dragon pipe in her car, claiming it had been stolen from *her.*

"You'd already given me the pipe, then you tried to take it back, which is bullshit. Besides, you can't hog an entire festival just because we met here."

As they start bickering I let go of Bugg's hand and back into a storefront selling a lot of strong-smelling soaps. I'm sure Bugg didn't drag me on this getaway for the possibility of running into Veronica and making her jealous, but suddenly my moon juice is too warm to drink and more than anything else I want to call Sara. When I look back warily, Bugg has her arms crossed and Veronica's voice is rising.

"You can't act like I'm what's wrong with you and if you cut me out of your life you'll be fine. I'm not the reason you had to go to treatment, Sally Bugg. I'm not the one who made you drink so much you tried to kill yourself, *you* are. When are you going to take responsibility for the things you do instead of pawning off your mistakes on other people?"

I don't wait to hear Bugg's retort. Instead I throw my cup into the grass, kind of hoping for a littering fine. Everything fun has to have some sort of consequence.

I walk back to the house and lie in the indoor hammock for so long the rope diamonds leave their mark. Bugg gets home half an hour after I do and apologizes profusely, reassuring me that this was all a bad coincidence. I feel cold toward her until she starts crying (I'm not a sociopath or anything). She makes another batch of cookies to make it up to me, though what "it" is exactly, I'm not sure.

Before we fall asleep she kisses my shoulder and I notice that despite the cookies and despite Veronica, when our bodies are touching I feel lighter or something, even though I'm the exact same density as before.

The next morning while Bugg brushes her teeth I look at my phone for the first time since we got here, when I told my parents I was safe.

"I don't want to go back and face the real world," I say, looking reluctantly at the black screen. By "the real world" I mean Sara, my parents, the looming prospect of returning to Harvard, and whatever label something like what Bugg and I are doing requires.

"I think you should reach out to Sara, though." Toothpaste foam squishes out of Bugg's mouth as she speaks. "She's going through a lot what with being cut from the tennis team and stuff."

"What?"

She spits in the sink more times than necessary. "Shit, I thought you knew."

"She got *cut*? She told me they were going to make her *captain* next year."

Bugg talks into her toothbrush. "I shouldn't have

said anything—I assumed that because you were her best friend...I think, she only told me because she got drunk at my house that night—"

"Well, now I *have* to call her." I hold down the home button and my phone lights up. I have three voicemails from Janet, five from my mom, and two from my dad, but nothing from Sara. I listen to my mom's first.

"Danny, please, PLEASE call me. It's urgent."

There's a bad feeling in my stomach as I dial. "Mom, what is it?" I ask when she picks up. "I'm sorry I missed all your calls this morning. I had my phone off."

"Danny," she says and then she starts crying, and not little whimpers either. Big, stinking sobs. I lean against the bathroom door for support. "How soon can you get to the hospital? Sara's here and it's critical."

My body turns to stone, but I will my mouth to move.

"Be there in an hour."

CHAPTER FIFTEEN

The whole car ride I'm thinking that even though it's critical, it's okay. Everything with Sara is perpetually okay. I take out my MCAT study book, which I snuck into my backpack, and try to commit some formulas to memory but nothing will stay in my head.

"Are you sure you don't want me to come in with you?" Bugg asks when she drops me off at the emergency entrance. She went at least ninety the whole way, which got us there in fifty-five life-threatening minutes.

"No, thanks. Not until I know what's going on."

"Okay, call me," she says, and I run in through the automatic doors.

Inside, everything is white and smells like old people and doughnuts and hand sanitizer. Hospitals are so depressing, it's no wonder people die here. I walk so fast my feet squeak on the ground, which would be funny in any other circumstance, and my hands clench in and out of fists with the tempo of my footsteps. I'm afraid to take my eyes off the orange exit sign at the end of the hall, as if without a single unmoving point to focus on, the world will spin entirely out of my control. I follow a sign to the waiting room, and when I turn the corner Janet is there, holding a Dunkin' Donuts napkin up to her face. There's mascara all down her cheeks.

"Janet—"

She pulls me into a tight hug and I feel her whole body shake. "You missed her." Her voice is hardly her voice at all.

"Who did I miss? Where's Sara?" Seeing other people cry has this domino effect on me, and tears roll down my cheeks too. "Janet, please tell me what's going on. Where's my mom? She told me she was here."

"She went," Janet starts, but she's crying too hard to get anything coherent out.

I try to flag down the three doctors who are coming toward us. They're all wearing the same green scrubs, which, I distract myself by thinking, makes them look unnecessarily like aliens. Don't they make any other-colored scrubs?

"Excuse me," I say. "Is there any way you can tell me what's going on? I don't know if you know anything about our situation, but we're here for Sara Collins, who's in critical condition so I need to see her, but I don't know where she is and I don't understand what's wrong, but if someone told me, I think it'd be much easier, you know, for me."

Janet clutches my arm until I feel like I'm going to lose all circulation. "Sara didn't make it," she says, but the last word comes out as a screech that echoes through the hallway of my ear like the longest and loneliest tunnel.

"Didn't make what?" I ask, but by this point I know. My mouth waters and I feel dizzy. Three-Part Pause-and . . .

But I can't remember how it is that I'm supposed to breathe.

Two of the doctors put their hands on Janet's shoulders and tell her to come with them, and the other looks like she's about to talk to me, but then my mom comes around the corner with a box full of Munchkins.

"Mom," I say, and I sound about six years old. "Mom, please, tell me what happened. Why won't anyone tell me anything?"

She hugs me so hard she drops the Munchkins.

"Careful, those are precious cargo." I pick the box up and stuff one in my mouth quickly, as if to put a stopper in it. I hardly feel myself chew, almost like something has snapped between my brain and my mouth, and they're not connected anymore.

"We're still waiting on the details," my mom says as I occupy myself with the doughnut holes.

"I don't understand how people our age end up in critical condition. Was it a car accident? Something with Ethan's boat?" The jelly from the Munchkin explodes in my mouth in a way that's sickening. "I need to know *something*."

One of the doctors approaches and leads us into the small windowless room where Janet is already seated. "She was at home, sweetie, having her tennis lesson," my mom whispers. "Come sit down; they're going to tell us everything they know."

I sit between Janet and my mom on the hard little bed, but the sheets feel weird and my face starts to get hot and my mouth waters again. The itchy feeling is moving into my brain, taking over my fingers, which now tap the bed in rounds of five. I shouldn't have eaten those Munchkins. I shouldn't have left for the weekend with Bugg. I shouldn't have compared Sara to a sponge. Some sort of sickness is growing in my stomach now, and I have to get it out.

Not an option, I remind myself. But I have to say it a few more times before I believe it.

I look at the doctors and wipe my lips. Powdered sugar comes off on my hands, which is sort of a surprise. My theory is that I am dreaming this whole thing.

"Can you please tell me what happened to Sara?" I ask the female doctor. Maybe it's not fair, but I suspect she's more likely than the two male doctors to feel sorry for me and therefore answer my questions.

"Sara was rushed here this morning after collapsing on her tennis court at home," one of the male doctors answers. "Her tennis coach called 9-1-1, but by the time the ambulance came, the complication with her heart had already rendered her unconscious. We tried surgery, but unfortunately it was ineffective. She passed about forty minutes ago."

My mom lets out a soft cry and hugs me closer to her body. I think I feel her tears on my forehead, but it's impossible to discern what's happening.

"I don't understand." I look left and right between the doctors, hoping the motion will keep my brain in my head. "Sara is healthy and plays tennis all the time."

"We're not sure what brought it on. We're assuming it was congenital, but we won't know for a few more days," the female doctor says.

At the moment, I don't know what *congenital* means, which goes to show you what a terrible pre-med student I am or else how slow my brain is functioning. I sit on the bed like a cardboard version of myself.

"We are so sorry for your loss."

I want to say something, but there's so much saliva in my mouth I think my tongue might drown. Which I guess is for the better. There's not a goddamn thing left in the world to say.

"Cal is on his way back from California now," Janet says, but she sounds dead or something.

"We'll stay until then," my mom says. The hot itchiness is narrowing my vision, but at the same time it's like I'm watching someone else with my hand reach for another Munchkin.

"No, let's all go," Janet says, her voice uncharacteristically calm. I wish she would sob uncontrollably, say something inappropriate, be just Janet. "There's no reason to stay here."

"But isn't Sara still here?" I ask. It seems wrong to leave her alone. What if they're taking her kidney out or something? Her new fake ID said she's an organ donor, so her regular ID probably says it too. "We can't leave her. We can't go. I'm not leaving." I feel the hysteria in my voice rising, snapping the last wire and shutting down my brain entirely.

"She's gone, baby," my mom whispers.

The word has an eerie thud to it. *Gone.* Like a metal pipe landing in a pit of dirt. No splash, no echo.

CHAPTER SIXTEEN

The hours afterward don't pass so much as solidify around me like Jell-O, trapping me inside. I wake up at three in the afternoon wondering why, as a swear, *fuck* is so much worse than *damn*. You'd think *damn* would be worse, considering you're sentencing someone to Hell for eternity, while *fuck* in the worst of scenarios is a stranger you'll never see again. I drink two servings of NyQuil (calories unknown) and pass out again until a little after eight, when the sun is setting so brightly through my window I think it's about to blow up. *At least let me have some cereal first*, I tell it, but when I go downstairs I can't choose between the almond or the coconut milk. Why, if not for the love of cows, are there so many milk substitutes? Aren't there any spare activists to save the soybeans? Of course there aren't. Not even an edamame has an easy life. Every living thing senses its mortality.

I pour Cheerios into a bowl, then get a spoon from the drawer. It's cool in my palm. Sara and I used to put them on our noses to see who could keep them there the longest, I guess to see who had the better spoon nose. I try to eat my cereal, but the o's are bloated with milk and float in the bowl like unclaimed life preservers.

And the rest of the night is like that: totally unremarkable. The world doesn't even have the decency to blow up. I send Bugg a brief text finally responding to all her questions about what happened and explain that I can't talk because I'm currently in outer space: Will text you when I return to my earthly body. Then I turn my cell phone off and put it in the kitchen drawer, mostly scared that I'll forget and try to text Sara something stupid, like a cat meme. At one point my parents come home and the three of us huddle on the couch, even though it's too warm for it. All night I sweat through my grief, staining every surface I touch, from the bedsheets to my sleeves.

I have no sense of time, but according to the clock, it's been forty-seven hours since Sara died. My parents and I are on our way to Sara's house, and I'm trying to prepare myself, but it's not the sort of thing you can sharpen your pencils for.

When Janet and Cal open the door, my dad hugs Cal and it feels weird to see them a) hug and b) cry. Conventional standards of behavior are falling apart, and I don't feel good about it. As we walk in, my dad puts his arm around me and whispers in my ear, "I'm so glad you're safe."

But safe is the last thing I feel. Honestly, it feels like I'm on the precipice of something very, very bad.

"Can I get you guys anything?" Janet asks as we take seats in the kitchen. The coffeepot is brewing but we shake our heads. She launches into it alarmingly fast. "Cal and I want to talk to you guys, mainly you, Danny, about what happened with Sara and the arrangements for the funeral."

"Please let us know if we can help in any way," my mom says, semi-interrupting her. When Janet thanks her, I wonder if she hates my mom because my mom still has a daughter, albeit a slightly fucked-up one, or if she feels jealous or if she feels anything at all.

"Two months ago, Cal was diagnosed with hypertrophic cardiomyopathy," Janet begins.

Meanwhile, Cal stands with his back to us, getting out mugs and pouring coffee in them. The one he gives to Janet has a picture of her and Sara on it from one of those kiosks in the mall. If all that's going to be left of Sara are things like Sara-inspired mugs, then I don't want to have any part of her at all.

"He'd been having chest pain, so we finally got him to the doctor, and luckily they were able to detect it. In most cases it's asymptomatic with a high rate of sudden death," she says.

"We wanted Sara to get tested too," Cal adds, stirring sugar into this coffee. "Because it's genetic."

It gets terribly quiet as all that sinks in.

"We tried to get her to go, but she didn't want to get tested," Janet says. "She didn't want to risk slowing down her game or stopping altogether. You guys know she was cut from the team, but she thought that if she could prove herself, she could get her spot back."

Well, actually, no, we did not know until Bugg accidentally said something about it, but I guess that's all irrelevant now.

"And I tried, I really tried to get her to go but she's an adult now, was an adult, and you guys know how it goes." Janet's voice starts to break and Cal puts his hand on her back, but he's staring into his cup.

"You can't blame yourself," my mom says. "It was a terrible accident." My dad and I nod. My mom is very good at saying the right thing.

"It was sudden, very sudden," Janet continues. "One

minute she was playing, the next she was lying on the court. Her coach did everything she could and those surgeons were excellent, but—" She starts to cry again and Cal takes over.

"We don't know how much of this, the background story, we're going to tell everyone. We'd like to protect Sara's and our privacy, but we wanted you guys to know the full story."

Again we all nod, but it's like they want us to keep their secrets, which I guess I should be fine with, but something about it feels slimy.

"We're going to have a funeral and a private burial next week," Janet says, again like this is some business proposition. "What we were hoping, Danny, is that you would write Sara's eulogy. Sometimes it felt like you were closer to Sara than even Cal and I were. It would mean so much to us if you would write something in her honor."

"Of course," I say because I'm not going to say *no*. The problem is public speaking gives me hives, and the tone of her voice and the expressionless stare of her red-rimmed eyes are giving me a cold-fish feeling in my stomach.

The coffeepot makes a final, exhausted cough and I hold my breath, hoping the silence will break quickly. It doesn't, and realizing there's nothing left to say, we all shuffle outside together for one final round of good-byes.

As soon as we're safely in the car, my mom goes off. "I can't believe they didn't make her get tested. What sort of parents—"

"Enough," my dad interrupts her, gripping the steering wheel like it holds the last of his sanity. "It's not going to bring her back."

"All I'm saying is you can't trust a kid to make decisions like that even if they *are* an adult. Look what we did when we found out about Danny: met with her dean, got her the help she needed. We were *involved*. It's called responsible parenting. She hated us at first, but you've gotten over that now, haven't you, Danny?"

"I never hated you," I say miserably. At least never as much as I hated myself for not being more discreet about everything. Still, at least Sara's parents had the decency to leave her alone.

"Kids may only be kids, but they have to work out their own problems."

I roll my eyes at my dad's hypocrisy.

"*No*, kids need protection." My mom turns to me. "We should work on the eulogy tonight," she adds, as if this is some sort of group project.

"I don't know what to say." Not in the eulogy, not about anything at all.

My dad gets off the highway and I look out the window at the most unfortunate moment because something big is lying in the road. At first I don't think it's dead, or I wish it weren't, but then we get closer. There's no blood, no tire marks, no disruption in the feather stuff, but the goose is certainly dead. Her head hangs from her neck at a ninety-degree angle, which feels like a bad omen or something.

"Why is everything dead today?" I ask as I look back at its contorted shape on the side of the road. *You're still alive*, I tell it. It doesn't move.

"It's a *Branta canadensis occidentalis*," my dad says, never one to miss a chance to remind us that he's a bird professor.

"*Was* a *Branta canadensis* whatever."

Because Janet made some Facebook status, I don't have to tell Kate or Liz or any of Sara's friends that Sara is, you know, what Sara is. I decide to deactivate all forms of social media because there's something very creepy about finding out about death on the same platform where you get live updates about people's cats. Besides, people are posting all these hokey statuses and sad pictures, and I don't have that sort of public display in me.

I retrieve my cell phone from the drawer and discover a million missed calls and unread texts, but Bugg is the only person I want to talk to. She picks up on the first ring.

"I've been so worried. Are you okay?" she asks. "God, that's such a stupid thing to say."

"No, can you come over?"

"Be right there."

I hear my mom let Bugg in, and when she comes into my room I'm tucked into bed with my dear friends: peanut butter, M&M's, and pepperoni. I haven't had this mutant snack concoction in too long, and my life has been severely lackluster because of it.

"Wouldn't this be an awesome-sounding name for a rap group?" I ask, pointing to my goods. "Especially if you abbreviated peanut butter to 'PB.'"

"You could be their manager," Bugg agrees, sitting on the bed next to me. We smile for a moment but as soon as she kisses my forehead I burst into slobbery tears.

"What happened, Danny?" she asks, and I'm glad she's whispering. It's the sort of thing you can't talk about, but if you have to talk about it, a whisper is all that feels right.

I try to say something but it gets lost in a great series of hiccups, so she pats my hair and waits for me to catch my breath. When I can finally breathe without gasping these weird seal gasps, I tell her everything Janet and Cal and the doctors told us.

"She knew she could have had it." I can hear how angry I sound. "She knew it and she didn't want it to ruin her chances of trying to get back on the team, which she told everyone about except for me. And on top of that she knew it could kill her because Cal got tested or whatever, and she never did anything. It was so fucking selfish." I dig the spoon into the peanut butter jar and watch the soupy crushed peanuts inch back to their source. "I fucking hate this peanut butter," I add because natural peanut butter is the grossest kind of peanut butter. "And I don't mean that, about Sara. If she knew, *really* knew that it were possible to die, she would've stopped playing. I know she would have. She never wanted to be a tennis martyr or something. She wouldn't have left me." I stop stabbing the peanut butter swamp and look at Bugg. Tears are rolling down her cheeks. "She was wrong, but I can't blame her for that. No one *actually* thinks it's possible to die."

"God, I can't believe it. It's so *chilling*." There are bags under her eyes, and it looks like she hasn't slept in a few nights. "Can I have a bite of that?"

I pass her the spoon. "I can't believe she didn't tell me," I say.

"Is it really that surprising, though? She was keeping her medical shit to herself," Bugg points out, "just like you were keeping your St. John's shit to yourself." I want to snatch my precious peanut butter from her, then dump it on her head.

"But I didn't tell her because that was *private*. And so embarrassing."

"Maybe it was embarrassing for her too," Bugg says quietly.

"But mine was way worse, way harder to talk about.

She at least had something physical, something concrete to deal with. Mental illness is like trying to follow along with a Houdini act."

I take Sara's tiny pink helicopter from the nightstand and stuff it into a drawer. Bugg bites her lip. "Yeah, but you both held each other to such an impossible standard that it seems reasonable to have a hard time telling each other about your quote unquote failures."

"Then why did you keep trying to get me to tell Sara the truth? As if I was the only one not holding up my end of the friendship bargain?" I can't even believe we're having a semi-fight at a time like this.

"I told her to tell you the truth too!" Bugg says.

For some reason that makes me feel more betrayed. "I thought you were with *me*. I didn't think you were playing both sides. You and Sara were hardly even friends."

"Come on, Danny," she says gently. "I wasn't trying to play anybody. Before I knew that *you* were Danny, Sara said she was going through a weird time with her best friend, so I offered to help."

"Well, yeah, friendship is like a river," I say angrily. "Sometimes it dries up a little, but that doesn't mean it's not a river anymore." I wipe my eyes. "And I hate this organic fucking peanut butter."

"Yeah, it's bad." She clicks her tongue on the roof of her mouth. "Really sticks to the back of your throat, doesn't it?"

"That's what she said."

Bugg laughs and so do I, which feels good. It feels terrible too, guilt-laden and inappropriate, but I guess so does being alive.

"I didn't mean that, about her being selfish or you playing sides. It's just so weird. I feel like I'm looking through a kaleidoscope, but it's not fun or colorful. It's dark and disturbed. Contorted, like. I don't know what anything means, so I'm sorry."

"Don't apologize," Bugg says. I lean in closer to her and get a little lost in her cinnamon and cigarettes smell.

"I have to write Sara's eulogy within the next week. Maybe you could read it over for me before I go word-vomit on however many hundreds of people are going to be there on Wednesday."

"You're not going to word-vomit. You're going to be great." She kisses me on the lips this time. "I'm supposed to help Cynthia out tonight, but I can cancel if you want to, like, do a weed run or crash a house party," she offers.

"No, no, it's okay. Faux-friendship duties call, meaning I should go see Liz and Kate. Besides, I think Sara's parents are having people over. My mom said something about bringing a tuna casserole, but you'd think that'd make everyone more depressed."

Bugg's face wrinkles. "Gross. Why do adults insist on eating the worst food?"

"Because they suck."

"Well, let me know when you're done and we'll work on the eulogy. You're also always welcome to sleep over," she says, which makes me want to cancel my whole life and move to Mars with her. Since there are no space shuttles in the vicinity, once she leaves I prepare myself for all the ensuing grief-stricken socializing in the best way I know how: by consuming about three thousand more calories.

CHAPTER SEVENTEEN

Being at Sara's house with all these people and all this food reminds me of the surprise party we threw for her fifteenth birthday and how when she walked through the door we scared the shit out of her. The sick thing is that I keep expecting her to walk through the door and scare the shit out of *us*, and I have to keep reminding myself that's not what dead people do. They don't walk through doors or attend surprise parties or do anything ever again. They certainly don't eat six pigs in a blanket (which are really cows in a blanket), like I just did.

"I can't believe there's a God if he'd do something like

this," I overhear Kate telling Liz. I feel like telling them God is the adult equivalent of Santa Claus, but I think this is supposed to be a time for us all to "come together." And I guess it *is* better than being alone, at least for Janet and Cal and forty of Sara's closest friends and family. I change my mind when Kate and Liz come over and try to talk to me.

"Oh, Danny, can you believe it?" Liz says.

"Nflsknviowe," I say, because my mouth is full.

"What?"

I swallow too much too fast and my esophagus freaks out. "No, not at all," I clarify after I've coughed.

"I don't know how you can even *eat* at a time like this," Kate says.

I narrow my eyes at her stupid, skinny face. "I must be an incredible human."

"It's so good you're becoming a doctor," Liz says. "I can't think of a better way to honor Sara than by saving other people's lives. Do you think you'll be a heart surgeon now or, like, a different organ surgeon?"

I squint at them and try to figure out where the logic in that sentence is. "Probably a plastic surgeon," I say, because it's just too easy with them. "Hit me up in ten years if you decide you want a boob job or something." It's beyond relieving when my phone rings. "Sorry, gotta get this." I deliberately take more food with me as I go outside to answer it.

"What's up, Stephen?" I ask. The night air feels good and quiet.

"Danny," he says and it kind of sounds like he's been crying. "I'm so, so sorry about what happened. I saw it on Instagram."

"Thank you. Thanks a lot." This has become my stock response. I used the shit out of it back there in Sara's kitchen, and I'll probably have many more uses for the double ingratiation in the days to come.

"I don't know if it's appropriate, because I only met Sara once, but I know how close you two were, so if you wanted I could come to the funeral. I figured since we were maybe going to hang out sometime this summer that we could do that instead. Not that that's a fun-hang-out activity," he adds quickly.

"Yeah, sure you could come. Thanks. Thanks so much."

"If you need anything in the meantime, let me know."

"Thank you. Thanks a lot."

After we hang up I notice a red plastic cup stuffed in the bushes near the tennis court. It could've been anyone's who was at the party that first night of summer, but the sight of it makes me feel uneasy. It's a relief to go back inside and feel the chaos of so many people talking and eating and crying. Every so often I look at the door, wondering if Bugg is going to show up. Part of me wants her to, but the other part of me thinks that after the whole sex thing happened between us, it's going to make our dynamic noticeably different. On top of everything else I don't need people asking questions about Bugg and me, which is why when she comes through the door I feel equal parts relieved and sick to my stomach.

She weaves through groups of people and introduces herself to Janet, who then gives her a hug.

"I was Sara's friend from yoga," Bugg says, and I notice she omits the "and I sold weed to her less than five times" part. "I was only just getting to know Sara, but I'm so sorry for your loss." I can't help noticing that, unlike nearly everyone else in the room, Bugg looks pretty when she cries.

"Her death was so sudden and unexpected. We can't believe it—no warning signs or anything," Janet says. Which is slightly untrue, but I guess we're all continuously lying for appearances' sake.

"I feel lucky to have gotten to know her even for a short while. She had the best energy. It was palpable when she walked into a room."

Listening to this conversation feels like how it would probably feel to watch your parents have sex, so I make a beeline for the bacon-covered scallops and lose myself in the magic that is fatty land and sea creatures combined.

When Bugg's done talking, she comes over to me and puts her arm around my waist, which I then turn into a hug so that no one will get suspicious. I give her a look that clearly says Please Don't Act Like You've Interacted With Me Naked and she whispers, "Sorry. I thought you might have changed your mind about PDA."

"No, not even a little bit. If anything, it's more

imperative than ever that we keep this whole thing under wraps," I say, licking the bacon dribble from my fingers. I'm a little annoyed she'd even bring it up at a time like this.

"Whatever you need, Danny." She helps herself to bacon-wrapped scallops.

The whole time we're talking I can feel Kate and Liz's eyes on us, not because I'm paranoid but because they're actually staring at us. I'm not psychic or anything, but I have a feeling it's going to be a problem. I break away from Bugg under the pretense of having to console Ethan, who is literally soaking the cheese and cracker plate with his tears. As I hold his muscles awkwardly (because we're hugging, not because I'm suddenly into jocks), I make a note to keep my Bugg life as separate from my other life as humanly possible. Unfortunately, Sara has made it exponentially more difficult and if she were here, I'd let her know what an inconvenient time it was for her to go and die.

It hasn't rained once all summer, so when it pours for a few days there's a sense of relief in the air. Water drips steadily from the gutter, and I feel something pool inside of me too. I should probably tell Leslie about it during our sessions, but my parents are concerned enough for the three of us, not that they know what's percolating in my screwed-up headspace. What they're reacting to is the full residency

I've taken up in my bed, with the AC on the Antarctica setting.

"Are you okay, Danny?" my mom asks the day before the funeral. She's standing in my doorway rubbing her arms for warmth. I'm in the middle of an epic journaling session, after having asked Cynthia to e-mail me extra prompts.

"I think so." I roll onto my side and pull my Harry Potter blanket up to my nose. "I think as long as we all stick to the facts we'll be fine."

"What facts, sweetie?"

"That Sara is dead. Sara died on Saturday at twelve fifty-three p.m. Sara died of a heart attack. You know, the facts."

"I think you're in shock, Danny, and that's okay," my mom says, inviting herself in and turning my AC down.

Well, of course I'm in shock, I want to shout. But the thing about being in shock is that even if you keep saying *I'm in shock, I'm in shock, I'm in shock*, it doesn't make you less in shock.

"I'm fine. I just need to focus on writing this eulogy. My friend from poetry class said she'd help me, so I'm going to shower, then go to her house."

"The pretty one who came over a few days ago?" my mom asks.

The problem with living with your parents is you can't easily sneak people in and out unless you use the window, but that starts to get dangerous, what with all those statistics about ladders and broken tibias.

"Yeah. She went to Brown." I know how to get my mom to want me to keep a friend around.

"Oh, excellent! What year did she graduate? It'd be so great for you to have a sort of mentor."

Shit. "Um, I forget." I quickly change the subject as my mom pauses with a pile of my clothes in her hands. "I can do that, Mom. Leave my sweaty smocks where I left them."

"You need to clean up in here, Danny. A tidy room reflects a tidy mental space."

"Fine, you stay and I'll go. I have to shower now or I'm going to be late."

She hands me my towel, looking hurt and confused.

When I get to the doorway I turn around. "There has to be one part of my life that gets to be messy, that nobody else tries to clean up. Even if you do my laundry and put my clothes away this one time, it's not going to stay that way unless I keep it that way. Okay?"

She nods but still clutches my clothes. I wouldn't be surprised if I came back and found her on her hands and knees scrubbing the floor.

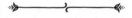

Bugg and I try to make out on her porch swing for a while, to get me inspired, but it feels wrong. Every time our tongues touch I remember the last time I saw Sara, which obviously wasn't the finest hour in our friendship.

I ask Bugg to read her "September" poem to me, the one that ends with "but their scent / is there any scent as sweet / as dying leaves?" I think she meant *leaves* as in the plant, but I like that it can be read as *leaves* as in "left behind." More things should be open to interpretation like that. It's nice to have something feel up to me.

"I can't believe we didn't get to resolve anything," I say when she finishes reading, and I make the swing rock with my foot. The rain has stopped, but it smells like it's still raining around us. "This eulogy is my only chance to apologize to her. It has to be everything."

Bugg lights two cigarettes, one for her and one for me, then puts her arm around me.

"If you put that much pressure on yourself, you're going to shit your pants."

"I don't *wear* pants," I say, wondering when I started to like smoking cigarettes.

"Ultimately, *you* have to forgive yourself. You already know Sara would." Then she pulls a pen and paper from her bag and ashes the cigarette over the arm of the swing. "Let's take down some ideas."

The things that come to mind are clichés that don't do Sara any justice. "She was a light in people's life" or "Her smile lit up a whole room."

"I don't want it to be one of those eulogies that lies, you know? The ones that say so-and-so was practically an archangel who descended from heaven by the grace of God's thumb, and we were all so lucky to be graced by her super-human presence while we trudged through our mortal, shit lives." I take a long drag, proud of myself for not coughing. "Sara wasn't more selfless or loving or kind than anyone else I know," I say through the smoke. "And a lot of times she was less. But what was great about Sara was that she was exactly Sara all the time. She knew what was impor-tant to her, and she didn't care if other people thought it was shallow or stupid or self-absorbed. She didn't act all heroic when she got cut from the team, she lied about it, because she was human and being human is way better than being anything else."

I sigh and watch the ash accumulate on the end of the cigarette. I can't say any of those things in front of a crowd of hysterical people who want to hear about how Sara was the brightest star in an otherwise dark, bumfuck galaxy, but it feels good to say them to myself anyway.

"I feel you," Bugg says. "You don't want to put her on a pedestal just because she's dead."

"Exactly."

"Well, what if you talk about who Sara was to you? If you keep it specific to your relationship, you won't have to worry about making any grandiose statements about her superhumanness."

"But," I say, and my lip trembles against my will, "it was such a shitty time for her to have to die. Our friendship was coming apart at the seams."

"I don't believe that," Bugg says. "What about friendship being like a river? You were experiencing a drought is all."

"I don't know." I get up from the swing and rattle the chains so hard that the birds roosting above us scatter from the roof and disappear into her perfectly manicured backyard.

"Well, hey, so what if it was coming apart?" Bugg gets up and stands next to me. "That doesn't mean you didn't have a good run of it. Or that you didn't love each other and give each other your tiny worlds while you could. Nothing lasts forever," she says, reaching the end of her cigarette and stomping on it.

"But we had The Plan," I say, rubbing my eyes and feeling a headache coming on.

Bugg shrugs. "You made a plan when you were kids, and it was sweet and a little weird, but isn't it also what started to destroy you? You gotta say fuck The Plan."

"It's not that easy to say fuck The Plan." I lean my elbows on the rail of the porch, as if it's suddenly too much effort to hold myself up. "We had our whole house built, and while I totally appreciate the words of wisdom even though you're only, like, two years older than I am, I think I should figure out the rest of this myself."

Bugg bites her lip and tries to put her hand on my hand, but I move it out of reach.

"I'm sorry, I didn't mean to make it seem like I know it

all. Obviously I don't know everything about your relationship with Sara."

"No, you don't. You came into it in the last two months. We've been going at it for the last fourteen years. I shouldn't have asked for any help with this. The eulogy is between Sara and me, and since it's the last thing between Sara and me, I have to get it right and I have to do it alone."

I don't know why I'm so angry, but I leave Bugg's house crying, which is getting exhausting at this point.

In an attempt to make everything better I stop at McDonald's. Something somewhere in my body is so hungry that it's threatening to make me crazy unless I eat every forbidden nonfruit in my fast-food garden. Six dollars later I take my burger to the ocean and eat it while the tide moves in and out.

As I sit on the hood of my dad's car, the burger and fries go about the task of filling up my arteries. It's a tasty process until I bite into an onion and think about how Sara only liked caramelized onions and how weird it is that she'll never be annoyed by regular onions again. I feel the hot itchiness establishing itself, and soon it's too itchy to handle. *Three-Part*, I start to say to myself, but I can't remember the rest of it. All I can think about is how I have to get this food out of my stomach or I'm going to burst into a million pieces. Besides, it's about progress, not perfection. Isn't that what Leslie keeps telling me? Throwing up one time in three months is much better than throwing up after every meal. So really I'd be *proving* my recovery by throwing up a tiny bit in this trash can over here, because no one is around and if a tree falls in the forest but no one is around to hear it did it make a sound and similarly, if I throw up just this once and no one is around to police it...

It's not that the act itself is particularly pleasurable, especially because nothing is digested yet, which sometimes makes it feel like you're going to choke on your own bad decision, but afterward...well, afterward it's this sense of emptiness and peace, and even though you need to brush your teeth, you feel a hell of a lot better than you did before. Really, you can handle anything. Even writing something as fucked up as your best friend's eulogy.

CHAPTER EIGHTEEN

In the hours before the funeral I let myself have carte blanche in the bathroom. It makes the time pass very quickly. You have to understand that these are difficult circumstances and being gentle with yourself is imperative. At least that's what Leslie told me this morning because my mom booked an emergency appointment with her. Since then I've been avoiding human contact. Kate and Liz wanted me to come to Sara's with them, but I'm too busy tending my garden of screwed-up eating rituals to really make time for group activities.

I'll see you guys tomorrow, though, I text them. It's very

weird to be in a group text with the two of them and not Sara. It's one of a hundred million things that feel wrong.

I also get a lot of texts from Bugg asking how I'm doing and apologizing mostly. It's not that I'm mad at her, it's that I don't want to talk to her. When I start indulging the hot itchy feeling, I don't want other people around because then they might notice and then they might put me on the first bus back to You-Know-Where.

Her last text is about the eulogy. I'm sure you have a lot written—(I have nothing written)—but in case you get writer's block Cynthia always tells me to write the worst possible thing I can that way I'll at least have something to work with. You can always do something with words. It's pretty hard to face a blank page. Thinking about you.

I can't think of a good response. It's too stressful having my cell phone on me. Whoever thought it'd be a good idea to be reachable at all times?

"Danny, come eat dinner. I made vegan lasagna," my mom hollers through my closed door. I don't have the heart to tell her veganism has gone shit out the window lately, so I join her in the kitchen and act delighted. It's all fake meat and fake cheese, but it's surprisingly delicious. Well, the first bite is delicious and the fiftieth bite is much less so, which makes me think that all of life is a series of diminishing returns.

"How are you holding up, sweetie? Your dad got stuck with students, but he is hurrying home," she says, cutting bite-size pieces of lasagna and moving them from her plate to her mouth.

"No worries. I'm fine. Still have a lot of this eulogy to write, so I should probably get back to it," I say, inhaling massive quantities of food.

"Leslie seemed a little worried."

"You talked to my therapist?" My fork clanks down on my plate too loudly.

"Danny, you know that's part of the deal we made when you were released on medical leave. The therapist, your dean, your father, and I have to be in communication so we can all be certain that you're healthy enough to go back. She's allowed to contact your father and me if she thinks she needs to." My mom pauses with her fork in the air.

Obviously I know this is part of the deal. It's the biggest reason why I don't tell my therapist anything. I could've mentioned that I don't feel okay at all, that the hot itchiness is taking over my body and I don't care because I sort of want to make a bag of popcorn and curl up inside it until all of this stops hurting so much. But that is not the sort of response that gets a girl back to college in the fall. In fact, that's the sort of response that lands a girl back in treatment.

"So what did she want?" I ask, taking a roll from the basket but not quite ready to eat it yet.

"To make sure that you're getting three solid meals a

day and not spending too much time alone. Janet invited you over for a get-together tonight, and you should go. It's important for you to be with people who loved Sara and want to remember her with you right now."

"I don't want to *remember* Sara. I want her to be here," I say, pushing the bread through the sauce on my plate. "I don't see how it could help to spend time with all these people I don't like anymore. Sara wouldn't want that."

Unfortunately, this makes my mother cry, which then makes me feel like the spawn of Satan. "I need for you to be okay," she semiwails as I help myself to a second serving. "You were doing so well, and I hope this doesn't ruin everything."

"Yeah, I can't believe Sara would go and die like that," I say, pushing a piece of impostor beef to the far end of my plate. "Talk about ruining what was otherwise going to be a perfect summer."

My mother stiffens and wipes her nose with a napkin. She takes to sarcasm the way I take to therapy, and on top of that can't stand anyone suggesting she's being insensitive. Or worse, *unmotherly.*

"Danny, I understand that you're angry right now, but please don't speak in that tone with me."

"Sorry," I mumble. Of course every mother's priority is her own child, but is it asking so much that she doesn't imply that Sara having died is soooo inconvenient for us? "If you want me to go over to Janet and Cal's for the pre-funeral get-together I will, but I still have to finish this eulogy and they're probably drinking a lot and I don't think that's a good environment for me to be around."

"I doubt it's a big party over there," my mom says coolly, which goes to show how little she knows Janet. "I'll go with you, and if it starts to feel unhealthy for you, let me know and I'll drive you back."

"Okay," I say miserably. I feel too guilty about my sarcasm to tell her I don't need a bodyguard. At least there will be good snacks.

I wake up the next morning in my parents' bed with a major bad-behavior hangover. I also have the chills.

"Thanks for letting me sleep here," I say to them a little sheepishly. Acting childishly encourages them to treat me like a child. But if I'm going to suffer all the inconveniences of living with my parents, I might as well reap the rewards too.

I have more missed texts from Bugg and a text from Stephen that's all, Hope you're doing okay, see you soon. I kind of forgot he was coming to the funeral (the problem with Stephen is he's a little forgettable) but it'll be nice to see him. It'll be nice to be with someone who doesn't remind me of Sara, because every time I remember Sara what I remember is that she's dead.

Before breakfast I make one final stab at Sara's eulogy. With my eyes puffy and head pounding it's hard to think straight, but these are symptoms of crying too much and not only symptoms of throwing up too much. Every so often a pain extends to my nonphysical body and it's so intense that I wonder if I'm going to die. When it passes I feel nothing until the pain comes back.

"Do you feel good about what you wrote?" my dad asks, straightening his tie in the reflection of the microwave and looking very un-Dad-like.

"Not really. I'm hoping that when I get up there it'll come to me, like, divine intervention or something."

He hands me the mug of coffee that says HARVARD DAD, and I take a sip.

"You're going to be great. Just remember how well you did at graduation day."

"You mean when I broke out in hives and had to drink a whole bottle of Benadryl?"

"But it was a great speech," he points out, hovering over me at the kitchen table. In the wake of everything that's happened I've stopped being mad at him for ignoring me in treatment.

"It's sweet of you to try, and thanks for loving me unconditionally, but I'm not a giver of speeches, Dad, and today will probably be no exception." I reach for the sugar in the center of the table and try to turn my coffee into something palatable. "The good thing is no one will be able to say anything bad about it because Sara is dead and that would make them look like a real asshole."

My dad kisses me on the forehead. "You feel warm, Danny. Do you feel okay?"

I nod, but I feel pretty lousy. When he leaves the room I rummage around in the cabinets and find a few dough-nuts in a paper bag. I don't know who was in charge of that operation, but unfortunately they're all cinnamon pow-dered. A few minutes later, my parents come in all ready to go.

"Sweetheart?" my mom says in a careful voice. She's putting tissues, breath mints, and other practical things into her pocketbook. Leave it to my mother to use a funeral as an opportunity to be overprepared.

"Yes?" I wipe some of the powder from my mouth and pour myself a glass of real milk, which hopefully doesn't have cow pus in it (it's organic).

"Are you almost ready?"

Do I look almost ready? Stained T-shirt, greasy hair, doughnut bits around my mouth... "I just need to shower."

"Go do that and I'll make you a real breakfast. We need to leave in twenty."

"Doughnuts *are* a real breakfast," I snap and stomp to the bathroom. I feel bad for the people around me, but I can't help it if my temper is suddenly on a half-inch fuse.

After I shower, my parents herd me into the car with a hard-boiled egg and a piece of toast.

"I don't think I can do this," I say from the back seat. We're already turning onto the main road.

"What'd you say, sweetie?" my mom asks. I can hear her typing away on her BlackBerry.

"I think I'm going to be sick."

She turns around to look at me. "Do you need us to pull over?"

I nod. I have to throw up, like, stomach-bug throw up. My dad pulls over and I open the door just in time to heave onto the curb. My mom is out of the car so fast you'd think we were doing a fire drill. She holds my hair back even though there's nothing left in my stomach. My dad leaves the car running and squats down beside her.

"There's bile in there," he says in his professor tone, as if he got a PhD in the subtleties of puke. I'm worried he's going to figure me out and ship me back to You-Know-Where, so I try to think of a way to explain that I'm regular sick, not Danny sick.

"I think I have some sort of food poisoning."

"Yes, that food was out all day at Janet and Cal's yesterday and then we ate some of it. No wonder you're sick. Poor baby." My mom strokes my hair, which feels both comforting and gross since it's still wet from the shower. My dad doesn't say anything, just asks my mom to take over and gets in the back seat with me. I put my head in his lap while my mom drives. His hand feels delightfully cool on my face.

"You *are* warm," he says finally, and I feel confident that I've assuaged any suspicion. "I should've checked if you had a fever before we left."

It wouldn't have changed anything, but it'd be nice to know how many degrees I'm deviating from normal.

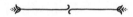

When we get to the church, there's a black puddle of people outside waiting for the doors to open. I hold my mother's hand at first but feel silly when I see Liz and Kate in their long black dresses and big sunglasses. They look chic and mature, while I look like I thought it was Halloween and thus dressed up as a black curtain.

We make our rounds and say hello to people, the worst people being Janet and Cal. I try not to cry because it seems like everyone has been coming up to them and crying, then Janet and Cal have to console *them*, which is a screwed-up order of things. It's so obvious that people are crying less for Sara and more for themselves.

The church bells strike nine, and the hundreds of people outside stop talking. The silence makes me feel woozy, but there's nothing good left to talk about, I guess. When the doors finally open people rush in for a good seat, which seems kind of funny to me because it's so inappropriate, so I turn to Liz and whisper, "Jeez, it's like Black Friday up in here." I want her to laugh. I wish someone would. But her face is steel. "Because everyone's stampeding each other? Plus, er, wearing black?" Jokes lose their funniness real quick when you have to explain them to people as thick-skulled as Liz, who could be Kate, given their identical attire and identical stupidity.

"That was out of line," she finally says. "Can't you take this one thing seriously?" But she sounds more scared than anything else.

I realize, as I shuffle behind the pew, that a) Liz has always been a fun suck and b) funerals are quite dependent on formalities. No one likes a code-breaker when things are already too spooky. And that's the only way to describe how I feel: spooked. I always figured the world was a math equation, albeit a long and complicated one, but one with predictable outcomes. Now it seems more like a strange and wild machine, prone to combustion and general mayhem.

"Sara wouldn't want this to be a sob-fest. Just because it's technically a matter of life and death doesn't mean we have to be so goddamn forlorn," I hiss at Liz, but I'm not in the right here.

The organ sounds and we stand up as the casket is carried in...as the coffin is carried in? Everyone is sad while I'm hung up on the difference between a coffin and a casket and whether they can be used interchangeably. Then we do all these prayers, but I don't know any of them. I always felt sorry for Sara when she had to go to confirmation and stuff, but now I feel a bit like an idiot. I can't even recite the Our Father, which everyone and their mother seems to know, so I try to average how many calories I've absorbed in the last few days. It makes me feel woozy, so instead I listen to all this talk about God receiving another angel, but it's too obscure to comfort me. Actually, it sounds like a load of crap.

"And now we will have Sara's best friend, Danny, say a few words," the priest says, and my heart does a nosedive.

I want to ask if I can bring my mom up with me, but I can't muster the courage, so I shuffle up to the podium and apologize to Whoever for being an atheist, and ask/pray/beg that I please deliver this speech without breaking out into a rash. I take my notes out and clear my throat, but as soon as I read the first sentence to myself I can tell it's all wrong, so I fold it back up and say what's already coming out of my mouth.

"Um, hi, good morning," I start, running my fingers over the carvings on the podium. "I thought I was going to get up here and say that Sara was a very special person in a world full of special people, and how she and I were practically sisters, and that my favorite memory of her is when we were nine and she meant to fart in the pool but then she pooped in it instead."

I wait for the weird chuckling to die down. In the very back of the church I see Bugg smiling and crying, which makes me want to smile and cry too, but I have to finish getting out what it is that I want to get out...which is what, exactly?

"It's not that those things aren't true, but what's more true is that Sara and I weren't in the best of places when she died. We were both keeping some pretty big secrets from each other, which I think happens in life all the time. You say you're going to tell someone something and you keep putting it off and putting it off until you finally woman up and do it." I stop for a minute because this sounds like a bad confessional on *Dr. Phil* and whoa, I do not feel good. Not nervous, *sick*. I've never been one to give pep talks so I forge ahead.

"I didn't realize that we might not get another opportunity to learn who the other person had become. And that's a shame. It would've been cool for Sara and me to get reacquainted."

I have to stop again because the chills are taking over my body, and I'm starting to visibly shake. The church is so quiet I can nearly hear the tears drop. Overall, I would classify the experience as remarkably uncomfortable.

"So I guess what I'm getting at is," I say, but then my mouth waters and I have no idea what I'm going to say but I know that if I do open my mouth it's not words that are going to come out, it's my breakfast. I put my finger up to the microphone like moms do when they're on the phone and their kid tries to tell them something important, mainly that they're sick and could they please have a paper bag because...but it's too late. I open my mouth and turn my head to the side, throwing up neatly into the tall plant next to the podium. For once my forays in discreet vomiting have paid off, and I wipe my mouth.

"Excuse me," I say into the microphone, then descend the stage in a state of shock. Truly this has been the greatest example to date of my total and complete failure to be not only a halfway decent public speaker, but a halfway decent best friend.

CHAPTER NINETEEN

"It wasn't bad at all," my mom says. We're in the handicap stall of the church bathroom and I'm staring into the toilet bowl waiting for something to happen. Now that we're in the appropriate location, though, everything seems hunky-dory down there in my stomach.

"I hope you're happy with yourself," I whisper to it as I smooth out my dress.

"Sweetie, you couldn't help getting sick." My mom flushes the toilet for me even though there's nothing in it. "It's no wonder too, what with something so disturbing as this. A lot of times emotional ailments present themselves physically."

"I'm super glad you were a hippie once, Mom, but it's not making me feel like less of an asshole." I undo the lock and try not to look at myself in the mirror above the sink as I scrub my hands viciously. "What, will these hands ne'er be clean?" I deadpan, but apparently my mom doesn't remember any high school English. Or maybe I'm 10 percent as funny as I think I am.

"You're not an asshole," she says gently. "Sara would've understood."

I dry my hands on the cheap paper towels for longer than is necessary, just to hear their crinkling sounds. "Sara would've thought it was hilarious, but Sara is dead, and now I'm never going to be able to face any of these people again."

Then Bugg comes into the bathroom. "Danny?"

The sound of her voice nearly triggers the nervous puke response, but I hold it together.

"How ya doing?" she asks, and the three of us stand there awkwardly. It's not great timing.

"Uh, Mom, this is Bugg. From poetry class."

"We met the other day," Bugg says. "Nice to see you again, though unfortunately under terrible circumstances. Anyway, Danny, the ceremony is over. You survived it!" Then she puts her hand to her mouth. "Not that 'survive' is a great choice of words or anything."

"We should go to the burial, Danny. I'll pull the car around. It was nice to see you too, Bugg. We've heard so much about you," my mom says warmly as she leaves.

When it's the two of us in the bathroom, I clarify, "Not *so* much," and Bugg gives me a long hug.

"You smell like alcohol," I notice, and her eyes are bloodshot too.

"I'm fine," she says quickly, but she's blushing. "You haven't been returning my texts."

"I know, I'm sorry. I didn't feel like talking to anyone."

"It's okay. I'm your go-to girl. Even if you just want to be friends for now—"

She's interrupted by her phone ringing, and Veronica's laughing face and blue hair illuminates the screen. It's such an up-close shot that it feels like she's in the bathroom with us, having just made a joke at our expense. Bugg pockets the phone after she ignores the call, and collectively we ignore the awkwardness.

"Like I was saying, even if you just want to be friends—" Bugg starts, but I don't have the capacity for this conversation right now.

"This isn't the greatest time to hammer out the logistics of our relationship." Despite my fever, my voice is chilly. "I kind of have something more pressing going on."

By the look on her face I can tell I've hurt her feelings. I wonder what it says about me, that it feels so good to hurt someone I love.

"Sorry. I didn't mean to make it seem like I wanted you to make a decision right here between the paper towel dispenser and the leaking faucet. And I don't know why Veronica called—"

I turn away from her, opening the bathroom door as a tear falls from her face and catches in her hair. "I'll text you when I'm done further fucking up these funeral arrangements."

I leave the bathroom and then the church, too blinded by the eleven a.m. sun to see what's in front of me.

The burial is a smooth, sad affair. It's official. Sara is dead. It's less official. I'm alive. The difference between "dead" and "alive" is only one syllable, but one I've shortened to a tiny utterance that hardly makes a sound. I want to go home and curl up with my journal, but afterward there's a "celebration" at Janet and Cal's. Why anyone would want to drag this sort of thing out is beyond me, but they're calling it a celebration because there's a slideshow full of happy pictures of Sara's life, and lots of food and expensive wine. They had a caterer make Sara's special grilled cheeses, but it's a shitty thing to have done; Sara is the only one who should be making them.

I show up with my parents but too many people are here: Ethan and his friends, anyone she ever played tennis with, acquaintances from high school. I am nearly delirious from the crowds, from hugging people and soothing them as they tell me how very sorry they are for my loss. Mothers seem to cry the hardest, overall. I feel bad for the ones who try to get away with regular eye makeup. They end up with clown faces and crumpled Kleenex, then an inevitable "excuse me" as they hightail it to the nearest bathroom. The number of bathrooms in Sara's house would be convenient under normal circumstances, but as I look at all the food, I feel sorry for myself; this stomach bug has ruined my appetite entirely. I'm almost tempted to try to eat something anyway, but the thing about being truly sick is it's hard to find even bacon appealing. I feel a hand on my back and I'm about to fake some pre-vomit noises when I turn around and see who it is.

"Oh my God, Stephen, hi," I say. His hug is the millionth I've received in the last hour but it feels better than the others, even though I end up inhaling his starchy tie. "I'm so sorry. I entirely forgot to find you before the funeral."

"Don't worry about it. You had a lot going on. Are you feeling okay?" He grew a stubbly beard since I last saw him, which works for him, mostly because it makes him look more like nineteen and less like twelve.

"Come on, let's talk outside," I say, grabbing hold of his hand and taking the long route out of the house so we pass

Kate and Liz. It's not that I'm trying to plant any ideas in their heads, but if they were to jump to conclusions, as gossipy people do, I wouldn't object. "Your hair looks nice, by the way," I add when they're in earshot. "You're very handsome in your suit."

"Thank you," he says and blushes. Ugh, I hate boy blushes. "You look beautiful as always."

I mean, I definitely wouldn't classify myself as an "always" type beauty. I probably have my moments, but usually I troll around in sweatpants looking prepubescent.

"How have you been?" he asks as we sit by the pool. I'm not sure how to answer him, but it feels good to be away from the constant bombardment of Sara memories. Out here it feels a little bit more like I can breathe. "Sorry, that's probably a stupid question. I've never been in a situation like this, so I have no idea what to say."

I decide it's kind of cute how nervous he is, in a fourth-grader-at-the-spelling-bee type way. "Don't worry, so far you're getting a solid A minus in Supporting Your Bereft Friend."

"No! Not an A minus. That's going to kill my GPA."

I roll my eyes at him. "Don't even talk to me about GPAs."

He and I share a knowing look, full of love and hatred for our 3.9 and 2.9, respectively, then I try to get serious with him. "I've been okay. I don't know. It's very weird. I'm here but not here. And when I do feel here it doesn't feel normal. It feels like I've been freshly submerged in an ice bath. You know, that caught-up, can't-catch-your-breath feeling."

He nods and lets me talk more.

"And life seems weirdly fragile. Before, I thought I was running around with a bowling ball, but it's actually a robin's egg."

"Yeah, I can't believe how unexpected it was," he breathes.

Since Sara's whole disease situation isn't public yet, I shouldn't tell Stephen what I've been googling. But since Stephen is also pre-med, I tell him about how Sara could have upped her chances of survival by getting tested once she knew Cal had hypertrophic cardiomyopathy, seeing as there's a 50 percent likelihood of a parent passing the disease down to their kid. After she got her diagnosis she'd have had to quit tennis, but she probably could have lived thanks to medication, surgery, and other marvels of modern medicine. But I guess to Sara quitting tennis felt like death itself.

"Wow," he says when I'm done. "I don't think I love doing anything enough to risk my whole life for it."

"Me either." I dig my heels into the grass and feel them sink into the soft ground.

"If someone said, hey, you have this weird block in your

brain and every time you study medicine you're at risk of an aneurism, I'd be, like, 'Later, med school.' And I've wanted to be a doctor since I was in utero."

I laugh. Stephen is one of those good guys who wants to be a doctor to save lives, and not just to get paid lots of money to save lives.

"Sara was more dedicated than anyone I know," I say, wishing I could loosen the collar of my funeral dress. "We were both really intense about the things we cared about and I think that's why we respected each other so much, but what I cared so much about pales in comparison to what she cared about."

He squints into the sun to look at me. "Well, what is it that you cared so much about?"

I don't even know how to describe it. Being the smartest, being the best, doing everything according to The Plan...there isn't one word for that. "I guess I wanted to be Valedictorian of Life. The best college was a big part of it, but then it'd be the best med school and then the best hospital, and on and on. For Sara it was tennis because she truly loved the game, not because she wanted to prove she was the best at arbitrary things."

A rogue tear rolls down my cheek and Stephen wipes it. *Wipes it.* It's the gentlest boy-action to date.

"There's nothing wrong with being driven, Danny. It's my favorite thing about you," he says, and then he does the weirdest thing ever, which is that he kisses me on the cheek. I become a statue, but he doesn't seem to notice and carries on with the conversation as if his lips usually occupy my face. "So are you excited to come back in the fall?"

I ignore the question and look out at the pool. "Oh no."

"What?"

"The beach ball." Instead of rolling cheerfully on top of the water, it's lying deflated and waterlogged in the shallow end. "Whatever, it's a *beach ball*," I console myself, but it still seems to capture how I feel.

"We could get a new beach ball?" he offers, puzzled, but I shake my head. It's not worth trying to explain how much more consequential the inconsequential things are now.

To change the subject, I ask, "So, what have you been up to?"

"Lots of volunteering at this hospital. I love it. I think I might want to do pediatric oncology."

"Isn't that the kiddy cancer?"

"Yeah, you'd love interacting with them, Danny. They're so sweet." Actually, I can't imagine *electing* to do something so depressing. "Anyway, should we get you back inside? I'm probably going to head out—don't want to take you away from your friends any longer. I'd like to, but it seems selfish of me." He stands up and I let the sun turn him into a silhouette. "I'm here for you, though, Danny, and I want to see you again before the summer ends." He

208

grins and I should qualify that Stephen *is* cute, in a nerdy puppy way.

He reaches his hand down to help me up, which is a very gentlemanly gesture. As I turn around I see Bugg watching us through the screen door, but when she sees me looking at her she looks away.

CHAPTER TWENTY

Going home is a relief. I don't feel sick anymore, which makes me think I *did* make myself sick with nerves, which, according to my mom, would be totally logical. As I plop down on my bed, I tell myself I'm ready to cry for real now. No more dainty sniffles and two-to-three small-to-midsize tears. I'm ready to hiccup and sob. But nothing happens. Bodies are so weird, not to mention annoying. Mine never does what I want it to. The longer I lie there, the more the hot itchy feeling starts to creep into my body. Or rather it creeps in at first, all gentle like, then takes over violently. I don't know what else to do, so I sneak into the basement and fill a water bottle with some of the vodka from my parents' liquor cabinet. They never lock it or anything because I'm an A+ kid, which feels a little shitty to take advantage of right now, but I think they'd understand. I'm just not going to risk it by asking them.

With my generous serving of inebriant, I sit down with my journal. I wish I'd started writing in it before You-Know-Where. I'd like to read about the night of my birthday, right after Sara slapped me in the face with the piece of pizza. It was buffalo chicken, by the way, and the spice made it sting even more. Instead I reread "Wild Geese" on the napkins Bugg wrote on for me. Mary Oliver is the sort of poet who not only makes you believe in poetry, but makes you want to be a poet too. Since I have Cynthia's class tomorrow I try to finish her latest assignment. I make doodles on the page in between sips of vodka but don't seem to get any closer to being able to adequately complete our final project. Honestly, I'm many things, but I don't think "poet" is one of them. This mentality changes when I'm halfway through with the drink I've poured, at which point I'm like, *Wait, am I a literary genius? Keats in disguise? Destined to die on a gurney of tuberculosis? Why, yes! Yes, I am!*

I finish the vodka, then the poem, and decide to send it to Bugg first in case I'm wrong about my newly appointed destiny as the greatest female poet of this millennium. I pause before I send it, though. It's a very exposed thing to have someone read your writing. You may as well invite yourself over to their house, take all your clothes off in their kitchen, and then wait for them to say something about it. Which sort of gives me an idea.

I get up and take my terrible curtain funeral dress off, then my bra and even my underwear. It definitely feels uncouth to put my bare butt on my bare desk chair but, honestly, nudity is an improvement over my usual granny-panty situation. I open Photo Booth for the hell of it—well, actually I do it because I have this sneaking suspicion that I, yes, wouldn't you know it, I look *good, really* good, which I think has something to do with my nipple-to-boob ratio and certainly not the vodka-to-empty-stomach ratio. Now, I know you're not supposed to take naked pictures because of dignity and stuff, but when I look this good I can't help myself. Besides, it's symbolic, what with the whole stripping of the soul thing that's going on with this poem. I put my MacBook camera on timer, back up a little, then wink, but since the timer is set to fifteen seconds, I have to close one eye for way too long to be sexy. Whatever, it's the thought that counts.

I attach the picture along with the poem and hit SEND before I talk myself out of it. With Operation Reveal My Truest, Sexiest, Most Badass Self complete, I wrap a towel around myself, tiptoe downstairs for a smidge more vodka, then hightail it back upstairs with my loot.

While lying naked on my bed and drinking what is certainly the drink of the gods, I realize that I haven't slept naked since I was born. Sometimes I take a shower in a bathing suit to avoid looking at myself in the mirror. I should at least start going topless, if not at the beach, then at least in the shower. But you know what, it's totally fine in Europe to be naked at the beach so why *is* America such a prude? "Fuck America!" I say cheerfully, then promise myself to never wear a shirt again.

I look at my bed but it's obviously absurd to sleep in it so I rip my comforter off and make a new, better bed for myself on the floor, like the animal that refuses to sleep in the straw that some Farmer Dude laid out for her because screw the Farmer Dude, I make my own bed, yes, I certainly do. One time my mother threatened that if I make my bed I have to lie in it, but I don't understand why that'd be such a grueling punishment.

I fucking *love* lying in my own bed.

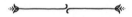

I wake up with the worst hangover I've ever had. For a second I think I'm dead, but nope, that pounding thing is my head.

"Holy moly of cow," I gasp. "Need. Water. Now. And why the *hell* am I naked?"

Feeling embarrassed, not to mention cold, I take an oversized collared shirt from my closet, button it as close to my eyebrows as I can, then throw a smock over it.

"What *even* time is it?" I ask myself, which is not the usual order of those words but my brain is vodka soaked and therefore borderline pickled. *Twelve thirty, stupid,* the clock says, and I stick my tongue out at it.

Luckily my parents are at work so I get to do some serious mutant snack concocting in the kitchen. I can't give away the complete recipe, but it involves bacon, ice cream, eggs, and chocolate sauce, which only sounds disgusting if you think about it. Everyone knows the whole purpose of eating is to not think about it. As I'm going to town on what will one day be featured only in the ritziest of restaurants, the doorbell rings.

"Come in," I shout, shoveling the last forkful in my mouth. I didn't check to see who it was, but certainly a burglar wouldn't announce himself first.

"Hello?" Bugg's voice calls.

"Hey, in the kitchen," I say, wiping my mouth quickly and trying to smooth out my hair. When I see the look on her face, though, I realize I must look pretty bad.

"You doing okay?" she asks. I'm a little disappointed that she doesn't try to hug me or touch me at all. Do I look *that* disgusting, or is she still feeling awkward from our subpar funeral interaction?

"I think so," I say. I try to squeeze her hand, but it's like a dead fish in my hand. "What's wrong?"

"Nothing." But she avoids my eyes when she says it.

"Are you lying?"

"Not really."

"Well, what is it?" I take her face in my hands, guiding her to meet my gaze.

"I was wondering who that guy was yesterday," she says, and for the first time I register something like jealousy on her face. I know people say that jealousy isn't the same thing as love, but they have to at least be cousins.

"That's Stephen. He's literally the only friend I made all of freshman year. Gold star for me, amirite?" I punch her playfully in the arm, but her face is as steely as the kitchen accents.

"Are you in love with him back?" she asks, and I feel my cheeks burn. Sara seemed to harbor this same suspicion that Stephen was into me, but I assumed she was desperately hoping I had a potential love interest.

"No, of course not. We're friends."

"Kate and Liz didn't seem to think so."

I'm feeling pretty good about having pulled off Mission Impossible until I register how upset Bugg is. I don't want to blow my own cover so instead I reassure her that Kate and Liz are gossipy ignoramuses. "Seriously, they pull shit out of their conjoined butthole all the time. You just gotta ignore them."

Bugg smiles and looks relieved, which in turn makes me feel relieved.

"Well, good. I was hoping you'd say that because I brought you something." She reaches into her tote bag. "Close your eyes."

215

"Ooh, a present? I've always wanted to have Christmas in July." I close my eyes and pray for a pony.

"Now open them." She's holding out a plastic pot with three long stems, the heads of which look like green spiky clams.

"A Venus flytrap," she says. "For you and your new-found love of vaginas. And for us, and our destiny to become Trappers."

It's seriously the freakiest plant I've ever seen. "I'm very touched," I say, taking the pot gingerly in my hands.

"Watch." She puts her finger in her mouth and I follow her lips as they close around the base of her pointer, right before the knuckle. She pulls it out slowly, then touches the inside of one of the green spiky traps. The plant closes around her finger. "Pretty cool, right?"

"*Very* cool." She might as well have touched the inside of my stomach, which reminds me that as nice as it was to see Stephen, nothing he did hit anywhere remotely near my insides. "Seriously, there's nothing going on between me and Stephen. Even if he and I didn't have the chemistry of candle wax, you'd still be the only person I'm interested in."

I set the plant down on the counter and she looks at it lovingly. "Me too, especially after that picture you sent me."

"What picture?"

She laughs. "What do you mean, 'what picture'?" She pulls up her e-mail, resting her phone on the kitchen counter, and shows me the most appalling naked photo of myself to date, and believe me, I was a *very* ugly baby.

"Where did you get that?!" I ask, covering her phone with my hand, but it's pretty obvious where it came from.

She looks at me a little confused. "What, did you mean to send it to your friend *Stephen* instead?"

"No! Seriously, Stephen and I are not like that," I say, peeking at the photo again, then closing her e-mail app. "But I have no recollection of taking that photo, let alone sending it to you."

She pulls up the poem I apparently wrote too, which I do recall writing but have no idea what it says. "Do you want to read your darling haiku or shall I?" Bugg asks.

"You do it," I say miserably, closing my eyes and slumping onto the floor. It feels like a million ants are crawling inside me.

"Ahem," Bugg says. "It's titled 'Ode to My Special.'"

I brace myself for a gooey heart-dump.

"'I have to tell you,'" she starts, and I check the syllables. Yep, five. "'You're so hot and I love you.'"

Dear god.

She ends with the final flourish: "'Cheeseburger pizza.'"

She bursts out laughing and I do too, very, very relieved that I didn't spill my heart to Bugg. Pizza can know my true feelings, but Bugg?

"I'd just seen a commercial for some cheeseburger pizza special," I say sheepishly, "and apparently got quite inspired."

While I'm patting myself on the back for getting the syllables of a haiku right even though I was shit-faced, the smile slowly leaves Bugg's face, and she looks at me seriously.

"Were you drinking last night?" she asks quietly.

"A little." But due to my liquid-inspired actions my credibility is entirely shot. "Okay, yes, a lot."

Bugg frowns and I realize that she doesn't look so good either. I almost ask if she's hungover too, but I figure I have no ground to stand on here.

"I don't want to tell you what to do, but drinking alone is *no bueno*, Danny." She looks unnecessarily concerned for me considering how many times she's been all for us getting drunk together.

"You've gotten us drunk, like, every day we've hung out," I point out.

"Yeah, but we were *together*."

"So you think I can't handle my drinking unless you're there to monitor me?" I pause for a couple of seconds, but she doesn't disagree with me. "I already have a helicopter mother. I don't need a helicopter friend too."

I stand up, and we face each other in a ruined silence. The sympathy flowers sent by friends of my parents cast a shadow on the green spiky heads, and side by side, you start to see how different they are.

I step closer to Bugg, too tired and too hungover to sustain a fight. "Look, it was one bad night. I'm not going to make a habit of it. I don't even like drinking. I'm Queen Frink."

She nods slowly. "I guess every so often it's good to do something by yourself that you don't usually do alone. Healthy even, like masturbating..."

"Well, thanks for stopping by," I say, interrupting her justification. In my hungover state I greatly overestimated how much food I needed and now I'm too full, for which there is only one cure.

"Aren't you going to come to poetry? I responded to your poem and sassy photo saying that I'd pick you up, hence why I'm here ten minutes before class." She points to the clock on the stove, which is mercilessly shuttling our lives along. "You said that was fine."

"Right." I rub my temples and wonder when the drunk blunders will stop. "I'm sorry, I need to call Sara's parents first, so can I meet you there?" I do not like the look on her face, but even less tolerable than that is the way the hot itchiness is expanding past my body in a way that feels like I'm filling up the whole kitchen.

"Whatever you need to do. I'll see you later." Her voice is kind, but it's starting to feel like what was once whole between us is becoming fractured.

I don't end up making it to poetry class. After the toilet and I do business for the last time I dig through the trash on my computer until I find the file labeled "Don't Eat." At

You-Know-Where they were pretty clear about not having files like this around, so I dutifully put them in the trash. The thing is I never got around to *emptying* the trash, and you know how computers are: They never let go of anything. It's pretty harmless, really—lots of superskinny girls running and drinking green juice and doing other skinny-people activities. It's like how an Olympic runner might have a picture of another Olympic runner up on her treadmill, you know, for inspiration sake. The folder also has tons of vegan propaganda with studies about how the standard American diet will kill you, if not via heart disease, then via the shame of looking less like a person and more like an osteoporosis-destined model. I haven't looked at any of this stuff in a while, and it's having the exact opposite effect that it used to. Instead of quelling my appetite, it's making me *ravenous*.

Since my dad biked to work, I get in his car and hightail it to McDonald's, where the golden arches embrace me like a long-lost lover. I order two small fries, two double cheeseburgers, an extra-large Oreo McFlurry, and an apple pie.

"Oh, and a Diet Coke please," I add.

"Eleven twenty-six at the next window."

I drive up, and as the acne-struck guy sporting a visor is about to hand me my loot, he goes, "Hey, didn't we go to high school together? Yeah, you were, like, surgically attached to that blond girl who just died. You two won class friendship."

I nod numbly.

"Whoa, I'm so sorry about your friend. Danny, right? It's Chris. We had ceramics class together."

"Oh, right." I can feel my eyes burning. "Sorry, but I'm late to pick up these kids I'm babysitting. This is their food so if we could—" I wave the twenty at him and he hands me my cure. I drive away without waiting for the change. As I try to manage opening a mayonnaise packet with one hand, I make the executive decision to stop at the grocery store too. Chris has permanently ruined my McDonald's for me, and the hot itchiness is spreading through my body faster than the plague.

Everyone else in the grocery store mills through the aisles and picks up products as if contemplating God. I, on the other hand, walk quickly under the watchful eye of a thousand fluorescent lightbulbs, weave through carts positioned like roadblocks, and avoid everything on the bottom shelf, which little kids are certain to have left a gummy residue on. Hershey's sauce is a must, as well as Cheetos, a four-pack of Boston cream cupcakes, precooked bacon—wait, two things of precooked bacon—and a liter of Coke. I double back and get a cake from the bakery. It's vanilla, on sale, and says HAPPY 10TH BIRTHDAY CHARLOTTE. I also get one of those platters of veggies with dip in the center just so that the cashier thinks all this food is for a party I'm throwing.

"I always do this thing last minute," I tell the woman as she rings in my items in the express line. "The party starts in an hour, but what can you do?"

She smiles and nods. She doesn't care. Nobody cares.

I get home excited and full of dread. When I get to my room, I realize that all of this would taste better with vodka. Wasn't it Sara who told me that a little more alcohol is the best way to cure a hangover? Yes, I should absolutely honor Sara, so I go downstairs and get some liquor. Back in my room I dump out half the liter of Coke and fill it the rest of the way with alcohol. A few sips and I feel much better, so I place the cake on the desk and remove its plastic lid. Poor Charlotte. I hope she had a good birthday.

"Look away," I tell the yet-to-be-named Venus flytrap that's sitting on my windowsill next to the picture of Sara and me. I use the fork as a shovel and guide the icing flower into my mouth. The sugar takes over. Then I break into the cake part itself: spongy vanilla heaven. I've hardly swallowed before I've started the next bite. And then I add the bacon, wrapping it around the piece of cake so that the frosting squishes out of my little roll-up. I am pretty fucking happy so I put some music on, cheerful stuff that Sara would've liked to dance to. It's loud and I have my food spread out around me and I'm happier than a pig in shit.

Except then the door opens, and I try to hide the cake

and the Cheetos and the bacon and the Coke full of vodka. I try to disassociate myself from the crime scene, but it's impossible and it's worse than being walked in on while masturbating. It's worse than being walked in on while masturbating to PBS Kids. It's my greatest fear actualized and there's nothing I can say, no way to cover my tracks. The proof is all over my fingers.

CHAPTER TWENTY-ONE

Bugg's head emerges first and then her body. "Danny?"

"No one by that name lives here," I say, running to my bedroom door and trying to close it.

"Danny..." She sounds exasperated.

"Beep...BEEP...BEEPBEEPBEEP."

"DANNY," she says, finally pushing the door open.

"You can't be here." I slump against the wood of the door and lick the frosting from my fingers. "You're supposed to be at poetry class."

"It just ended. I was worried because you never showed up."

I watch her take in the components of the crime scene.

"Well, you have to get out," I say rudely, hugging my knees into my chest and trying to shrink to something microscopic. Even though I'm being the worst host/sort-of girlfriend ever, she doesn't leave.

"Danny, it's okay." She sits on the floor across from me.

"No, it's not." My voice breaks, and the next thing I know I'm crying like an idiot. "You weren't supposed to see. No one can see this."

She reaches into her tote bag and hands me a piece of scrap paper. "You have a bat in the cave," she says, and I proceed to blow my nose into the most painful substitute for a tissue.

"Well, just so you know, a study was done very carefully that adhered to all the rules of the scientific method and it showed that bacon enhances the flavor of every food." I sniffle. I'm so deep in my own world that the edges of the real one are fuzzy, no matter how many times I blink. "Every. Single. Food. So it's not weird. None of this is weird."

"I don't think it's weird." Bugg's voice is so tender I can't bear to look at her, especially not when she's surrounded by all my wrappers.

"But it's gross."

"I don't think it's gross."

"You don't have to lie about it." I get up and plop face-down on the bed, trying to blend in with the comforter. My mom has this book that says the whole secret of the universe is visualization: If you picture something long enough and hard enough, it comes true. So I stare intently at the pillowcase and imagine my body flickering itself invisible. Wouldn't you know it, not a goddamn thing happens.

"Don't sweat it. Everyone does weird shit when they're alone. That's why life should come with a Clear History button. Can I have a sip of this?" she asks, picking up the Coke.

"No!" I take it from her quickly. It's not that she hasn't had a drink in my presence before, but I never know when it could be a problem. Besides, I told her about fifty minutes ago that I wouldn't drink. "It's not just Coke."

"Danny," she starts, then grabs the bottle from me and sniffs it. It's exactly the tone of voice my mom uses. "You're drinking in the middle of the day? After blacking out last night? I know you're going through a hard time and I can't even begin to imagine what it's like, but you can't let yourself spiral out of control."

This is a side of her I didn't think could exist, because it chafes against the image I have of her, smoking a cigarette in her tutu and smuggling weed to high schoolers in tampon applicators and getting drunk a few months out of treatment when she's "technically not supposed to be drinking."

"What about your manifesto?" I demand. "What about fun and being carefree and not having all these rules?"

"There's a distinct line between carefree and dangerous."

"No, there's not! You draw the line as you go and expect me to walk it with you."

She gets up and the dark liquid sloshes against the sides of the bottle, but I think I feel it in my stomach. "Can I dump this out?" she asks.

"No, I'll do it later. You should team up with my mom, though. She loves trying to impose order on my life." I'm antsy with anger, and Bugg walks over to the flytrap and provokes it heartlessly, offering her finger then retracting it as soon as the plant bites.

"No need to, bitchy mcbitch bitch," she says.

"Bitchy mcbitch bitch, *really*?" I point toward her. "Will you stop doing that? Plants have feelings too, you know."

She puts her hands in her pockets and looks at me. Her hair is greasy and more limp today, or maybe I've just never noticed that she's prone to dirty hair like the rest of us.

"I want to be Team Danny, your ride-or-die, go-to girl. But I can't be around you if you're drinking all the time. It's bad for me and I can't risk going down that road again. I can't let you drag me down."

When she says this I remember Veronica yelling at Bugg during the moon festival. "It's exactly like Veronica said," I say, shaking my head. "*You're* the one who's gotten *me* drunk the last couple of times, and now you're trying to use one bad day against me, because it's easier to blame me than to take responsibility for yourself. Well, I'm not falling for your hypocritical bullshit."

"Do *not* bring Veronica into this." Bugg's voice is like ice. "It's one thing to drink at a party or with another person, but you're not drinking for fun, Danny, and when I drink alone I get into some shit, *real* shit—not just eating by myself in a room and maybe throwing it up." She says it like we're in a competition to see who has it worse. As she swipes a lick of frosting off the cake, I decide I hate her.

"Get out," I say, but she's already opening the door.

"Gladly."

CHAPTER TWENTY-TWO

Over the next few days my mom notices that something is up: She catches me hoarding snacks from the cupboard in my room, then doing the elliptical at odd hours of the night. Even though I tell her I'm swell, she mandates that I see Leslie every day instead of twice a week. To avoid talk of medication I try to be obedient and hold it together. The one caveat, and maybe it's not a caveat at all, is I'm doing this for my mom and not for me. I lie to Leslie and tell her I've been doing all the normal things, like eating, when in fact it's been thirty-eight hours since I've consumed anything besides a Tic Tac. I sprinkle our conversations with funny memories of Sara and do not let on that I am petrified because I don't actually know what "dead" means. The one problem with trying to hold it together is that probably at some point you can't hold on so tightly anymore.

A week after the fight with Bugg, my parents and I are having dinner. Well, they're having dinner and I'm having lettuce, and they decide to bring up Harvard stuff, which is so insensitive of them. On top of everything else, do they think I want to discuss the precarious nature of my academic future right now?

"Your dean called to let us know you haven't registered for classes yet," my mom says. It marks the hundredth time this summer that I've regretted agreeing to the terms of my medical leave. Literally no one else's parents are as overinvolved as mine are. Most parents don't even know *where* their kids go to college, let alone have play dates with faculty members. "You only have a couple more days to make the cut for fall term."

"Right. I'll do it tomorrow," I say, and dump balsamic vinegar on a piece of lettuce, hoping it will drown. "Don't worry," I add half-heartedly.

"It's our job to worry about you," my mom says, which makes me want to say, *Well, if that's true, why do you keep getting paychecks from these places claiming to be your employer?* "It's because we love you," she adds. "And you need to eat something more than lettuce, Danny, please."

"I told you I had a huge lunch. It's not healthy to eat when I'm not hungry." I pierce a stem and it makes a satisfying crunch.

"She's right," my dad pipes up, which makes me feel like a pile of poop for lying. "Hey, how about you and I spend some time together after dinner? I want to clear up some, uh, treatment, stuff with you." With everything that happened with Sara I'd forgotten all about being mad at him until, oh, right now. In six seconds he goes from my favorite half of the parent team to the absolute worst.

"There's nothing to talk about," I say flatly. I extended the olive branch of forgiveness weeks ago; what else could he have to say about it?

"We have to talk about Harvard," my mom says, slamming her water glass onto the table. "If you're not feeling up to registering for classes, you're not going to last a minute on campus and you're going to end up having to take more time off. Jim, tell her what Leslie said." She doesn't wait for my dad to say anything. Her snowball of anxiety is so tangible I can almost feel it hit my chest. "She thinks you're concerningly depressed."

I squint at her. I don't know if that's an actual diagnosis or if there's a version of "depressed" that isn't "concerning," but my parents, as you can imagine, look concerned. My dad rubs the top of my mom's wrist with his thumb and that seems to calm her down.

"Leslie has spiritual warts and not going back to

Harvard isn't an option," I say miserably. Don't they understand what a failure that'd make me? If I don't go back now, I never will. "I can't live in this weird limbo any longer. I won't be able to stand it." It's so tense at the table that even the utensils are sweating. My parents look at each other and share one of those annoying looks that makes me think they telecommunicate 86 percent of the time.

"We thought you might say that, which is why we'd like you to be open to talking to a psychiatrist about medication. It's another thing we were talking about with your therapist, and she thinks it could help." My mom reaches for the salt as if this is a dandy time to adjust her pasta seasonings.

"I told you guys the medication made me feel weird. I don't want to go on any medication. I don't *need* medication. My best friend just died. I'm sad. I'll live."

I throw my napkin down and hate it for landing so softly, so imperceptibly on the table. Despite my compelling argument, my mom starts listing the medications the therapist apparently thinks I'm bat-shit-crazy enough to require. Why can't everyone accept that I'm just another person aged eighteen to twenty-four who's miserable as balls?

"So she'd have you treated for each disorder," my mom says. "The obsessive-compulsive thoughts, the purging—"

I cut her off. "It seems to me," I begin, "that as a technique, separation has become rather popular. Take the business of dairy." My voice is calm and my whole body is still, but something about it feels dangerous, like being stuck in the eye of a hurricane. "You go to any grocery store and there are all these different types of milk: nonfat, whole, one percent, two percent, half and half, light cream, even nonfat cream, but all it does when we divide everything up is trick us into feeling more secure, like we have some agency the milk gods don't."

My parents are no longer nodding.

"We separate it, homogenize it, fix it to our liking, right? And the same goes for bulimia, anorexia, depression, anxiety, and what is it now? Eating Disorders Not Otherwise Specified? Fucking stop it. It's compulsion wearing different colored riding hoods. It's dis-ease, disease, destruction. I wish you'd leave me alone in mine."

The sweat is all around my armpits. Somehow I've moved from my seat at the table to the windowsill, where I'm gripping the ledge and looking out at the stupid neighbor walking his stupid dog as if life is one long stroll.

"I probably had orthorexia or whatever before I got treated for bulimia and then what happened? They kept trying to fix me by fixing whatever label they'd slapped onto me, and it hasn't worked yet. You know why? Because of the octopus."

"What octopus?" my mom interrupts, as if an octopus is as unfeasible as a UFO.

"I heard once that dealing with craziness is like trying

to make an octopus go to bed. Just when you think you've done it, another tentacle wakes up and pokes out of the covers: depression, overeating, mutant snacking. I live with her, this giant octopus with infinite arms. She wants to get me the hell out of human reality, which by the way, means being sad some of the time. You think she cares how I do it? She thinks you're hilarious, you and all your therapies and treatments and bedtime stories. Guess what, she wins that way. She *wants* to remain in disguise so that she can entirely overtake my body, but it's not going to happen because I'm onto you. I'm fucking onto you." I swipe my dad's keys from the counter in an angry rush before they can try to stop me. "If you'll excuse me, I have some business to attend to."

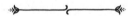

The only reasonable thing to do at a time like this is have drinks with Sara. I mean Sara's gravestone. The minor obstacles are 1) the cemetery is closed at night, so 2) I have to break in when 3) I'm scared shitless of ghosts, so now I also have to be scared of 4) authority figures. Luckily, I'm angry enough that the adrenaline gets me to park the car, hop the fence, and find my way to her little swatch of earth. Less luckily, when I sit down the adrenaline evaporates and I'm sufficiently creeped out. The trees are so moody and the stones are so grave. I uncap the cheap booze I bought at the only liquor store that doesn't card and take a few sips. The empty-stomach-to-eighty-proof-vodka ratio makes it so that I'm feeling pretty groovy in a matter of minutes.

"You won't believe the fight I just had with my parents," I start. It's strange to talk out loud when no one is around. My voice sounds too deep at first and then too high. I can't stop feeling self-conscious, so I keep talking, self-conscious and all. "I won't bore you with the details of my unraveling, though. How are you?" I pause and try to picture her response, but when the Spirit of Sara doesn't speak to me, I go on. "If we're being honest, I'm scared for you," I say in a stage whisper. "The way I see it you're either in heaven being fed grapes by a hundred beautiful men, or you're in the process of being reincarnated into the future champion of Wimbledon, or, and this is the worst-case scenario, you're nothing. Absolutely nothing at all."

A cricket chirps and I nearly fall over. "Don't interrupt me, this is very important," I say to it, then clear my throat, close my eyes (my vision is blurring anyway), and continue. "I think besides my gravestone reading 'tried and failed to lose the same twenty-five pounds,' my greatest fear is that when we die there's nothing, not even a hole to suggest we might have once conducted a mediocre life here. Isn't that why people try to write epic novels and compose famous symphonies and build monuments and put human debris on the moon? To avoid oblivion?"

I take another sip while adjusting my smock, in case the spirits might be offended by my heinous undergarments. "Socrates, or some other boring guy in his time period, said we shouldn't be afraid of death because death is like one of those deep, dreamless sleeps, which everyone knows is the best night's sleep, so really being afraid to die doesn't make any sense at all. What I'd add, *Socrates*, is that if death is just good old oblivion, it's basically the same thing as drinking so much you can't remember anything, amirite or amirite?"

I pour the rest of the vodka into a cup and dump a packet of red Kool-Aid into it. "So here's to not remembering," I say, holding the cup up to Sara's rock slab. "Here's to death and here's to dying." It's the sorriest cheers to date, but I have to know that oblivion won't kill us. I drink half the cup for me and half the cup for Sara, then wait.

Eventually I lie on the ground, mostly because it's too much work to keep my body upright. It's kind of wet and I don't feel any less stupid talking into it, but I've come this far; I might as well make my sad apology to the smell of fresh-cut grass. "I should have told you. I'm sorry I didn't tell you any of the things I should have told you. I'm sorry that I sometimes hated you. I'm sorry for not letting you copy my geography homework in seventh grade. I'm sorry for telling you Billy Taylor fingered me on prom night when he didn't. I'm sorry for leaving you to go to college and I'm not sorry too, if that makes sense. I'm sorry we put so much pressure on each other that we couldn't tell each other the truth." I wipe the snot from my nose, which is running down my face and dripping on her grave. I am the most sappy, most sentimental drunk. "But above everything, Sara, a thousand times over, I forgive you."

CHAPTER TWENTY-THREE

Beeping noises. Why are there beeping noises? It's not that I'm against the beep as a noise per se, but I have a feeling that being plugged into a vital signs monitor with an IV jabbed into my arm isn't the best way to start the day.

"Oh, thank God," my mom says as I blink my eyes open. She's hovering over me, and from what I can glean we're a hospital room. "Let me text your father. He was getting more coffee. Oh, thank God, you're all right." She kisses my face and I try not to let the panic set in. The thing is I had the craziest dream...

"So, uh, what happened here?" I try to ask casually.

My lips are so chapped they burn, and my joints are achy. I have a very bad feeling about all of this. My mom scoots her chair closer and holds my hand. I try to hold her hand back but she has such a death grip on me that I'm kind of losing circulation in my fingers.

"Your father and I were worried sick last night when you still weren't home by midnight," she says, and I register the bags under her eyes. "We were going to call the police because you wouldn't answer your phone and Janet hadn't seen you, and neither had Bugg—"

"How did you even—"

"—and we had no idea where else to look. But then we got a call from the hospital and they said they'd admitted you. One of the groundskeepers at the cemetery found you passed out in there, and when they couldn't wake you up they called 9-1-1."

"Well, that was a neighborly thing to do," I say cheerfully. "The world is full of Good Samaritans."

"Danny, this isn't a joke. You had to get your stomach pumped twice. Your blood alcohol levels were four and a half times the legal limit, not to mention that you're underage. You could've gotten into some serious trouble." My mom starts to cry into the stiff cuffs of her blouse. "You could've been really, really hurt. You could have *died*." I feel her trying to peer into my soul and figure out if that's what I was trying to do.

"I'm obviously too scared of death to try to kill myself, Mom."

My dad walks in, and he looks relieved but also worried, which in turn makes me feel stupid. What will become of me, I want to ask, but it's not the sort of thing they or anyone I know can answer.

"You fell on your face too," my mom says, which sounds funny until she hands me her makeup mirror.

"Dammit." The universe is *definitely* not Team Danny. There's a cut on my chin and my lip is split open and filled with dried blood.

"We don't know what to do with you, Danny," my dad says, and then he starts crying too. Dad tears are the worst kind of tears. They make you want to do a quick operation on yourself, remove all the screwed-up parts, and sew yourself back together real quick. Good as new. Better than new, even.

The door opens and a nurse with a name tag that reads BILL comes in, asking my parents to leave so that he and I can go over some things. My parents look like they want to reattach my umbilical cord, but with a little coaxing they go. Bill is probably in his sixties and he writes things on his electronic chart with his electronic pen in such an enthusiastic way that this couldn't be his first career. Men like Bill are the reason people think this country is progressing. He pulls the roll-y stool over and sits by my bed. "So, how are you feeling, Danny?"

"Pretty exceptional, considering."

He takes a read on the equipment. "You got lucky, kid.

Two stomach pumps and an IV later and your blood alcohol levels are out of the danger zone. You might get a few second glances with your lip, but other than that you're relatively unscathed."

He goes on to tell me that my parents told him my best friend of fourteen years just died, which is probably why I'm "acting out." This then prompts him to tell me about all the resources the hospital has, mainly a really depressing-sounding grief support group for teens that has free coffee, free doughnuts, and a biannual grief-stricken dance.

"Thanks, but I'm more of a go-it-alone-type gal," I say.

He caps his pen and touches his white mustache. "Listen, no one can make you take care of yourself or keep you from hurting yourself. Your parents probably think they can, judging by how they're hovering at the window—"

I look up and wave and they duck out of sight. Those sneaky bastards.

"But it's up to you. If you choose not to get help that's fine, but then that's your *choice*. It's not something that happened to you." He gets up and puts his hand on the doorknob. "Do you see the difference?"

I nod and he leaves me to the arduous task of gearing up to face another day. Once I have my grass-stained clothes back on, my parents and I walk into the parking lot like a defeated army traipsing back from war. It's so bright my eyes are bleeding, and it's rather insensitive of the sun to be shining so insistently on a day like today. A little girl passes us with a neck brace, which means she has to stop and turn her whole body around to stare at me, which I guess means my bloody lip is not as subtle a fixture on my face as I'd hoped it'd be.

"Mommy, look," she says, and I glare at her. Kids can be real assholes.

My parents have to go to work, so they drop me off in front of the house. "Please have a quiet afternoon, okay?" they say, and I half expect them to call a babysitter for me.

"I will."

"Promise?"

I'm about to roll my eyes when it occurs to me that I forfeited the right to sass them indefinitely. "Yes, I promise." Looking at them, I wonder when they got so old.

"We have lots to talk about at dinner," my mom says, and my dad nods.

"Can't wait," I mutter.

As they drive off I hear a flapping sound in the garage, and since I have nothing better to do I go see what's up. "Shit," I say under my breath. One of the birds that comes regularly to my dad's feeders is trapped inside, fluttering against the window and frantic to get out. The sound of its feathers against the windowpane is like nails on a chalkboard. I try to get closer to it, but its skittish movements make me skittish too. "Would you cut it out?" I hate birds, which is yet another way I probably break my father's heart every day.

It rests on the windowsill for a moment and I grab the broom to try to point it in the direction of the free world, but it seems dead set on keeping itself a prisoner. I look at it helplessly as it flaps against the glass, getting a few feet off the sill, then landing with a stomach-turning thud.

"You know you belong out there, don't you? It's where you want to be, isn't it?" I ask, ignoring the fact that I've officially lost my last marble. The problem is that the bird's disoriented, too close to see that the glass of the window is an illusion and not really the way out. "It's a trap. A barrier disguised as freedom," I say, but I'm clearly not the bird whisperer.

I can't watch it bang its body against the glass anymore, so I get my mother's gardening gloves and sneak up behind it. The next time it lands on the sill to catch its breath I clamp my hands around its body in my stealthiest maneuver to date. It tries to flap its wings and the movement against my hands makes me think I'm holding a beating heart.

I run into the yard, crouch into the grass, and open my hands. At first it looks at me stupidly, and for the first time I notice the tiny swatch of red on its wing. "Well, go on," I say. It takes to the sky uninjured—a little shaken, but alive.

CHAPTER TWENTY-FOUR

I can't say much on behalf of those who die, but I hope they don't suffer as much as we do. Being left behind is like being one of those rare isotopes of nitrogen that you hope scientists never unearth because it could blow up everything south of the sky. Not to mention that this is the worst hangover of my whole life, which I know I've said about my last two hangovers, but it gets truer every time.

I've drawn a cool bath to try to combat the hot itchy situation that has become my whole body, and I'm entirely submerged except for my right hand, which holds a stick of salami, and my mouth, which receives said salami.

The salami helps for a minute, but then the black hole in my stomach yawns even wider. I'm midbite when the bathroom door opens, and I drop my precious salami in a frantic attempt to whip the curtain closed and salvage my dignity.

"Jeez, ever heard of knocking?" I say, fishing the salami out of the tub and giving it a mini eulogy in my head.

"Sorry, your mom let me in." Chills take over my body and a lump develops in my throat. I peek my head out from around the curtain, careful to keep my lip concealed. I hadn't expected to hear Bugg's voice. "That's the biggest bathtub I've ever seen."

"Yeah, you can basically host a frat party in it. So what-cha doing here?"

She's wearing suspenders and a mustard-colored skirt and I'm trying to tell by the look on her face if we're still in a fight. I'm not mad anymore, but she's my Achilles' heel whereas I'm not sure if I'm part of her anatomy at all.

"Your mom called me last night and said you were missing, which scared the shit out of me. I don't even know how she got my number." She leans against the bathroom counter, and the mirror reflects the frizziness of the back of her hair. It's weird to have her in the bathroom, and I feel hyperaware of the fuzzy toilet seat cover and how it probably smells like vanilla and poop (scented spray never de-scents perfectly).

"My mom belongs in the CIA. I stashed my phone in

a drawer after Sara died, and I think she went through my contacts then. She's overinvolved like that."

"No kidding." Bugg starts rummaging through the top drawer and helps herself to some of my deodorant. As she swipes it on, little white balls stick in her armpit creases and I decide we are officially not in a fight. "So are you okay?" she asks. "You're still hiding behind that curtain."

"Yeah, I'm okay. Are you?"

She starts to nod, but then it becomes a slight shaking of her head. "Not really. I've felt off since the funeral and it got worse after our little tiff. The blinders came back in the corner of my eyes." Her voice is flat and she doesn't sound that much like Bugg.

"What blinders?"

"It's a darkness in my peripheral vision that happens when I'm starting to spiral down. You were right when you smelled alcohol on me at the funeral. I've been drinking again." She sounds embarrassed, but I'm confused.

"What do you mean 'again'? I didn't know you'd ever stopped drinking." I feel the frustration rise in my voice. "I don't get what you're supposed to be doing or not doing with alcohol."

"That makes two of us." She helps herself to my makeup too, turning around and swiping mascara onto her lashes with her mouth slightly open. I watch her reflection so long my fingers and toes start to wrinkle under the water. "I was supposed to be sober for the first couple of months after treatment, but it's so *boring*. I thought that if I could distinguish between when I was drinking to have fun and drinking to hurt myself, then it'd be okay."

"But it's not okay?"

"I don't think it's okay."

"I don't think I'm okay either." I peel back the shower curtain and show her my lip. At first she gasps, but then she starts laughing when I tell her how it happened.

"That is nasty," she says. "I bet you woke up in the hospital feeling like quite the idiot." Then she tells me about the stupidest thing she did when she was drunk, which was the time in college when she peed in her roommate's bed because she thought it was the bathroom.

"No wonder you never went back."

"Seriously. Can I join you?"

"Yeah, but lock the door so my mom doesn't wander in."

She takes off her shirt and I watch her ease her bra off. Her nipples are pink sunsets and I'm curious what the night could hold. I scoot to one end of the tub and our toes touch when I extend my legs.

"Let's make it hotter," she says, turning the faucet on and entirely defeating the purpose of my cool bath. As the water is running she moves closer to me and I grow new nerve endings. I close the distance between us and her mouth tastes like nicotine and coffee.

"Ugh, I can't do this, Danny," she says abruptly, pulling away and scrunching her eyes closed.

"What do you mean? You can't get in the tub with me and then decide two seconds later that you can't. Watch, it's easy." I kiss her more.

"Look at us. We're hot messes."

"We did meet in the loony bin, but that's a good thing! We kinda get each other's crazy."

She takes a deep breath and puts her head under the faucet, then turns the water off and I listen to her hair drip into the bath. "It's one thing to get each other's crazy and another thing to impose my shit on you."

"It's not imposing. I want to be imposed on by your shit." A tear makes itself known on her lower left eyelid. I will it to go back where it came from because there's nothing to be sad about because she and I are completely fine.

"It's too much shit," she says, and I don't know if she means my drinking or my emotions or her drinking or her emotions or generally the clusterfuck of doom we've found ourselves in. "I know myself well enough by now to know when I have to go back to treatment."

The emotional iceberg hits hard and my heart starts its epic, *Titanic* sink.

"You can't leave me," I say selfishly, looking at the soggy piece of salami and wishing my entire life up to this point was different. "What if I quit drinking too? I promise I can handle whatever shit you think I can't handle. What I can't handle is you leaving me."

"I'm not leaving you. I'll still be here for you, but as a friend. A friend at St. John's."

"We've never been friends."

"Well, we can start now."

"What if I don't want to be your friend?" I ask. This time the tears are presenting themselves on my lower eyelids but I have no consolation for them. There's everything to be sad about.

She gets out of the tub and dries herself off. When she turns around her face is blotchy and my mascara is running down her cheeks.

"What about being Trappers?" I ask. "What about all the things we haven't gotten to do yet?"

"It's postponed for a while," she says, and I'm so upset I'm not consoled by what she says next. "Haven't you heard that love is like a telephone? If you can't answer it, you put it on hold for a second."

I should say something, I know I should say something, anything, but my brain is solidifying like bacon grease. I feel myself drifting into outer space. She leans over the tub and kisses me on the forehead, then walks out of my life in the six steps it takes her to cross the bathroom. When I no longer hear her receding footsteps, I touch the place where her lips were, half expecting to find a scar.

CHAPTER TWENTY-FIVE

That week, after doing a quick inventory, I realize I have nothing left. Nothing except my $600 hospital bill, which my parents fully expect me to pay them back for. In a way, a breakup is like a death but worse, because you could still technically touch the person, if only they'd let you. Even though Bugg texts me in a friendly way asking how I am, I ignore her because it's too confusing to talk to ghosts. I spend the days drifting like a balloon that's lost most of its helium, feeling very sorry for myself beneath the layer of emotional frostbite that's numbed my entire system.

I don't bother looking for any more internship opportunities. My one self-imposed duty each day is to get fresh flowers to bring to Sara's grave, which I buy at the supermarket with my parents' credit card, except today I failed to do even that because I couldn't choose between the baby's breath (which, mind you, looks nothing like any exhalation I've ever seen) and the carnations, which were corny.

This is why I'm in my room with a ski hat on, simulating the polar regions via the AC when I get a phone call and suddenly remember—of *course*, I'm not *entirely* alone in the world!

"Stephen," I say, probably too eagerly. "What's up?"

"Hey, how are you doing?"

I picture him in scrubs walking to his car after a long shift as the most caring volunteer on earth. "Oh, you know," I say, trying to silently unwrap a Twix bar so that I can rewrap it in prosciutto. "So-so."

"Well, hey, I don't know if you have any plans tonight, but my parents decided to leave for a few days and I have this embarrassing fear of staying home overnight alone. So if you wanted to get away for a little while, I thought maybe you could come stay with me." I mute the phone so I can take a bite. It's too good to resist. "We have a guest bedroom," he adds quickly, then, "Um, hello?"

"Hi, sorry, I'm here," I say after I've swallowed.

"So what do you think?"

I try to get a read on my body, but all the mechanisms that generally keep it functioning have entirely shut down due to the aforementioned emotional frostbite. Still, it's not like I have anything to lose by going.

"Yeah, okay. Let's do it." Then I add, "Like, let's hang out."

He laughs. "I knew what you meant."

After we hang up I wait to feel something, but I've officially become Cardboard Cutout Danny. It's pretty fine really, except who knew cardboard cutouts could be so hungry? When I tell my parents I'm going to see Stephen, they sound less than thrilled about it. I think they were planning to ground me or something after the hospital fiasco, but once I relate to them how hard it is to be in this town-slash-world without Sara, they take pity on me and let me go.

"Don't you look nice," my mom says when I come into the living room. My lip is still swollen but I finally brushed my teeth and put on a little mascara. "Is this boy your *boyfriend*?"

I don't know why I do this, but I tell her, "Yes. Yes he is." I guess I want something to be easy without needing any sort of long-winded explanation.

"Well, good. You deserve something special in your life. It's been such a hard few months." She gathers the mail not so discreetly in front of me, where a letter from Harvard sits on top.

252

"It has been hard, hasn't it," I say, kissing her on the cheek and deciding to ignore Harvard until later. "But Stephen is a wonderful..." I can't decide if I should call him a boy or a man. Neither sounds right. "...guy? Well, see ya later!"

"No drinking," my mom calls, but I'm already out the door. Besides, I'm so hungover from my pity party last night (sponsored by Grey Goose) that I can't even smell hand sanitizer without my stomach turning.

In the car I play the country music Sara liked so much, which kind of makes me feel like she's cheering me on. She'd been hoping for this for a while—it's all she would talk about after she got drunk on my birthday—so I figure it's the least I can do. You know, for Sara.

An hour and a half later I pull up to the address Stephen gave me feeling a lot less confident than I'd been earlier. "Maybe he doesn't even want to hook up with you," I remind myself. "You're not winning any beauty pageants over here."

I respond to myself in the visor mirror. "Yeah, but why else would he wait until his parents are gone to invite me over?"

He comes out of the house, which forces me to stop second-guessing myself and to get out of the car. When he hugs me I notice that he smells weird, like sports deodorant—except Stephen doesn't play sports. We at least have that in common.

"What happened to your mouth?" he asks.

"I fell in the shower. I'm *so* clumsy. Face-planted on the side of the tub. Who knew ceramic could be so dangerous, amirite?" I tug down my smock and try to figure out if it feels tighter than it did when summer started.

"That's terrible," he says, leading me into the house and asking me to take my shoes off at the door. "Well, I made carrot soup for dinner, so hopefully it won't hurt too much to eat. Don't worry, it's vegan," he adds.

"Oh, phew." I kick my sandals off and smell my breath for hints of the cured pig parts I ate for lunch.

Over some of the blandest soup I've ever tasted (like, if I put twigs in hose water it would've tasted better), Stephen and I talk Harvard stuff. I don't mention that I have seventeen hours to register for classes or else I can't come back in the fall. Instead I tell him I'm doing swimmingly, excited about my class selections and very eager to get a fresh start. By "fresh start" I mean I'm praying for a case of selective amnesia to wipe the last six months from my poor, tortured memory.

"You must miss Sara," Stephen says quietly, talking mostly into his soup. "It's funny 'cause when she came to visit she was never who I would've pictured your best friend from home to be."

"Yeah." I'm eager for the chance to put my spoon down and stop eating this orange sludge. "She's not nerdy at all and I'm not athletic at all, but I think that's what made us so close. We weren't ever competing for the same things, so it was easy to want each other to slay shit."

Stephen finally looks up at me, but his thick eyebrows are furrowed together like he's about to ask me for my kidney. "I've been curious about this," he starts, and I hold my breath and nod. "Why did you guys fight when she came to visit?"

I exhale with relief, not sure what exactly I thought he'd be asking, but this is easy enough. I stir circles into my soup that disappear each time another stroke interrupts the last swirl. "I guess on the surface it was about me ditching this plan we had and going to a different college than she did. It wouldn't have stung so much if I'd gotten into Harvard when decisions first came out, but getting in off the waitlist after Sara and I had spent a whole month before graduation picking out furniture for our dorm room sucked. That and I was a mega asshole about it and didn't tell her for another whole month after *I* found out, which was shitty. I don't know. I think we were both scared of being apart and growing up." I rest my spoon down and the soup settles.

"I'm still scared to grow up," Stephen says, and I can tell he feels a little embarrassed talking about it. Our conversations are usually deep, but in a cellular sense: mitochondria, not mighty feelings.

"Ditto, but I've basically hit pause on all that anyway. I think if I come back in the fall, I'll still be a freshman."

"'If'?"

I curse him for being too perceptive for his own good. "I mean, 'when,'" I correct myself quickly, but if I'm being honest with myself, that Freudian slip felt pretty damn good.

"Do you even want to come back?"

"Of course I want to come back. Harvard is one of the best colleges in the world. How could I not go back?" I'm looking at him too probingly. It's not a rhetorical question. Maybe if he could give me a step-by-step response, I could consider not going back.

He puts his sweaty boy hand on mine. "Well, I'm relieved to hear it. We're going to have a great year together. Do you want to try this after-dinner drink I've been wanting to make?"

I nod and the hot itchy feeling makes itself known in my stomach. I pray that the thought of alcohol hasn't turned my face a light shade of green, but the alternative is to sit back while the hot itchiness takes over my body.

Stephen takes a fancy bottle and two glasses from the dark wood chest in the corner of the dining room. While he fixes our fate I take in the chandelier and the wall of family photos. Each one proves time has passed and the smiling faces have aged some. It spooks me thinking there won't be any new pictures of Sara to add to Janet and Cal's wall collection.

My thoughts are interrupted when Stephen hands me a glass of brown liquid that smells like it could tranquilize an elephant. "Here you go."

"I thought you were going to make, like, a martini sundae," I say, trying to talk myself into this whole night.

His face falls. "I'm sorry, I don't think I have any chocolate liquor."

"Don't apologize, I'm sure this is delicious." I smell it again and my eyes nearly cross. "What is this exactly?" I take too big of a sip and my chest lights on fire.

"Cognac."

"Delicious," I pant. "Just delicious."

The silence feels charged, but only 12 percent sexually.

"Want to go upstairs and listen to my dad's old record player?" he finally asks. It's better than listening to each other breathe, so I follow him upstairs. The only problem is that it feels like we're on a second-grade play date, but with booze. I'm sure the choo-choo train wallpaper in his bedroom isn't helping any sexy causes, but it's more than that.

Hope you're happy, Spirit of Sara, I say in my head. It's completely unfair that I can't tell her about any of this. She would know how to make it hilarious. Stephen puts a song on the record player and I bob my head like every other terrible dancer trying to survive in the modern age. "This is my favorite song," I say, downing the last of the elephant tranquilizer.

"Is it really?"

"No, I've never heard it before." I like his face best when he smiles.

"You're hard to read, Danny." He offers to refill my glass by holding up the entire bottle. I nod and he sits closer to me on the bed. I study the stubble of his beard and wonder how often he has to shave to keep it that length. "I never know when you're telling the truth. Just when I think I've figured you out, you say something that throws me off entirely and I second-guess myself." He tucks my hair behind my ear and I get goose bumps in spite of myself. "You're my favorite mystery."

"I'm not a mystery." I pretend to have an itch on my leg to avoid outwardly cringing at his rom-com-worthy line. "What you see is pretty much what you get."

"No, you're complicated, maybe a little unavailable, but I know who you pretend to be and I think I know who you really are. I like you both ways." If only *I* knew who I really was, then we'd be in business. He inches his hand toward my thigh. "And after Sara's funeral, I knew I wasn't imagining something between us." Fluffernutters. "I wanted to kiss you then but it seemed wrong, and I want to kiss you now but I feel like it's still wrong. Will it hurt your lip?"

It's undoubtedly shitty to have deliberately led him on

while it was convenient for me, and while I don't feel the sexual pull I feel toward Bugg toward Stephen, for the first time ever I do feel a little curious about him. This granule of curiosity probably has more to do with the elephant tranquilizer than with any legitimate sexual chemistry, but isn't that why people drink in the first place? To enter a different kind of reality?

"This is what I mean," he says, and I watch his eyes move back and forth, trying to read me. "You're being so quiet right now, but I know there's a lot going on in there." He taps my head like I'm a robot who's been floundering around on earth only pretending to be human.

"Try it anyway. Kiss me," I finally say. Then recalling what Bugg said to me, I add, "If it hurts too much, the code word is 'ouch.'" I close my eyes and he comes on a little too strong. "Ouch."

"Oops, sorry."

"How about a little less like you're trying to break into my mouth. No offense," I add, and it's better the second time.

I lie on top of him, which I hope doesn't collapse his lungs (he's kind of a skinny dude), and even though it's sort of nice, I can't stop thinking that my mouth is the same mouth that Bugg's tongue touched, and the tongue in my mouth is the same tongue that touched Bugg's mouth, except it's also Stephen's tongue and Stephen's mouth, which makes it feel way too crowded here in my mouth.

"Let me finish my drink so it doesn't spill," I say, even though the glass is safely on his nightstand.

"I'll have the rest of mine too." He holds up his glass to me. "You don't know how long I've wanted this. To us," he says.

Dear lord.

"Cheers," I say miserably. It goes down easier than it did at first. "How about one more? For good luck," I offer.

He grins. "I've never seen party-Danny before."

"What can I say?" Bugg's voice floats into my head. "'I contain multitudes.'"

Everything that happens next happens very quickly, which is the nice thing about being drunk. It's like existing in time-lapse. We finish our drinks, make out a bit, then try to, you know, do it. We give it such a valiant effort, we really do, but he doesn't know how to touch me and the whole time I keep wondering what all the fuss about boys is. I haven't been missing *anything*. One time in second grade I got strep throat and I couldn't go to the zoo and Sara sat with Jenny Cho on the bus ride there *and* the bus ride back, and that still feels like a greater loss than not having done any sexy business with boys up until, well, this very instant.

"Um." I don't think I've quit anything in my life, except maybe T-ball and my second semester at Harvard, but this won't do. "Hey, Stephen," I whisper, but he can't hear me over his animal sounds. "STEPHEN."

"Shit, yes, what's wrong? Are you okay, baby?"

My body recoils. I hate how that word sounds in his mouth.

"No, I'm not okay. Nothing about me is okay." I try to blend in with the sheet as he rolls over. I talk to the thirty or so Stephen King books on his shelf to avoid having to look at him. "I've been seeing someone but then this person broke up with me and I thought that maybe if I gave you and me a shot, it would fix everything and we could, like, go to med school together and have a stethoscope-themed wedding, but now I think that was a bad idea. Not to freak you out," I add. "But I had a lot of time to think things over in the past few pumps and, well…" I try to find an inoffensive spot on his body to make eye contact with, but his eyes are too hurt and the rest of him is just as naked. "Look, I don't want to do any more naked activities together. I have someone to do that with already, or at least I did, until she broke up with me, but I think I can fix that. Actually, I'm sure I can fix that."

And in my cognac haze it seems totally likely that if I clean my act up a bit, Bugg will be so inspired that she won't have to go to treatment at all. She'll come back and pick me up right where she left me, on the longest and loneliest metaphoric road.

"'She'?" Stephen asks, and he sounds all sorts of confused because I'm a drunk idiot who can't even keep her own secrets a secret. Again. "You've been seeing a girl?"

261

I feel my cheeks flush and then suddenly all the tears that have been playing hooky on me for the day show up at once. My eyes are barely big enough to hold them all.

"Oh, shit, Danny, why are you crying?" he asks, sitting up and awkwardly patting my head.

"It's not you," I wail. "It's everything." I pull the sheet up around my chin. It smells like Cheer, but I'm too upset to laugh at the irony. "I went to college with a very clear idea about who I was. But then life went and bulldozed my entire plan, and now I'm standing in the dirt without a single slab of sorry cement under me. Do you know how scary the bulldozed place is, Stephen?"

He pats my head harder, and it gets kind of annoying.

"I have no foundation anymore. And I really wish we would both put our clothes back on."

He sighs, so I scramble to collect our dignity and then we sit side by side on the bed together, but not in a sexy way at all this time.

"Well, do you want to tell me about her?" he asks, but he doesn't sound that pleased about it.

He gets up, pours another drink, downs it in a mouthful, and makes a face. I wonder how much he hates me.

"Her name is Bugg." Even though he probably doesn't want to hear this at all, I have to say it out loud to keep her real. I could tell him that she went to Brown, but it doesn't define her the way it defines everyone else who goes to schools like that, how she's the type of girl who can't disconnect one type of wanting from all the others. When she craves a piece of gum it could easily become an afternoon of making out upside down on her bed, or smoking a cigarette or eating potato chips because all the things she wants at any given time extend like a cord from her deepest center, but aren't really about the thing at all, if that makes sense. She's just a wanting type of person, exactly everything I couldn't imagine letting myself be.

But I don't tell Stephen any of that because the thing about love is it's almost more about you than it is about the other person. So, instead I say, "She makes me feel like I'm not myself and more myself at the same time. She devours me in the best way and kills me in the worst way, but I'm happy to be killed by her because she's heaven too."

I take a deep breath. My head is spinning, and I do not feel well. "I don't know. I'm a terrible sappy drunk. It's probably not like that at all, I just love her."

I realize that Stephen hasn't said anything or tried to pat my head awkwardly. He's basically gotten pretty cold toward me, but I don't even care. It's actually the greatest thing in the world not to be the only person who knows my own secret anymore.

"Well, this is shit for me, Danny. You shouldn't have sent me mixed signals or acted like you wanted to hook up tonight." He looks at me like he wants an apology, but I'm really not liking his accusatory tone.

"Regardless of what I did before, mixed signals or not,

you don't get to bitch at me for deciding I'm not into this right now."

I raise my eyebrow as he gets up to pour yet another drink. I don't want to be the one cleaning up his vomit later. "Actually, they weren't *mixed* at all," he says, and his face puckers as he drains his glass. "You entirely led me on. Or did I make it up that you were flirting with me at Sara's? Am I so self-delusional that—"

I cut him off. "No, no, you're not delusional. I *was* flirting, or trying to. At Sara's I needed my other friends to think I was into you so they wouldn't suspect anything about Bugg, which was really shitty, and I'm sorry."

He rubs his eyes for a long time, so long that I wonder if I should go sleep in the shed, but then he says, in a voice entirely devoid of emotion, "If you love her, you should get her back. I've seen plenty of romantic comedies with my little sister. It doesn't look *that* hard." He opens the door and stumbles out.

"Where are you going?"

"To pee."

"You're not going to tell anyone about Bugg, are you?" I call as he pads down the hallway to the bathroom. I start to follow him but the sound of him peeing stops me in my tracks.

"Shit, let me delete the Facebook status I was crafting," he says sarcastically. Then his voice softens. "I care about you, Danny. I wouldn't do that. Besides, with any luck I won't remember this whole night tomorrow."

He comes back and his cheeks are flushed from the alcohol. "I kind of hate you right now," he says thoughtfully. "But I can't be mad at you either. I wish I could be what you need."

We stand there in the doorway and I have no idea what to say to that. I don't like being pitied, but I'd also like for my one friend at Harvard not to hate me, so finally I ask if he wants to take shots. He does and we do and it's not that things are good between us, but I think maybe our friendship can still be salvaged.

"Am I the first person you've come out to?" he slurs. We're slumped against the wall in his room under a shelf of spelling bee trophies. Initially he'd put the record player back on, but watching it spin was making me nauseous so he turned it off.

"I'm not *coming out*. All I know so far is I have this feeling for this girl. I haven't gotten any further than that." The last thing I need is an invite to yet another club, because as soon as you're in a club you have to be some sort of spokesperson. I declined in treatment and I'll decline here, thank you.

Later we crawl into bed next to each other as if the last few hours of trying to make use of each other's bodies didn't happen. Within a few minutes Stephen is snoring, which is another reason I made the right choice in not choosing him. When Bugg sleeps her breath flutters like a butterfly doing ballet; meanwhile, Stephen is single-handedly taking down the Costa Rican rain forest.

I fall asleep anyway, feeling tired and right with myself, the way you do when you realize your suspicions about the Big Hunger were correct: There really *is* only one person who can make it stop.

CHAPTER TWENTY-SIX

On the ride of shame home, I get a call from Kate. The problem with cell phones is they make you so accessible.

"Hello?" I rasp, holding the steering wheel with one hand and putting the phone on speaker with the other. I'm so hungover even sounds are making me nauseous.

"Hi, Danny, it's Kate."

"Yeah, I have caller ID on my iPhone."

"*Okay*, well, I'm at the Coffee Place with Liz and we're wondering where you are 'cause you're thirty minutes late." I swerve around an unidentifiable piece of flattened detritus, thinking it probably looks better than I do.

"Shit, I'm sorry, I entirely forgot about meeting today." They texted me a couple of days ago about planning some fancy tennis tournament in Sara's honor, and I said I'd go because I can't *not* go, but come on. How am I supposed to remember all of my commitments?

"Well, can you come now?" I can tell she's making a bitchy face, even through the phone.

"I guess so. I'm twenty minutes away but I'll be there then." I hang up and slow at a yellow light for once in my life, stopping before it turns red.

When I finally get to the Coffee Place and sit down at their table, they look clean, put together, and not hungover, which pisses me off.

"Hi, sorry," I say, wishing I had a piece of gum to mitigate my cognac breath. "I got caught up with something."

On top of not looking impressed, they're staring at my lip like I had some sort of butchered plastic surgery. "What happened to your face?" Liz asks, swirling her green juice.

"Long story; let's get down to business." There's a threatening pause and I adjust my smock.

"Danny, no offense, but—" Kate starts. Worst. Way. To. Start. A. Sentence. Ever.

"We don't think you're taking any of these things surrounding Sara's passing very seriously." She straightens out the napkin dispenser and looks at me expectantly.

"What are you talking about?" I ask, eyeing their water glasses enviously. My mouth is as dry as Death Valley.

"Well, the eulogy—"

"I had a *stomach bug*."

"—and showing up late for this meeting. The tournament is going to be special, but it's going to take a lot of work and a lot of planning, and Liz and I don't think you're being supportive, which is messed up because Sara was your absolute best friend. You can't abandon us right now."

I look back and forth between their faces. They both have lip gloss on. Who has the energy to put lip gloss on in a time like this?

"Look, I'm sorry that I was late for planning this tournament. I'm sorry I got stage fright and threw up all over Sara's death day. I'm sorry that I don't want to have a tournament because that sounds hot and sweaty and awful for someone who hates sports. And I guess I'm sorry that you feel 'abandoned.'" I realize after the fact that the use of air quotes is unforgivably condescending. "But you can't tell me how to grieve."

"You're not even wearing the bracelet," Liz says and holds up her wrist. It's one of those terribly unfashionable but fashionable rubber band things. This one says w.w.s.d.

"I don't even know what that is," I say too loudly, and a couple from the next table over stares at us.

"Yeah, because you disappeared off the face of the earth the past couple of weeks," Kate hisses, turning hers so the letters face me.

"It stands for What Would Sara Do," Liz adds, like I'm their intellectually challenged substitute version of a true friend. "We think you should be thinking more about what Sara would want."

I reach for Kate's glass and help myself to what is clearly not mine. I'm trying to swallow "what Sara would want," but we can't live out our lives in a perpetual quandary about whether Sara would or would not have done whatever we're doing. She's gone. We're not.

"Look, I'm sorry that I'm not as strong-stomached as the rest of you. I'm sorry the second that bad shit happens I lock myself in my inner closet and don't come out." Kate and Liz look at me with bewilderment, as if they couldn't fathom any sort of closet besides the one housing all their shoes. I feel something swelling up inside me and I don't know where it's coming from, but it feels right so I go with it. "The thing is, I don't want to do social things with everybody and talk about how Sara was our hero. I need to do this my way, and I'm sorry if that *offends* you, and even though I could probably try a little harder to do things your way, I *like* who I am and I *like* doing things my way."

I stand up and walk out of the Coffee Place before they can argue. It's probably a stretch to say I like who I am, but maybe if I say it enough times, it'll be true.

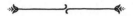

When I pull onto my street, I'm feeling good with myself and bad with myself at the same time. I definitely took some sort of stand with Kate and Liz, but fights are shitty. Also, full disclosure, I ate a shitty breakfast sandwich then threw it up in a shitty convenience-store bathroom before I met them. I shouldn't be hard on myself, though. I was just hungover. A lot of people throw up when they're hungover. Just ask a lot of people.

When I go to pull into my usual spot in the driveway, there's a minivan already parked in it. It's weird to fathom my parents having a friend, but I walk into the living room fully prepared to be as social as a hungover antisocial person can be. That is, until I realize that their "friend" is Leslie, my therapist, sitting on the couch with my parents, looking like she's about to deliver news about the impending apocalypse.

"Hey, guys," I say, clanging the keys down on the counter just for something to break the silence.

"Hi, Danny," they all say in unison, which has this eerie artificial intelligence feel to it.

"You're kind of creeping me out. Are you robots impersonating your true selves? Should I be worried? IS THIS THE FUTURE?" Nobody laughs. I've been getting some tough crowds recently.

"Come sit down," my mom says, and my therapist nods

her usual nod, which is literally the only thing she's capable of doing. I eye the couch next to her and try to figure out where the trap is. Something about all of this seems very, very sketchy.

"What's up?" I ask as I sit down and my mom puts her hand firmly on my knee, as if my patella will fall off unless she holds it in place.

"We wanted to get together to let you know that we know," my dad starts, and that's when I get this awful pit in my stomach because what if they somehow found out that the failed attempt in Stephen's bedroom was a cover-up for my real feelings about Bugg and now we're all going to share our feelings on my sexuality, followed by a Q&A mediated by the damn therapist, who probably has loads and loads of textbook wisdom to convey. Just as I'm about to begin vehemently denying any sort of action involving my lips and Bugg's body, my dad says, "That you're not doing well in terms of your eating disorder."

I sigh. True, this is the preferred topic, but now I have to vehemently deny any and all lost meals of the past week, and there are a lot to account for.

"This, combined with excessive drinking, which we think is a new behavior, has the three of us really worried." He says "the three of us" like they've been spending spring break in the Caribbean with *Leslie* for the last nineteen years.

"We care about you too much to watch you go down this path," my mom adds, and that's when it dawns on me.

"Is this an *intervention*? Like, the shit they do for drug-addicted teens on MTV or whatever?" Suddenly, it feels way too crowded on the L-shaped couch. My dad stands and takes a knee in front of me so that we're at eye level.

"This is the people who love you begging you to please consider going back to St. John's for treatment," he says, and I concentrate on the smudge on his glasses.

"So, yes. This is an intervention," I say, looking among them, and they blink in unison like the robots they truly are. Well, except Leslie, who's been trained not to blink. "I can't believe you'd suggest that I go back there. You know how much I hated it. Or maybe you didn't, since you never visited." I get up from the couch and turn around to stare at them with my hands on my hips, hoping I'll look like someone who is capable of being in charge of her life.

"It was your mother's idea—" my dad starts to say, taking my seat on the couch.

"Not helpful, Jim," my mom snaps.

"Let's try to use kind words," Leslie offers, with her pen poised over her notepad like she's taking field notes.

"*Fine.*" My mom stands, sounding annoyed. It delights me to hear that I'm not the only one who finds the therapist's condescension insufferable. "Danny, of course you can know it was my idea to intervene." She adjusts one of my dad's taxidermied mallards so that it won't fall from the shelf and die. Again. "We're doing this to save you from getting any further into a deep hole."

"I don't need you to save me," I say quietly. Everything in the room holds its breath: my parents, the therapist, the cuckoo clock on the wall opposite the TV, the fake fireplace, the other taxidermied ducks, the shelves and shelves of books. They're waiting for me to say something, but I don't want to have this conversation with all parties in the room. "Can you give us a minute?" I ask Leslie. They all look at one another, my parents communicate telepathically, then nod, and she leaves the room. "Look, I'm not some cute teenage pattern who you need to sew up with your fancy wisdom. You had absolutely no right to bring Leslie into this and stage a coup on me."

My parents try to get closer to me, but I back away until I can feel the handle of the sliding door. It's comforting knowing the whole world is only a pane away.

"Danny, it's part of the deal we made," my mom says. She's wearing a blazer and looks a lot more formidable than I do. Also her breath probably smells like a Tic Tac whereas mine smells like a dive bar. "We are involved in these conversations together so that you're ready to go back to Harvard in the fall."

"I'M TECHNICALLY AN ADULT," I yell, but the tears are hot in the corner of my eyes. It's not like I forgot what I agreed to—they remind me every damn minute—but I thought we were all on the same side. "JUST BECAUSE YOU BIRTHED ME AND PAY FOR ALL MY SHIT DOESN'T MEAN I DON'T HAVE THE RIGHT TO PRIVACY."

I try to take deep breaths. I rack my brain for a time that something good has come from me being very angry and shouting at the people I love, but I can't come up with a single instance.

"Danny, we love you," my dad says, his eyebrows merging into one above the frame of his glasses.

"We're scared for you and wouldn't have been able to live with ourselves if we didn't intervene," my mom adds.

As she stands next to my dad and they look at me pityingly, I wish so much that Sara weren't dead and that Bugg hadn't broken up with me. Besides not having anyone to go to the movies with, it's pretty shitty having no one left on your team to say what you can't say for yourself. It's so profoundly lonely being the only person in the universe that I think my head is going to spin off, but then I realize that it's also very quiet when you're the only person left. So quiet, in fact, that you can think for yourself.

"Look at what Sara's parents are going through," my mom continues, walking over to me and trying to give me a hug. "Can you imagine? If only they'd stepped in."

"But at least Sara got to live a life that was *hers*." I inch away from my mother in hopes of still being able to hear myself think. "She made a choice and the choice was hers, entirely, irrevocably hers." I look out at the garden and the white plastic goose has gotten dirtier since I tripped over it. God it feels like a million lifetimes ago. "Isn't there some dignity in that?"

"Now isn't the time to get noble," my mom says. "If it's between your well-being or your so-called dignity, I'd prefer to lose the latter."

"You're being such vampires," I mutter, then lean my forehead against the cool glass of the window, feeling like this is some sort of prison. I can nearly feel my pulse in the tiny molecular crystals of the glass.

"Danny, we are one hundred percent on your team," my dad says, but he sounds like he knows he's lying.

The therapist pokes her head in. "Is everything okay in here?"

"Yes, *Leslie*, we're fine," I say.

"I think we could use some assistance," my mom pipes up, and I bite my tongue so hard I think I draw blood. "We want you to get better, Danny."

And Leslie chimes in with, "It's my professional opinion that you're headed down a dangerous path if you don't get some help. Though our sessions have been illuminating, they're not enough, not after everything that's happened with the passing of your friend. Luckily, there's an immediate opening at St. John's that we were able to book you into."

My jaw drops so low it grazes the carpet.

"We need to know you're going to be someplace safe," my dad says, and he looks truly sorry. My team, my ass.

"So just to clarify, I don't have any say in this at all? This whole intervention was a puppet show to get me to agree with you? You know that's even more screwed up than telling me straight up that I should go back to St. John's." My parents are nice people and they don't like to come off as fascists, but when they *are* being fascists, I think they should own up to it.

"Well, we think—" my dad starts, but my mom cuts him off.

"No. You don't have a choice, Danny. As your parents we have chosen to step in. Start packing up your stuff tonight and we're going to head over on Saturday." My mother buttons her blazer as if that's that.

"Hell no. If you think I'm going back to that shitty—"

"Danny, language, please."

"Let's try to use kind words," Leslie says again.

"Oh, fuck off," I say, pulling my smock down and walking past them. "Look, I get that you have to do your parental duties and I'm so glad you decided to have a kid, but I really fucking hate you. All three of you." Before I leave the room I turn around and add, "No offense."

CHAPTER TWENTY-SEVEN

"SHIT," I yell into my dad's car. "FUCK. SHITFUCK-SHITFUCKSHITFUCK."

I wish I were a guy, or an animal, or something unfeminine that's allowed to lose control. I want to break shit and not get labeled crazy for it. I want to punch a wall and leave a Danny-size hole in it. Instead I drive a little too fast and flip people off when I cut them off.

The way I see it I have two options. Either I march over to St. John's like a brainwashed soldier or I offer myself up to NASA and prepare for life on Mars. Both options sound terribly lonely, and I don't know which is more life-threatening. Regardless, I should certainly start drafting my Craigslist ad: a once-bright future, now yours for just $30.

"FUCK," I scream again.

"I'm sorry, I didn't get that," Siri says, and I jump in my seat then consider throwing her to her death, but really I need her much more than she needs me.

"At least make yourself useful," I say, removing her from the console and positioning my mouth close to the phone. "Siri, should I run away?"

"Calculating the—"

"Oh, shut up."

I open all the windows and try to air out the shit feelings. Then I take the exit for the beach and let the car idle in the parking lot.

"What *would* you do, Sara?"

But I don't see how that's going to help me. I've spent the majority of my life wondering what Sara might do, and the only thing it left me with was a string of unanswered questions about myself. No, if I'm going to get anywhere, it's going to be by doing it my way, whatever that means.

I get out of the car with my journal, which I grabbed from my room before I left, and lean on the hood. The parking lot is scattered with people and there's the faint smell of sunscreen and salt around me. I start by rereading some of the things I've written this summer as part of Cynthia's exercises, then I flip to the page where I've hand-copied "Wild Geese," which is also where I stashed Bugg's napkins the last time I read them. Cynthia is always telling us to let poems speak to us.

Even though nothing I've read has developed lips or anything corny like that, I can kind of believe that language goes deeper than mouths, so I lay out the napkins on the hot metal of the car and try to find something in "Wild Geese" that maybe I've been missing. I go through the poem line by line—I think about goodness and knees and deserts. I touch my stomach and feel its softness. I think about despair and rain and geese and what it might mean to go home.

Just as I'm wondering about calls and my place and things, a vengeful gust of wind comes out of nowhere and blows the napkins from the car. Their white tissue is suspended in the air for a second, then they scatter in different directions. At first I try to chase after them, but then it seems right to let the remnants of St. John's get away from me. Besides, it was never the napkins or even the poem that was important. It was the person who wrote them.

And that's when I call Bugg.

"We have to go someplace new, like we did before Sara died, where I don't have to feel like myself or suffer all the self-inflicted pressure that generally comes with being Danny. It's time to stop talking about it and actually become Trappers, because I want to see things and do things and eat things and be alive for once with no preconceived notions about what that should look like. Do you know what I mean? Maybe you have to go someplace entirely unfamiliar to finally get familiar with yourself, or maybe that's some new-age bullshit, but either way I want to be with you." I try to think if there's anything else that simply must be said, but I'm probably almost out of time. "Anyway, sorry to leave this whole long thing on your voicemail—you're probably at yoga or selling herbal remedies to minors, but will you call me when you're done? I need to know if you're in, and it's kind of time sensitive."

My foot taps and then my fingers start up too. The MCAT study book is glaring at me from the passenger's seat. "What are you looking at?" I ask its glossy cover. I grab it by the throat, get out of the car, and throw it on top of some soggy French fries that are piled on the nearest trash can. I linger guiltily for a moment because it could technically be recycled. Luckily, there are no Harvard students around to attack the size of my carbon footprint so I leave it where it belongs: with the garbage. There's also no one around to see me house a pulled-pork burrito from a nearby food truck, which turns out to be the best six dollars I've ever spent. As I sit on the hood of the car and wipe my mouth with my hand, I notice the time on my cell phone, 2:08 p.m., which means it's officially too late to register for fall classes. I lie down and feel the heat of the metal against my back. I should feel overwhelmed, I should maybe want to kill myself, but instead I smile like a cat and curl up in my spot of sun.

Bugg doesn't get back to me that night, so the next day I decide to show up at poetry class for the first time in weeks. "It's so good to see you, dear. We're practicing our final assignment today," Cynthia says, but I'm busy looking around the room for Bugg. Unless she saw me and hid under the table, she's not here yet or not coming at all.

"Cool," I say and take a seat with a good view of the door.

At one o'clock we get started even though Bugg isn't there. Cynthia passes around something by Jack Kerouac, a list of suggestions for writing and life. Irene reads them out loud and afterward Cynthia gives us a minute, "for our bones to settle." I close my eyes mostly because the last few days have been exhausting, and then Cynthia tells us about the in-class exercise: "Now you're going to write your own list of suggestions, which will hopefully launch you into your final assignment, the credo," she says cheerfully. I look up at her and raise my hand.

"You don't have to raise your hand here, dear. Go ahead." She puts the same collection of pencils on the table again.

"I know I should have asked this earlier, but what is a credo exactly?"

"It's what you believe, your guiding principles. 'Belief and Technique for Modern Prose' is a great example of someone's credo, so in this exercise you're going to write your own list of guidelines for modern poetry or modern life or anything you want, whatever inspired you from Kerouac's list." I nod but I don't know where to begin or what that would look like, despite having done all the exercises and assignments Cynthia suggested this summer. Luckily she's all about "setting the mood."

"Now close your eyes," she says, and I do. "And picture the last place you were truly happy." I almost throw up a little bit in my mouth. This is exactly the sort of touchy-feely stuff they tried to pull in treatment. As if reading my thoughts, she adds, "It's only corny if you believe in corniness. Otherwise it's a damn good exercise."

I dare myself to let go a little bit, and what comes to mind is a whole series of things, most of which make me want to cry: floating in the ocean with Bugg, sleeping next to Sara on the Fourth of July when we were eleven and we could see the fireworks from her room, reading "Wild Geese" a lot of nights when I should have been sleeping, waiting in line at midnight for the last Harry Potter book, the sound of biting into a perfectly golden grilled cheese...

"Now let go of the memories themselves," Cynthia

instructs. "And write through what's left—the pure emotion of—"

But I've tuned her out. I'm moving the pencil up and down the page of my journal slowly and steadily. Somehow, without telling myself to write anything, the words are flowing out of me, like when you tip a jar of honey into your mouth and you don't have to will it or anything, it comes out because it has to. I'm sure the phenomenon is due to something scientific, like gravity, but it still tastes good.

When the timer goes off, Cynthia asks me to read. I look down at my paper but it's not something I want to share with anyone. I feel the sets of eyes on me—Irene's thick lashes, Philip's dark eyeliner, Larry's wrinkled eyelids.

"Dandelion Theory." Looking down at the page, I feel like it'd be a crime against myself to share this with anyone else. "Dandelion Theory," I say again, hoping that repeating the title will get me to go on. But then I become the only person in the universe again and I hear myself say, "No, I'm sorry. I can't do this."

My heart is pounding. I've never denied a teacher in my life, but if I don't start respecting the little things I know are true, how will I ever be worth my own company?

"No problem. Are you okay, Danny?" Cynthia asks.

I reread my poem, feeling the energy gather in my body, then pull my chair back and stand up. "Yes, I'm fine." Maybe even great.

As I look out the window, a million tiny black birds

land on the lawn then take flight at once. Rosebushes blow in the wind and their thorny stems do too, but I'm not close enough to see them. You have to be very close to see the details that make a rose a rose, and when you can't get that close you have to trust that they're there.

"I have to get going now. Excuse me," I tell the room of confused faces as I pack my bag and close the door behind me. I can't wait for Bugg to tell me if she's in or not. I can't spend my whole life waiting for people to okay my decisions—not Stephen, not Kate and Liz, not my parents or Leslie or Cynthia. There's something in me that knows something, and it's imperative that I listen. Either that, or I'm having very bad indigestion.

As I cross the lawn to my dad's car, I pause and crouch down in the garden, pricking my finger as I grab hold of a rose. No, I'm not crazy, there is something there. It's been waiting to be acted upon.

CHAPTER TWENTY-EIGHT

I'd like to go home and change into something ceremonious, maybe some all-black stealth-mode attire, but a) I don't have that sort of attire and b) if my parents see me they're going to try to talk to me, and since I'm never going to talk to them again, it's better that they don't see me. These are the reasons why I show up at Sara's house in the mustard mom smock, the worst of the whole bunch, prepared to start the execution of Operation Free Bird, which I named after hearing a certain song on the radio on the way home. When I go to open the door it's locked, which has happened exactly never in the history of the Collins household. I don't know where Janet could be, but it's weird taking the spare key from the top of the door and letting myself in. It's even weirder when I open the door to Sara's room, which seems like it's been shut since the last time she was in it. I take a deep breath, not a Three-Part Pause-and-Blah breath, but just an honest stab at getting some air into my lungs.

Sara's bed hasn't been made and the pillows are crumpled, and when I get closer I see there's a long blond hair on one of the sheets still. Seeing it makes me want to get the hell out of there, stat, but I have to move carefully so I don't step on the clothes on the floor or knock over the glass of water by her closet. I think the hair is the worst thing she left behind, but it's hard to top the general feeling that she was *just* here. The longer I stand there the longer I remember miscellaneous snippets from our childhood: when she sprained her wrist and I tried to concoct an IV of Gatorade to get her through the summer, how she stood before her closet before prom trying to choose between the short dress with the blue ruffles and the long dress with the yellow tulle, and on and on. I'm afraid that if I don't leave, the memories will continue flooding me like a montage from a movie you can't turn off. I grab what I need to and go, otherwise I might believe she's in the bathroom or something—someplace she could come back from. I don't say bye when I close the door softly behind me, but I feel the significance of leaving.

I put our house in the passenger seat and buckle it in. Mostly I do this because the seat belt sign will ding if I don't, but also it feels right to give it a little extra protection. As I drive away, I weigh the pros and cons of a) setting it free in the ocean or b) setting it into the stratosphere via six or so helium balloons. The problem with the ocean is someone might find it and form their own twisted Plan, thinking it's fate or something. The problem with the stratosphere is the same problem as the ocean. I guess a third option is to bury it, but I'm not in the best shape to be digging holes in eighty-five-degree weather (ninety-five if you count the humidity).

"Hello, calling on the Spirit of Sara. How do you want me to dispose of this?" I've always been soft-spoken, so I'm not surprised when she doesn't answer me. (It's not that she's ignoring me. She's not mad anymore, trust me.) I decide the option with the least karmic consequences is to burn it—not that I believe in karma but it's good to take precautions, and luckily my family is like all other suburban families in that we have the possibility of fire in our backyard. Though it's not ideal to be within a hundred square feet of my parents, really *nothing* has been ideal in the last ten months.

I don't wait for it to be dark out because the golden window of opportunity happens to present itself when my parents go to the gym, which I know because I've staked out the house. After my mom's car pulls out of the driveway, I get a starter log and some newspaper from the garage, then drag the fire bowl to the very edge of the lawn, as far away from my parents, the vampires, as possible, in case they come home. I run into the house and take my cardboard cutout from my nightstand and bring it outside with a box of matches.

It's a sweaty affair in the late afternoon sun, trying to get the logs to catch. When they finally do, the smoke from the fire curls into the air and the smell fills my nostrils in a way that reminds me of something I can't remember. That's my favorite type of nostalgia, though, when you can't pinpoint the memory but the feeling swirls in your body and escapes you like smoke.

As the fire does its fire thing, I hold the cardboard house and try to get a read on my body. I'm not as sad as I thought I'd be, but I do feel nervous. We had a good run, Sara and I, and it was sweet thinking we could plan our whole lives out. It's also sweet that some people want to get all sweaty and play, like, a marathon of tennis in her name, but this feels like a truer way to release her. Less popular, sure, but I couldn't give less of a damn about whether Kate and Liz think my coping mechanisms are appropriate or whether my parents think I need to be babysat by six to twenty accredited doctors. I may not have much left, but the one thing I do have is some agency over how I handle my shit.

I sit in the grass and put the house in my lap. "Aw, look at you!" I say, reuniting our cutouts and holding them against the sky. They're giddy and hopeful because they're thirteen and two-dimensional—the right criteria for a rigid plan. It's harder to apply that same plan to a three-dimensional nineteen-year-old. What felt good at first ends up eating you whole.

"Well, a plan is pretty stupid, don't you think?" I ask Cardboard Cutout Sara. She nods with a little help from my finger and I place our house delicately into the fire. It's a little macabre watching the flames lick the cardboard windows, but it feels right too. It's definitely harder to throw Sara and me in (again, I hate feeling like a serial killer), and I'm almost tempted to Scotch tape our hands together but that seems cheesy and/or homicidal so finally I do it—no speeches, no apologies, no attempts to fix her poor butchered eulogy. Some friends don't need to say sorry, and though it would've been awfully nice, it doesn't change the stuff between us, that good old July river flowing between God knows where and God knows what. "You're going to be fine." And I'm talking a little bit to Sara, but I'm mostly talking to me.

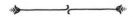

Holding a dead girl's cell phone is like holding her hand, I mean, if I was the sort of person who could read palms. Ironically, I have to plug the phone in because it's also dead, but as I sit in my room waiting for the lights to come on, I wonder if I should do this at all. I don't know the answers I'm looking for exactly. Besides, anything she texted to Bugg or Ethan or Liz/Kate, any drafts in her e-mail that she was maybe going to send to me, aren't my business. I can't violate her privacy because she's not around to yell at me. Those are the cons. The biggest pro is that I miss her, and if she was right last year when she said a piece of her soul lives in her cell phone, then isn't this the best way to see her again?

The bitten apple lights up and panic takes over my chest. I throw the phone on the ground, stare at it like it's about to blow up, then grab it and turn it off as fast as my clumsy fingers can. I lean against the wall afterward, relieved my moral compass hasn't entirely shit the bed. The problem now is that I don't want to keep her phone around. I could throw it away and pretend to have never taken it, but—*No. If I don't stop lying, I'm going to need a nose job before I'm twenty.*

I end up bringing the phone to Sara's house. The universe does not reward me for doing the right thing because as soon as I pull in on my bicycle (I need at least a little exercise), Janet comes out and chitchat is unavoidable. She ushers me into the kitchen.

"Want a glass of Pellegrino? It's the champagne of water, you know," she says as I sit at the counter among vases and vases of flowers. It smells so fragrant the kitchen could double as a florist, in a nauseating way.

"Why the hell not?" I take the glass she's already poured for me and she perks up. Ever since Janet told Sara she feels like the cool mom when we swear around her, I've been trying to do my part.

"I'd offer you something with more spunk, but I've decided to quit drinking." She points to the bracelet on her arm, which is the same as the w.w.s.d. ones that Kate and Liz were wearing. "Sara was thinking about quitting too, and we had some great conversations about it. Well, we had one conversation one night when we were both pretty drunk." She laughs as if this is normal mother-daughter behavior, then her face turns serious. "Don't you think Sara would be proud of me?"

"Very proud." I'm about to tell Janet that she was a good mother, but in the new vein of not lying, I go with, "Sara really loved you."

"I know she did. And I loved her and she loved you. Actually, it's perfect timing that you're here, Danny. Cal and I want you to have Sara's car."

I choke a little and the sparkling water starts to come up my nasal passageway. The tingling sensation is exacerbated by the bubbles, and I pinch my nose, anticipating a sneeze.

"Her car?" I say, sounding nasally and confused. I don't know the protocol in these sorts of situations, but a Range Rover seems like an absurd gift from a dead friend's parents.

"Yes," Janet says firmly. "And here, you need a Sara bracelet."

She leaves the room and I put Sara's phone in the electronics drawer, feeling a little guilty but nothing I can't live with. When Janet comes back, she puts the rubber bracelet on my wrist for me. "We don't need three cars now and I can't stand looking at it in the driveway any longer, thinking she's home. Besides, you're a second daughter to us." She fills a cup with water at the sink and refills the vases. They're plenty full but I can see that she likes tending to something. "I won't accept no for an answer," she adds.

And that's how I leave Sara's house with her keys in my hands and my bike in her trunk.

"Well, don't be a stranger, sweetie," Janet says as I adjust the seat and mirrors. "You know you've always been part of the family." She leans through the window and gives me a Chanel kiss, then tells me not to wipe it off. "Also, there's something for you in the console. Take a look when you're home."

I figure it's a card or something and forget all about it, because the moonroof works, the car smells new, and I've just figured out how to fund Operation Free Bird.

CHAPTER TWENTY-NINE

Back in my room, I get out my biggest backpack and try to narrow my life down to the necessities: four pairs of my sturdiest granny panties (there will be frequent hand washing), three of my darkest smocks (the rationale being that they'll be the least likely to show food/dirt), my journal + two awesome pens, the water bottle that filters itself through its own straw, computer + computer charger, and finally, a letter I wrote Bugg. I survey the situation, determine I'm not a very exciting person, but decide that's okay. Us boring people have our own ways of having fun. It's about four o'clock, which means time did not graciously slow down for me while I was getting my affairs in order. "Very well, *clock*, I'll pick up the pace a bit."

The first stop is the DMV, where I do all the tedious stuff involved with making Sara's car my car. It's insanely boring, but there are lots of free lollipops. Score. The second stop is the dealership, where I park Sara's car (it should technically be classified as a bus) and try to find whoever is in charge. This turns out to be a red-faced man named Lou.

"What can I do for you, sweetheart?" Lou asks.

I *hate* men who call women *sweetheart*. You don't know the sugar content of my heart just because of the genital parts you assume I'm sporting beneath my smock. "I'd like to trade in my car over there," I say, pointing to where I parked. "For cash."

"All right, I'm going to need to see the paperwork proving you own it, then it'll need a thorough inspection, which should only take a couple of days—"

"Oh no. I was hoping I could have the money now."

Lou laughs and pats my head. *Pats my head.* "It's gonna be at least a week, sweetheart. What are you in such a rush for? Not escaping the law, are ya?" He winks and slaps me on the back.

I burst into tears. "I...need...the...money...by... tomorrow," I gasp. "Or...else...I'm...screwed." I swear I didn't mean this as an act, but his face crumples like tissue paper and you know he has a daughter who's gotten herself into a snafu once or twice.

"All right, don't cry now. Let me see. How about you give me the keys and the registration stuff and I'll take it for a quick spin right now. If it seems okay, I'll front you a couple grand and send you a check in the mail as soon as we've cleared it. Sound good?"

I sniffle and nod. "Thank you. Thanks very much. It's only two years old because my best friend always got the best new things and I wouldn't even be in such a hurry about it except it's an emergency, kind of a long story—"

"Hey, it's none of my business, sweetheart. Just the car is my business."

I hand him the keys, and he hands me a check for two thousand dollars. It's the most money I've received in one sitting in my whole life. Actually, it's the most money I've received in my whole life ever.

"Cool," I say, then remember Janet telling me there was something for me in the console. "Wait!" I dig around the console until I find an envelope with my name on it. I'm too tired to read any sappy stuff from Janet, so I grip it in my sweaty palm and start home.

I spend the next day avoiding my parents, which is easy at first because they're at work, but much harder when they get home. They come into the kitchen looking the worst combination of sad, guilty, concerned, and eager to win back my affections. It's the sort of culpable look where I could probably leverage a puppy, if I wanted one.

"What can we make you for dinner on your last night here, Danny?" my mom asks, as if it's not disgusting that she'd like to do something nice for me now that she's decided my grueling fate.

I try not to grimace, though. It's imperative that I seem cooperative about traipsing off to prison tomorrow, lest they suspect my hidden agenda. "You know what I'd like? One of Sara's grilled cheeses."

Upon hearing this my mother bursts into tears. *Tears.* "It's so unfair that she was taken so young," she sobs.

"I don't think *unfair* is how you can describe it." Because do any of us really *deserve* anything? It seems to me that things happen in a tits-to-the-wind type fashion. If you get a life lived out into the monotony of old age and orthopedic shoes, well then, good for you, but it's certainly not *deserved*.

"You're being so strong, Danny," my mom says, and I sort of break out in hives where she kisses me. "If you want a Sara grilled cheese, that's what we'll make."

My mom breaks away to blow her nose, and my dad touches my elbow. "Come on, let's go get supplies," he says.

I take a deep breath. I only have to survive the next sixteen hours without blowing my own cover. Really, how hard could it be?

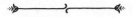

When we get to the grocery store I'm about to thank my dad for rescuing me from my mom's heart-to-heart when he goes, "Seems like a good time to talk, now, doesn't it?" We're parked in one of the various strip malls that has both an actual mall and a grocery store in it.

I muster all my courage. "Okay, what do you want to talk about?"

He kills the engine, then puts all the windows down. I keep my seat belt on as an emotional precaution, although nothing could protect me from the whiplash that follows him reaching into his pocket and pulling out a pack of Marlboros.

"What are you doing?"

"Sneaking a cigarette. You don't see anyone we know, do you?"

I look at the pack in his hand then back up at him. "Certainly no one I recognize."

Who is this mysterious man posing as my father? As he takes a cigarette from the carton it occurs to me that I don't know *that* much about him, considering we share a hot water supply.

"I've been wanting to tell you this for so many months, and now that I finally have your attention I'm getting stage fright," he says and sucks on his cigarette. I help myself to one too, and he opens his mouth to say something, then smiles, probably realizing there's absolutely nothing he can say.

"It's okay, Dad. You've, er, got this?" But I'm nervous too. I have no idea what I'm in for.

"All right. I'll give it a go and if it gets bad, cut me off." I've never seen my dad nervous. It's kind of sweet, in a weird parents-are-human type way. "The reason I couldn't visit you in treatment wasn't because I was disappointed in you, Danny," he says. The pause is enough for six pregnancies. "It's because I *was* you."

The seat belt suddenly feels very tight around my body. I light the cigarette and blink through the dirty windshield as a plastic bag comes into view, blown slowly across the gravel by the wind.

"I had an eating disorder, for as long as I can remember," he says, then launches into this story about how he used to diet and binge and throw up—the whole nine yards. "It wasn't until I was married to your mom and she walked in on me one day that I admitted I'd been doing that for years. She made me go into treatment, and since our whole marriage depended on it, I went."

I'm trying to listen to what he's saying, but sometimes someone says something that hits so close to home, you end up feeling homeless.

"But I didn't want to get better, so for the first couple of years nothing happened. Then one night I hit a new bottom. I was sick of being so sick all the time. I was sick of hating my body. I decided I didn't care if I was three hundred pounds, I couldn't keep dieting and bingeing anymore. So I went back to treatment for *me*, and that's how I got better."

The plastic bag continues to drift across the parking lot like a ghost of things bought. I clench and unclench the seat belt, trying to control my anger by thinking about absolutely fucking nothing.

"It was too painful to see you in treatment," he continues, "suffering the same way I did. I couldn't bear it." He looks at me for too long and accidentally blows smoke directly into my face.

"Jesus, Dad," I say, waving my hand in front of my face, even though I'm smoking too. "Jesus Shit Christ."

I want to run until I am someplace new, where no one is pretending and nothing is kept secret and no one is nineteen.

"Do you know how many hours I spent wondering what was wrong with me? Why this shit came out of nowhere? If I'd known it's probably *genetic*, I could've at least slept peacefully after I threw up my dinner." I undo my seat belt and open the car door, then get out and slam it shut with so much force I half expect the window to break.

"I'm so sorry," he says, following me out of the car. "Danny, please, where are you going?"

I chase after the plastic bag I saw through the windshield, stomp on it, then crumple it into a ball.

"Besides feeling like an idiot for having this random, stupid thing wrong with me," I shout, "don't you think it would've been a nice thing to know that you weren't ignoring me in treatment because you were *disappointed* in me? Do you have any idea how much less confusing and painful this would have been if you'd just told me?" I start walking toward the nearest trash can with the plastic bag safe in hand. At least one of us can be saved from a life of aimless drifting. "I hate you," I yell back at him, then scrunch the plastic bag into a tighter ball, probably burrowing a million plastic bag diseases into the creases of my palm. "I fucking hate you."

When I get to the trash can, I start crying because it smells bad and life is stupidly complicated and I've never sworn at my parents so much as this summer and I'm probably going to get grounded for this. I wipe the snot with my wrist. You know what? My dad ought to be grounded too.

"I'm sorry," he says again when he's caught up to me. "But you of all people can understand how easy it is to keep avoiding important conversations."

I turn around and glare at him. "But you're the adult! You're supposed to be better at doing the right thing."

"I know, I know. I'm sorry," he says miserably, and standing there with his hands in his jeans he looks about ten years old. It occurs to me that just because adults have age on their side, doesn't mean they're any older than kids. "I want to tell you what worked for me so that you can get better too. Even though I'm late, I might not be too late."

I stand there for a moment, not knowing what to do. "I'm going into the mall to wash my hands now," I say, pointing toward the glass doors of the most dismal place on earth. "I'll find another ride home."

"Danny—" he starts to say, but then the mall doors open and a woman with tall hair and too much perfume comes swirling out. Even after she's walked away my dad and I are left standing in her sugar scent, like her eau de toilette crop-dusted us.

"God, we're all trying to mask *something*," my dad says, looking bitterly after her.

And I don't want to, like, I risk drawing blood by biting my lip to avoid it, but despite my best efforts I let out a suppressed laugh that gets stuck in my throat and makes me cough.

My dad looks delighted. "You liked my little joke," he says, way too pleased with himself.

"You're not off the hook," I tell him, opening the doors to suburban hell. "That was a shitty thing to do, Dad."

And it was, but as much as it feels like I got punched in the boob, it also feels like a weight has been lifted, because maybe I didn't go and give myself an eating disorder. Maybe my shit genetic luck had something to do with it. And honestly, I think that's the truth about truth: It knocks the wind out of you, but surely that's a fair price for making you freer too.

"I don't know how to make it right," he says as we go inside.

We pass the pet store and I point to the closest puppy in the window. "You could start there," I say. "I'll name it Dog."

My dad puts his arm around me and I let him, mostly because the AC is so high I feel susceptible to the flu. Then he starts to try to convey, like, a life's worth of eating disorder wisdom onto me, saying things about "loving your body" and "feeding your soul." It's a relief when we get to the bathrooms.

He waits outside while I wash my hands. There's something disturbing about how many times I can put my hand under the dispenser and it still shoots pink antibacterial liquid into my palm. It's like it never learns or never remembers that we've been here before—ten seconds ago, in fact. I slap it with my hand a few times before realizing it's not the soap dispenser who needs changing.

"I thought you might have fallen in," my dad says when I come out.

"I know what you can do." I stand across from him tugging at my smock in a way that does not suggest confidence. "Convince Mom that going back to St. John's is a waste. You said it yourself. You can't get better until you want to get better, and I *do* want to get better. I don't *like* being so obsessed with food and veganism and how I look and all that stuff. But since I know St. John's isn't going to help me, I've devised a plan that will."

My dad looks down at his man-sandals. "I wish I could prove to you that there's a whole world out there beyond hiding who you love, beyond this whole obsession with food."

"Hold the phone," I say, kicking one of the mandals. "You can't sneak that in there. You're supposed to let *me* tell *you* unprompted if I want to share any details about who I love."

He looks at me all deer-in-the-headlights, and even though my heart is beating outside of my chest, I'm secretly glad he pried the door open. Now I can own up to it real quick and we'll never have to talk about it again. If the cat is already out of the bag, what difference does it make if I pet it or not? "You're right, okay? I've been lying about who I love. Stephen isn't my boyfriend. Bugg is. I mean, my girlfriend. I mean, she *was*."

His eyes bulge out.

"Oh, Danny, I had no idea," he says.

"WHAT DO YOU MEAN YOU HAD NO IDEA?" I shout, and a startled mother steers her two children to the other side of the mall.

"I was talking about *pre-med*," he says, semiwhispering.

"*PRE-MED?*"

"Yeah," he says hurriedly. "You don't have to pretend that you like your pre-med classes and want to be a doctor. Your mom and I have suspected that you hate it, and we wouldn't be mad if you wanted to pursue a different career path. Hence why I said you don't have to hide what you love."

"I THOUGHT YOU SAID *WHO* I LOVE."

At first I'm so mad at him and at myself that my face gets all tomato-like, but then I burst out laughing, because how did someone as dense and idiotic as I am get into Harvard? Off the waitlist, but still.

My dad is *howling* at this point, leaning against the pet-store window for support. When he finally catches his breath enough to talk, he ruffles my hair, which would be fine if I had a crew cut, but really ruins the ponytail thing I've got going on. "You know your mother and I love you no matter what. We're *very* progressive people, not to mention progressive *parents*."

"Correction: You're progressive people and *helicopter* parents. But thanks. I know you don't care, it was just a weird thing to have to tell you."

Because it's not that I ever thought they'd give a shit, but it's still hard to say, "Hey, I know you thought I was one way but actually I'm another way entirely." Maybe the hardest person to say that to is myself.... No, it's definitely harder to tell him, here outside the last stop for those poor creatures at the puppy mill. *I'm sorry*, I mouth to them. Then I turn to my dad with my best impersonation of the cutest one in there. "So will you do it? Tell Mom I don't have to go?"

My dad sighs and looks longingly at the puppies, probably wishing he'd agreed to Dog. "Well, what will you do instead?"

"Like I said, I have a plan," I assure him. He looks at me expectantly, as if I'm going to lay out Operation Free Bird for him. "You know I can't tell it to you, Dad. That'd put you in a bad position with Mom. And besides, how do I know you're not some sort of Benedict Arnold?"

He laughs, but I can tell he thought we'd made enough progress in this heart-to-heart to be true confidants. What can I say? My best-kept secrets are still the ones I keep with myself.

CHAPTER THIRTY

When people you love die, you're supposed to
become a better version of yourself. Sure, you're
supposed to cry a little, but after that it's
assumed you'll have nothing less than an epiphany.
You'll start flossing, tell the people you love how
much you love them, develop a creative hobby
like basket weaving, and shortly after, you'll free
yourself from your own brain prison. I think it's
called exaltation. Well, predictably I've done none
of those things and less, which is why I'm going.
New place, new me. I hope you'll come with me.
If you can't, I understand, but, like, please?

That's how I've ended Bugg's letter. It's folded up and safe in the envelope with the plane ticket I bought her. Check-in time: twelve hours from now. I lick the envelope and take my bike from the garage, hoping I don't pedal all the way to her house and all the way back for her to say no. I'm a little pissed she hasn't responded to my super endearing voicemail, but it's hard to love someone and be mad at them at the same time. You'd think one feeling would be strong enough to override the other, but I guess that's the brilliant thing about being human: nothing you feel has to make any sense.

The only hiccup in my original plan of leaving the letter for Bugg in her mailbox is that when I get there, Bugg is already outside, standing by her mailbox.

"Danny," she says, and she sounds happy to see me. "I've been so worried. You haven't been answering my texts."

"What texts?" I say, stopping my bike next to her and nearly overdosing on the smell of cinnamon and cigarettes. "I called and left you a voicemail."

"Oh, damn, I never got it. I dropped my phone in the toilet a couple of days ago and it's been weird ever since."

"Yeah, iPhones aren't exactly suited for those conditions."

She smiles and I try not to let my heart erode. It's not fair for her to wear a yellow silk kimono and peacock feather earrings if we're just friends.

"You going someplace?" I ask. "That's not exactly lounge-around-the-house attire." It's only been a week since I've seen her, but it feels like my whole life.

"Dinner with Cynthia." The wind blows her peacock earrings back and forth. She looks totally fine and totally like she doesn't need to go back to St. John's, just saying.

"Cool." I feel like a barbarian on my stupid bike so I get off.

She takes out a cigarette and lights it. "So what did your voicemail say?" I watch the smoke escape her lips, jealous of their departure point.

"I'm, uh, leaving town tomorrow."

"What?"

I try not to take too much pleasure in the hurt look on her face. "Yeah, my parents staged an intervention." I give her a few of the gritty details. "They really want to put the octopus to bed."

She gives me a confused look and I explain what I yelled at my parents seemingly forever ago, about all the tentacles and how when you think you've taken your life back, another one wakes up.

"Oh, Danny, I'm so sorry." Her eyes brighten. "But it could be kind of cool to go back to St. John's at the same time? We couldn't *date* or anything but…oh, shit, what if it's awkward or—"

"Don't worry, I have no intention of going back, and I don't think you should go either." I hold the letter up to her. "Everything's explained in here, along with a terrible poem I wrote when you weren't in class the other day, but I can't say it out loud or I'm going to chicken out. So do me a favor and read it tonight and don't text me or call me or anything, but, well, there's instructions in there if you're interested."

Before she says anything I lean in and kiss her on the lips so hard it sort of hurts my mouth. Then I hop back on my bike and try to pedal off quickly, but given the tingling in my lips, my overall nonathleticism, and the less-than-ideal leg-to-pedal ratio, I don't get very far.

"Hey, Danny," she calls. I stop my bike and look back at her standing in the middle of the road, a bright mess framed by perfectly groomed shrubs and flower bushes.

"The octopus is my favorite creature," she shouts. "Want to know why?"

"It always figures out a way to escape the zoo?"

She steps on her cigarette then runs up to me. "Because it can love harder than anything else."

I raise my eyebrow at her and rack my brain for the last romantic comedy I saw starring an eight-tentacled monster.

"Haven't you heard?" she asks. "The octopus has three hearts."

Then she kisses me back and the bike sprouts wings, delivering me home in a dream.

I'm too nervous to sleep that night so I read Janet's card because it's that or the back of the ibuprofen container. I sit in bed and break open the envelope, but I recognize the handwriting as Sara's. The paper becomes as heavy as a heart in my hand, and I start shaking so badly I drop it. It'd probably be more effective to use my feet, but I force my fingers to cooperate and open it along the fold.

Dear Danny,
 I hope you're not reading this. If you ARE reading this, then shit, I'm sorry. I'm so sorry. If you're reading this, then you already know the news I got today about my dad and his stupid broken heart and that I might have one too. Not broken, malfunctioning? You're the pre-med one, you'll figure it out.
 Maybe if you had your phone on I would have called you when I found out, but honestly I probably wouldn't have, so it makes no difference that you're unreachable due to finals. Not telling you is all on me. But if I tell you, then it's real. If I go to the doctor, then it's real—the possibility of never playing again is real, and that sucks too much.
 Besides never playing again, I can't afford to stop playing now because (and I should have told you this before too) my spot on the team is on the line (I thought you'd like that pun). My tennis game sucks, but I lied to you

*because I had to. I'm not good enough, Danny.
It turns out we were wrong about me and my
dreams. I'm probably going to be a high school
tennis coach instead of a famous Wimbledon
player, but who fucking cares. No one can
take away my game. At least, not unless I get
the official diagnosis, which will make me
another person with a disease, not Sara, but
diseased Sara. Do you see the problem?*

I do, I want to shout. I do. Of course I see the problem,
of course, the world wants to put you in a box so small you
couldn't possibly be in its way. That's why people have labels
and diagnoses and even rigid plans, to stuff you into a box
meant to hold, like, Tic Tacs or something. And I'm not
blaming the world; I've done it too. I'm just saying anything rigid ends up swallowing you whole in the worst way,
until you're reduced to something about as interesting as a
breath mint.

*I know there are risks involved, mainly
that there's one BIG risk involved, but I
saw this Tumblr post that said if you're not
living on the edge, you're taking up too much
space. I know you'll think that's stupid. I
kind of think it's stupid too. I want to take
up TONS of space. I want my life to be big*

*and extraordinary, but whatever. You get what
I'm saying, and I don't think you'll think I'm
crazy. My parents are nearly out of their
tree, but they know how much my game
means to me. Like, if someone asked me to
hand them a diorama of the world, I wouldn't
give them anything green and blue that spins
in your living room. I'd give them a tennis ball.*

The paper is splotched with my tears and I draw my
knees into my chest. I wish I loved anything this much.
I wish that instead of spending my whole life trying to be
Valedictorian of the World I'd learned how to really do
something. *Passion* is such an overused word, but that's the
command I keep hearing in my head. *Find yours, find yours.*
I don't bother telling the hippie-dippie voices to shut up
because it's not a hippie-dippie voice. It's the rubber bracelet still on my wrist. It's what Sara would do.

*I'm going to find this letter one day
and read it to you, and we will laugh at it
together. But in case that's not true, I had
to have something in writing for you, my
Dandelion. I'm terrible with good-byes, but
just so you know I'm waving stupidly at you.*
                                        xoxo,
                                        Sara

Then a little way down the page:

> *PS—I'm sorry I wasn't more excited for you about Harvard. You're Einstein but fuckable. Don't change.*

I turn the page over, hoping for more. I flip it over and over, then read it again and again. It doesn't say everything, but it says something and ironically that makes her feel more gone than she felt before.

I turn the lamp off and the hot itchiness starts creeping in, bringing with it all the usual thoughts—about eating something and throwing it up, about how I'm not good enough in any capacity, about how I probably peaked at seventeen and should resign myself to a life of too many cats. But I have another thought too, which is that maybe none of those things are true. Maybe this feeling is just a bad place, like when you walk through a fun house and everything gets distorted, but when you come out you're completely fine, because you realize the real world isn't actually this way.

"The Undiagnosable Place," I whisper into the dark, feeling much less crazy to have a name for the madness. It gets hotter and itchier, and instead of scratching I fluff up my pillow and fall asleep in it.

At four a.m. my alarm goes off. Sara's letter is resting on my face, and it's all I can do not to read it again. It seems like if I keep reading it I'll be able to conjure her from thin air. Actually, that's a creepy thought, so I put the letter back in my backpack, splash some water on my face, and get dressed for the first day of the rest of my life.

"Oh, dammit. Stephen," I say, looking down at my phone and finding a text from him. Why is it that I consistently forget Stephen? I have a few extra minutes, so I leave a note for my parents on the counter. It's one part explanation, one part apology, and one part I love you so please love me back even though I've vehemently disobeyed you, told you I hated you, and called you a slew of curse words I did not mean. Then I tiptoe out of the house, and sit on the curb with my backpack a little way down the street. I call Stephen with the phone pressed against my face.

"Hello?" he says groggily.

"Morning!"

"Jesus Christ, what time is it? Is everything okay?"

"Yeah, yeah, it's totally fine." I pull my smock down so the gravel of the curb stops making an imprint on my butt. "Erm, it's four seventeen a.m., which I know is a tad early, but I have to tell you, because I'm probably not going to have cell phone service, that I'm not going to be around this fall."

"You're not?" He sounds more surprised than disappointed. "What changed?"

"I don't know exactly," I say, looking up in the sky and trying to find the moon.

It's too complicated to explain or maybe too simple. "I'm taking care of my shit, curating an adventure to cure myself or whatever. Like in *Eat Pray Love*."

"I think my sister made me watch the movie."

"Well, I'm going to do it too. Except not pray. Just eat, eat, and love—well, if Bugg decides to pick me up, but I'm pretty sure she's going to pick me up." I locate the moon, and for some reason, knowing it's there makes me feel like things are going to be all right. At least the world hasn't blown up if the big cheese is still orbiting it. "I wrote Bugg a very nice love letter and it's going to be great. Besides being a slightly less catchy title, I'm going to embrace my love of nonvegan food and learn how to eat like French people do: with gusto and an accompanying cigarette."

"When?" he asks, and he doesn't sound nearly as excited as I want him to. I picture him in the ugly pink elephant boxers he wore the night I slept over, being like, *What idiotic thing is she getting herself into* now?

"Approximately four and a half hours from now. My flight for Paris leaves at nine a.m." I can almost see his eyes bulge through the phone.

"I'm only half awake, so definitely don't hate me, but doesn't this seem a little erratic? I know you're upset about everything with Sara, but why are you doing this?"

I sigh. Stephen will be a great dad to someone else's kids someday. "You know, I don't really know, because I don't really know why I do any of the things I do."

"But, how are you even going to afford it?"

"Well, I sold Sara's car, which her parents gave to me, and I know it sounds weird, but I have a feeling that this is what I have to do. It doesn't make a whole lot of sense. It just sounds fun, and I think that's what I need more than anything right now." I stand up, because despite the layer my smock provides, the gravel is definitely leaving an imprint on my precious ass cheeks.

There's radio silence, then he finally says, "Well, you can always e-mail me if you need anything. I'll only be a whole ocean away."

I see Bugg's headlights turn onto my street, and my heart does the entire routine for *Swan Lake*. "Thanks, Stephen. Look, I gotta go, but I'll probably keep a travel blog or something, so I'll send you the link, okay?"

"Bye, Danny," he says, and he sounds relieved to go back to sleep or maybe to not have to deal with me for a little while.

"It's going to be great." But when I look at my phone I realize that he's already hung up. I get into Bugg's car and hope I'm right.

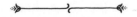

"I gotta say I'm impressed," Bugg says as she gets on the highway. "I thought I was the queen of planning how to run away, but you totally usurped me."

"Nice SAT vocab word."

She pulls out my letter, *while she's driving*, and reads off the things I told her to bring. "My favorite was 'two sporks.' You know they have silverware in France, right?"

"Yeah, but it's important that we bring something of our own to this culinary experience." I put my feet up on the dashboard, and the early morning air raises the hairs on the back of my neck. It feels like more than one new day is beginning.

"Also, I don't own a beret, and you realize people in France don't wear berets, right?"

"Duh, but I wanted to give you a hint about where we're going."

She laughs. The clock on the dash reads 4:31, but regardless of the numbers there seems to be so much time. "Do you think I'm so dense that I couldn't read the plane tickets? Also, that was a sly move, including your ticket in my letter too. Then I had to come."

I give her my most conniving smile. "I know, but aren't you happy I did?"

"You know, I am. As long as we both keep our heads on straight, I don't see why we can't be Venus Fly Trappers together right now, like your letter said." I put my hand on her hand, which is holding the clutch, and pretend we're driving the car together.

"I promise. I won't need to drink or throw up or anything if you're around. You make me feel okay."

"I bet your friend Stephen will miss you," she says.

Now would be a fine time to tell her about the small incident involving his penis—pun intended—but the lightening sky is too pretty to dig up old news. "I'm so glad it's just you and me," I say.

"We've constructed the perfect plan," Bugg agrees. "Will you tell it to me again?"

"The plan goes like this." I lean my head against her shoulder, feeling a little drowsy. The city skyline is ahead of us, and the way the highway turns it looks like we're going to drive head-on into all those buildings. "Two girls meet in kindergarten," I start, but suddenly something black hits the window. Bugg screams and I yell, "Jesus Christ!"

Then I clamp my eyes shut and pray sincerely for the first time in nineteen years as she swerves, in torturous slow motion, off the road.

CHAPTER THIRTY-ONE

"Sara, is that you?" I ask, feeling around and making contact with something warm and squishy.

"Shit, Danny, stop being morbid and open your eyes. It's me."

I peek my eyes open. Sure enough it's Bugg, and I'm groping her face. "So just to clarify, we're not dead," I say, looking at my hands and at the highway, where the occasional car zips past.

"No, we're very much alive. That bird on the other hand..." Bugg cranes her neck around to look at it, and I do my best to breathe. Even though we're nestled safely in the breakdown lane with no scratches and no blood, my heart is racing and not in the fun way it usually does when Bugg is around.

"I want to see it," I say with my voice shaking.

"The bird?"

"Yeah."

We get out of the car and I find it a few feet behind us. Its wings are bent back and even though there's no visible blood, it's clearly a goner.

"Not you too," I say, and start sobbing, which is a confusing response considering how little I like birds.

"Hey, it's okay, Danny," Bugg says. "I know this is jarring and upsetting and admittedly not a very good omen—"

"I don't *believe* in omens."

"Still."

I wish there was something nice I could say to the bird, but having blown one eulogy already, I figure silence is the best thing I have to give. I look at it for a minute and decide we should move it off the highway, not to give it a funeral, but so that it's not a spectacle for oncoming traffic. I don't have any gloves, and since I don't have a hankering to die of something as ignoble as the bird flu, I end up leaving it right where it is until Bugg comes back with a stick from the other side of the guardrail.

"We should go, or we're gonna miss our flight," Bugg says quietly, holding out the stick to me and trying to help me mop my face of tears and snot.

"I'm afraid I'm going to forget her." I focus on the gravel and how hard it looks compared to the bird's feathers, which move softly every time a car whooshes past.

"What do you mean?"

"I'm afraid that my life is going to keep happening while hers doesn't and that I'm going to forget," I say, taking the stick in my hand and smelling its earthy smell.

Bugg crouches down next to me and the damn bird seems to get more dead by the minute. "You won't forget, Danny. Your life will fill up with new shit, but that's a good thing. We all deserve brand-spanking-new shit."

"What if I can't live without Sara?" A truck barrels past us and I suddenly feel too exposed. I turn my back to Bugg and lean on the guardrail for support.

"You can. It's probably gonna suck for a while, but you can do sucky things."

"I suck at doing sucky things. I don't know if you've heard of this great rehabilitation center for fucked-up teens."

The sound of her laugh comforts me, and I turn around. "You're doing the right thing by not going. You're following your octopus hearts," she says.

"Gag me." I take the stick and move the bird off the side of the road gingerly. As I do, I notice a flash of red on its wing. I stare at it for a minute, trying to remember where I've seen this type of bird before.

"Come on, we gotta go," Bugg calls, and I hear her car

door open. I take one last look at the bird, still not able to place it, but when I get back in the car something is different. It's not that I want to take the bird home and get it taxidermied, but there's something back there that I need to take with me.

"You okay, Danny?" We're speeding now to get there in time.

"I'm okay." I look out the window and it dawns on me: It's the same type of bird that was stuck in the garage, the one that kept banging her head against the glass, thinking it was freedom. I turn to Bugg. "What was it you were saying, right before the bird accidentally suicided itself on your windshield?"

"I think I said something about our plan being a good one and that you should tell it to me again?"

"Oh, for fuck's sake," I breathe, because then I remember what *I* said. But Bugg and I didn't meet in kindergarten. Sara and I did.

I try to get air into my lungs, but I can't. The déjà vu is setting in hard. Didn't I just learn my lesson about concrete plans built around lofty ideas? Haven't I retained a single goddamn thing my entire life?

"Are you sure you're okay?" Bugg asks.

I don't want to say it, but I have to say it now because what if I've gotten so good at lying to other people that I don't know when I'm lying to myself? Also, practically speaking, I have to say it now because coming up on our left is one of those connector roads where for a few seconds you're not going anywhere, not toward or away from where you thought you were, but in a space somewhat perpendicular to the two.

"Turn here," I say quickly, and by instinct or miracle she slams on the brakes and turns the car hard to the left. I pummel without abandon toward no place in particular because for the first time in my life, nowhere is where I have to go. If I'm right, it's the place where I'll find everything.

"Jeez, what did you forget?" she asks, straightening the car out and accelerating again. "We're really going to miss our flight now."

"We can't go eat, not-pray, and love," I say quietly. "We can't be Trappers together. I'm trying to run away in a plan again."

She turns her head to look at me, which gives me heart palpitations seeing as she's operating a motor vehicle.

"I don't understand," she says, and her face is a wilted flower.

"This is the same exact thing I did with Sara but with you. The place I have to go isn't mappable, like, there's no longitude or latitude for it." I close my eyes and lean my head against the seat. "The place I have to go is the Undiagnosable Place."

"The what?"

"It's the hot itchy feeling. The thing that makes me

act crazy, basically the heart and soul of all my shit coping mechanisms."

"Oh, *that* place," Bugg says, and I know she knows what I mean. "But what exactly are you going to do? Or go? Or whatever?"

I look at the highway sprawling in front of us, indefinite and ugly with its metal guardrail and white dotted lines and potholes. It keeps going and going. Maybe there's a spot where the road ends, but I don't know where it is.

"I have no idea," I say. "I have no idea what the next move is or what I have to do or even how to get to the Undiagnosable Place. All I know is I can't fix it by going back to St. John's or reenrolling at Harvard or even succeeding at veganism and losing twenty-five pounds."

"But what about yoga? Yoga's all about inner journey shit," Bugg offers. "We can do it in France 'til we're blue in the face if we have to." She slows as we pass a cop, then looks anxiously in her rearview mirror to see if he follows us.

"No. I've done yoga, and yoga doesn't do it for me. Yoga makes me want to murder people, which is the exact opposite of what yoga should do." Thinking about it makes my smock feel rather tight around my neck.

"Maybe you haven't given it enough of a chance."

"I've given it plenty of chances. I don't know what it is, but whatever it is, I have to do it alone." I look over at Bugg, who's crying. "I wish it were different. I wish we were past all the shitty hard stuff we have to figure out on our own. But I can't fix you and you can't fix me." I don't even know if *I* can fix me.

Bugg nods and I check that the cop isn't following us. It appears that today we've been spared.

Bugg takes out a cigarette and keeps her eyes looking straight ahead. "You're right. I should've stuck with what I knew I had to do, which is go back to St. John's, but sometimes I fly into you and that's the end of me, you know?"

I do know. It hurts to watch another brilliant plan hit something as cold and hard as reality.

"How is it possible to be so infantile after twenty-one years on this godforsaken planet?" Bugg asks, pounding her fist into the steering wheel.

"And what the hell are we supposed to do now?" I ask. "Go home?"

"I guess so."

We're quiet for the rest of the ride, each maybe stewing in our shit worlds. After she gets off the highway she idles in front of my house. "I don't want to leave you yet," I tell her, then she undoes her seat belt and kisses me. I don't think she had time to brush her teeth this morning, but I even crave her bad breath. "Will you take me to the ocean, designated driver? The sun is about to come up, and I think we get one last hurrah."

CHAPTER THIRTY-TWO

There are too many things to say. "I love you" would be a fine start, but since she probably already knows that, it's superfluous to bring it up now. Besides, you should never say everything you want to. Then you'll have nothing to talk about. A few feet from the shore Bugg starts to take her clothes off.

"What are you doing? Don't you realize that this is a public beach? Exposing yourself after eighteen isn't a cute little crime."

"Oh, come on. It'll be *fun*," she says, pulling her T-shirt over her head and making me gulp. She takes my face in her hands and it seals us off from the world entirely. I like it better here inside our space, which is another universe altogether. "Dandelion," she says, and I get goose bumps, but in a sad way.

"Sara's the only person who's ever called me that," I whisper. "I know it's what my parents wanted for me and all, but I think I have to keep it that way."

"Okay, how about Dan, then?"

I laugh and look into her eyes, trying not to blink. Even though I'm sad to leave it, it's nice to know our world existed. Maybe someday if she's there and I'm there, we'll be able to get back to it.

"Arms over your head, please, *Dan*," she says.

"Oh my God, *no*. We are not calling me 'Dan.'"

"Fine, Danny, arms over your head!"

I put them up and she takes my smock off, leaving me standing there, feeling petrified but calm about it. As we step into the water, the sun breaks over the horizon like an egg (I'm hungry) and we let the future stay suspended for a few minutes. I know it's going to be hard. I know it's going to be lonely, but I don't think there's any other way out. Truthfully, I don't think there's ever a way out, only a way through.

"On the count of three run in with me," Bugg says. She holds my hand and I hold it back. We walk in up to our ankles.

"Why does it have to be so cold?" I ask. "My poor nipples could cut steak."

There's a honking sound above us, and we look up as a pack of geese flap on through our moment.

"I bet they don't even know where they're going," Bugg says, squinting up at their haphazard formation.

"They don't have a clue," I agree. She gets a running start then dives headfirst into the legal definition of an ice bath. Before I follow I add, to the ripples reverberating from her splash, "And they end up there anyway."

dandelion theory

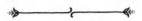

1. stop feeding yourself ideas in mirrors
2. don't wait in ugly dresses for your confidence to grow
3. if the fancy strikes you, this is your advance permission
4. keep diary, named *journal*
5. in praise of being last place: costume parade of the human race
6. no time for grades, just exactly what is
7. be hungry, then eat
8. believe in the compass genius of your starry heart
9. nothing that you know, but something that you trust
10. without a label for this, whatever it is, of jars and happened things
11. know how much time is left on the bombs you carry, the not-said, no-words bombs you carry
12. throw away your dreams
13. don't believe everything you tell yourself
14. feel your wild fingers breaking in
15. how the prison bird flies from its room in your chest
16. and sings

A NOTE FROM THE AUTHOR

Dear Reader,

I want to clarify something before you resume your life beyond this book. While I believe humor is great medicine, and I hope Danny's story made you laugh and feel something true, I also want to make sure that finding the humor in such heavy-hitting topics as mental health, eating disorders, sexuality and sexual identity, grief, and substance abuse doesn't obscure the gravity of the topics.

Danny is one imaginary person dealing with many of the hard things that nonimaginary people deal with, and she doesn't always deal with them well. She'd be the first to admit she's not the poster child for anything. Her sometimes flippant attitudes about such topics as binge drinking, fat shaming, and drug dealing may be inconsistent or even misguided at times as she grapples with her own inner conflicts and personal experiences in the context of societal and cultural attitudes. When writing this book, I intended to create a character who feels real and relatable, but not necessarily exemplary. Just because she doesn't believe in pharmaceutical treatments for her mental health issues doesn't mean that's not a viable path for many people. Just because she doesn't want to label her sexuality doesn't mean that others don't benefit tremendously from the community that comes with a defined identity. Just because she finds a way to laugh at herself as a coping mechanism, the severity of her behavior shouldn't be overlooked. If you or someone you know is struggling with any problems similar to Danny's, on the next page is a list of resources for help. It's not comprehensive, but it's proof that there's a lot of support available out there—and you're not alone.

Writing a story with so many sensitive issues created dialogues around topics that I wouldn't have engaged with otherwise. I'm so grateful to have learned a lot in the process and I'm excited to continue to learn. I think fiction provides a unique opportunity for honesty and connection, one we can't always muster in real life. And that's my biggest hope for *Love*.

Until next time,
Florence

RESOURCES

Eating Disorders

National Institute of Mental Health: http://www
.nimh.nih.gov/health/topics/eating-disorders/
index.shtml

National Eating Disorders Association, "General
Information": http://www.nationaleatingdisorders
.org/general-information

Eating Disorder Hope: http://www.eatingdisorderhope
.com/information/eating-disorder

Body Image/Body Shaming/Body Love

TED Talk, "Ending the Pursuit of Perfection":
https://youtu.be/GR_hq7OVzHU

About-Face: https://www.about-face.org/

The Body Positive: http://www.thebodypositive.org/

Grief

National Alliance for Grieving Children: https://
childrengrieve.org/

The Dougy Center: The National Center for Grieving

Children and Families, "Help for Teens":
http://www.dougy.org/grief-resources/
help-for-teens/

What's Your Grief: http://www.whatsyourgrief.com/

Alcohol Abuse

Screening for Mental Health, Drinking Screening:
http://howdoyouscore.org/

National Council on Alcoholism and Drug
Dependence: https://www.ncadd.org/

Substance Abuse and Mental Health Services
Administration: http://www.samhsa.gov/

Mental Health

National Suicide Prevention Lifeline: 1-800-273-
TALK or 1-800-273-8255 or http://www
.suicidepreventionlifeline.org/

National Alliance on Mental Illness: https://www
.nami.org/

American Psychiatric Association, "Warning Signs
of Mental Illness": https://www.psychiatry
.org/patients-families/warning-signs-of-mental
-illness

LGBTQIA

It Gets Better Project: http://www.itgetsbetter.org/

The Trevor Project and Lifeline: 866-488-7386 or
http://www.thetrevorproject.org/
American Psychological Association, "Lesbian, Gay,
Bisexual, Transgender" and "Understanding
Sexuality": http://www.apa.org/topics/lgbt/
index.aspx

ACKNOWLEDGMENTS

Special thanks to:

Mom and Dad for never suggesting I pursue a "stable" career (lol, what's that?) and for your endless and unconditional love and support.

Leigh Eisenman for being the first person to believe in *Love*, and for Dartmouth College for connecting us.

Danielle Burby for your relentless work on every aspect of this book over the last two years. To say I'm lucky to have you as an agent is to greatly understate my gratitude for having you on my team.

Andrea Spooner for being a force of nature with your editorial prowess and fourteen-page single-spaced revision letters. I am beyond fortunate to receive your guidance and could not dream up an editor I'd be more honored to work with.

Hallie Tibbetts and the entire team at Little, Brown Books for Young Readers for the countless hours you spent editing, publicizing, copyediting, marketing, and turning *Love* into a real, honest-to-God book.

Teresa Lotz for dedicating your free time to reading *Love* and providing such helpful feedback. I appreciate the time you took to offer your unique perspective.

Kheryn Callender for your thorough read through of *Love* in its final stages. It was a big endeavor to include so many weighty issues in this book and you came at the manuscript from every angle without skipping over a sentence. I learned so much from your notes.

Anne Lamott for introducing me to the idea that recovery is like putting an octopus to bed.

Friends—Erin, Laura, Dario, Alex, Lindsey, Carolyn, Nikki, Ellie, Becca, Mallory, and Alec—for all your help along the way, from sharing stories about growing up LGBTQIA to reading excerpts of *Love* to helping me think about what it means to write from a perspective that is different from my own—thank you.

And finally: the TA who told me I should probably quit chemistry, Thora for giving me "Wild Geese" on my nineteenth birthday, Gretchen for getting me through a most turbulent adolescence, and most important, you, reader, for giving a shit.

ABOUT THE AUTHOR

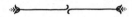

Florence Gonsalves, a recent Dartmouth graduate who dropped pre-med to try her hand at poetry and fiction, lives in Plymouth, Massachusetts. This is her first novel.